PROMISE ME

"You've been over that computer for nearly an hour." A.J. wrapped his fingers around the tightly corded muscles of her shoulders and began to knead gently.

"Mmm," Cara sighed with pleasure.

He sucked in his breath as if he'd been punched in the gut. For the second time that day, her graceful neck drew his attention. Trying to subdue his lascivious thoughts, he continued to work the muscles from the slope of her shoulders to the sensitive area just behind her ears.

Cara made another satisfied murmur, letting her head fall back against his chest. "Where'd you learn to do that?" she asked in a husky voice.

The sensuality of her tone made A.J. bite his lip, hoping the pain would chasten his libido. He wanted to go slower. She needed to know she could trust him. "The Tower Vista gives the best stress-relieving massages I've ever had."

"Ooh. If it feels half as good as this, I'm there."

He couldn't take any more. A.J. had to taste her lips. Slowly he swiveled her chair around until she faced him, then he bent to his knees until their faces were level.

Their lips touched and his control started slipping again. It had been a lifetime since their first kiss. Making love to Cara would be hotter than anything he'd experienced with another woman. Cara guarded her heart well and he was glad. Passion like hers shouldn't be squandered on just any man.

SENSUAL AND HEARTWARMING
ARABESQUE ROMANCES FEATURE
AFRICAN-AMERICAN CHARACTERS!

PROMISE ME

Robyn Amos

Pinnacle Books
Kensington Publishing Corp.

http://www.pinnaclebooks.com

PINNACLE BOOKS are published by

Kensington Publishing Corp.
850 Third Avenue
New York, NY 10022

Pinnacle, the P logo, and Arabesque Reg. U.S. Pat. & TM Off.

First Printing: October, 1997
10 9 8 7 6 5 4 3 2 1

Printed in the United States of America

This book is for my mother, Rosa Thomas,
who gave me the strength to pursue my dreams.

ACKNOWLEDGMENTS

Thank you to the members of my first critique group, Yvonne Yirka and Jill Sauder, who got me started on the right foot. And to those who supported me along the way, Julia Canchola, Eileen Betancourt, Bridget Collins and Vanessa Darby.

To the people who continue to lift me higher and push me further than I imagined possible, Judy Fitzwater, Ann Kline, Barbi Richardson and Vicki Singer.

Special thanks to Barbara Cummings, who gave me that extra push that got me over the top, to my agent, Karen Solem, whose support has been invaluable and to my editor, Monica Harris, who made the dream complete.

Chapter One

"Control is the most important thing," Cara Williams instructed her sixteen-year-old client. "You need to control your body throughout each movement. Wendy, are you paying attention?"

Though the plump, red-headed girl nodded in agreement, Cara's gaze followed Wendy's across the trendy health club to a man pumping iron in a tank top that covered little more than suspenders would have.

Cara shook her head in amusement. "Okay, this exercise will strengthen your triceps." Tossing the black rope of her French braid over her shoulder, she selected two five-pound free-weights from the rack in front of her. Cara demonstrated the exercise by bending her knees and elbows, then extending her arms behind her. "Now you try it."

Wendy awkwardly took the weights, but her attention clearly centered on a golden Adonis doing chin-ups a few feet away.

"Concentrate, Wendy." Since their training session had

begun, Cara hadn't received more than half of the girl's attention. The other half, Wendy gave generously to any well-muscled man in her field of vision. But Cara wasn't upset. This was only their first session, and she knew the novelty of being around so many men would soon wear off. Not even the most impressively muscled physique could turn Cara's head anymore.

Wendy slightly bent her knees and flung her arms out from her body in one wild motion, nearly belting a man behind her in the stomach.

"Wendy! Watch out!" Cara called too late.

Wendy released her grip on the weights, dropping one on the man's foot.

Cara rushed to help the tall mahogany-skinned man to one of the benches lining the mirrored walls. She knelt at his feet. "Are you okay?"

"Yeah, I'm okay. Just feels like I stubbed my toe . . . on a freight train," he said, trying to smile through his wince when she touched his foot.

"Let me have a look at it." Cara rested his injured foot on her thigh and gently removed his shoe and sock, as Wendy stood silently behind her.

Cara swallowed a gasp. A dark patch had already begun to form under his big toenail. She raised her gaze to his face and awareness crumbled her composure like a wrecking ball crumbles a building. Dark eyes watched her intently as she took in his strong features and a well-groomed mustache, which was complemented by a sexy five-o'clock shadow.

Cara lowered her head, trying to refocus on his injury. The soft hair covering his muscular leg teased her fingertips as she cradled his foot. Her cheeks burned. Suddenly, the contact seemed far too intimate.

"Ya need some help?" Her brawny co-worker, Matt, knelt beside her. "It's okay. I'll take over, now."

In her haste to move aside, Cara dropped the injured

man's foot roughly to the floor. Wincing, she apologized as Matt escorted him to the club's first aid center.

Cara had no time to brood over her uncharacteristic loss of composure. When she turned around, she saw Wendy clamp down on her lower lip and blink rapidly, trying to avert her face.

Cara reached for her arm. "Wendy? Are you okay?"

The girl simply stared back, trembling as tears silently trickled down her hot-pink cheeks. She raked her fingers through her frizzy red hair, becoming more agitated by the minute. "I'm sorry . . . I didn't mean to . . . I was—"

"It's okay. He'll be fine. It was just an accident."

Wendy continued to fret, and Cara folded the younger girl into her arms, surprised by how tightly Wendy gripped her in return—like a five-year-old who'd fallen on the playground. Sabrina, Tower Vista's manager, had warned her that Wendy was a bit immature for sixteen, but considering what Cara knew of the girl's parents, Wendy's fragile state wasn't surprising.

Earlier, Sabrina had told Cara to work on a fitness plan for Wendy Townsend at the request of the girl's influential parents. Apparently, the Townsends were high-society types whose overweight daughter didn't fit their image of all-American perfection. Cara had grimaced. The parents told Sabrina that Wendy had been placed on a strict diet. They expected her personal trainer to monitor Wendy's eating habits so she couldn't sneak any junk food while at the club.

Cara hugged Wendy closer. Personal trainers and nutrition courses were ridiculous for a teen-aged girl. Wendy was only slightly overweight, and a light workout routine would melt away those few extra pounds in no time. Thanks to the Townsend's tyrannical behavior, Wendy was so insecure that a little accident turned her into a basket case. They should have helped her become comfortable with who she was, instead of trying to mold her into their idea of perfection.

"It's okay, Wendy. Everything is going to be fine," Cara murmured. "Why don't you go to the bathroom and wash your face?"

Wendy nodded and started toward the locker room.

Cara sat on a bench to wait. *Finally, I can take a breath.* Then a face flashed in her mind. An attractive face with a sexy five-o'clock shadow. Cara frowned. *Wendy's bad habits must be rubbing off on me.*

Anthony-James Gray had chosen Tower Vista Health Club specifically for its modern conveniences. It was located on the top three floors of Bethesda, Maryland's lakefront Tower Building and specialized in comfort. It was the largest facility of its kind in Maryland, D.C., or northern Virginia, and the club's wealthy patrons wanted for nothing. In addition to state-of-the-art equipment, private gyms, and two heated swimming pools, the club had its own sportswear shop, exotic juice bar, cafeteria, *and* first aid facility. But he'd never expected to need it.

"So, how did this happen?" asked the sports doctor who examined his foot.

A.J. grinned at the top of the older man's head. He hated to admit he'd been laid out by a teenybopper. "Uh, someone dropped a free-weight on my foot." He winced as the man prodded his toe. "So what's the verdict, doc? Will I live?"

The tow-headed man faced him with a smile. "Fortunately your toe is only bruised, but it'll be tender for a while."

"Will this affect my workout?"

"I'd go easy on it for a week or two, but you can still do stationary exercises. No jogging or aerobics."

A.J. grinned in relief. He didn't know what he would

have done if the doc had said he couldn't work out at all.
He needed to blow off steam when the pressures of his
computer consulting company got to him—like now.

For weeks, pursuing the Ross, Locke & Malloy account
had kept tension high at Capital Consulting. Now that they
had the account, tension was even higher. Never before
had Capital secured a contract as big as the international
law firm. If everything went well in the D.C. offices, the
firm would contract Capital to work on their systems all
over the country. That kind of business could convert Capital from a growing consulting firm to a multimillion-dollar
corporation.

The business was doing well, but A.J. had his hands full
trying to keep everything together. It wasn't the business
itself that made things difficult. As Capital Consulting's
president, he welcomed responsibility. He never shirked
a duty, and he *never* let anyone down. He knew how to
handle pressure. It was his partners, Whittaker and Parker,
who tested his limits.

Today, after giving presentations to three different
departments of the law firm, A.J. had had to cater to Whittaker's obsession for detail. Did he review the budget
changes? Did he enunciate his words? Was his breath fresh?
A.J. rolled his eyes. He wished the old man would lighten
up. But that was nothing compared to what Parker had
put him through.

That afternoon, A.J. had driven all the way to southeast
D.C. to have Parker sign some papers that were three days
overdue. A.J. had sent the man three different sets, each
of which Parker claimed to have misplaced. When Parker
saw the forms that A.J. hand-delivered, he'd had the nerve
to say "Oh, those papers!" as he pulled down a wrinkled
set from a bulletin board on his wall.

A.J. clenched his fists and narrowed his eyes. He'd never
know how he'd managed to get out of there without strangling—

"Whoa, what are you thinking about? You look like you're about to kill someone," the doctor said, placing a final piece of tape on A.J.'s toe bandage.

A.J. blinked back to attention. "Just thinking about what a rotten day I've had."

The doctor smiled at him. "I guess this free-weight business didn't help any."

"Believe it or not, by comparison, this is a picnic." He remembered the stricken expression on the face of the little redhead who'd clobbered him. Maybe he would have been more upset if the poor kid hadn't looked so stunned, and her trainer so sexy.

A.J. grinned. Having the lady trainer examine his injury had been the high point of his day. He could still feel her soft, cool hands gliding over his leg, and he could still see the concern in her large, almond-shaped, brown eyes. He was never in too much pain to appreciate an attractive woman. She had a narrow, oval face with a smooth, honey-brown complexion, and full, berry-colored lips. Sensual lips. And her body. Unlike some of the overworked bodies he often saw at the gym, the trainer's figure, well toned and defined, was still feminine and curvaceous. He'd seen many women wearing the same blue and green Tower Club tracksuit, but he'd never seen *her* before. He would have remembered *her*.

He shifted uncomfortably. His thoughts were getting out of hand. He looked up at the doctor. "Am I all set?"

When the doctor nodded, A.J. left the first aid center and headed for the auxiliary gym where he used to teach tae kwon do class. It had been a while since he'd stopped in to visit the kids. His workout had been shot to hell anyway.

A.J. caught a glimpse of blue and green from the corner of his eye, and his head snapped around to follow it. He had to laugh when he realized what he'd done. Why was he thinking about her? He wasn't usually attracted to athletic women. Glamorous cosmopolitans were more his type. A.J. paused in the doorway of the martial arts room, remembering the trainer's elegant features and the sassy braid she'd kept tossing over her shoulder. *It was time to get a new type.*

"Girl, you drank that like it was a shot of tequila. What's wrong?" Veronica Howard, Cara's best friend since high school, frowned at the empty glass of orange juice she'd just poured for Cara.

"I hate the evening shift, Ronnie. I'm halfway through my first day on this schedule, and already I want to go back to the morning shift." Cara leaned back in her chair across from Ronnie at Tower Vista's exotic juice bar, The Big Squeeze.

"What's wrong? It can't be that bad. I can tell you right now, the men who work out in the evening are a helluva lot sexier than the old men you find here during the day. Look at that guy working out on that thingamajiggy over there. He is *fine!*"

Cara followed her friend's gaze. "You mean the guy jogging on the *treadmill.* Ya know, Ronnie, you really should take your workout more seriously," she said, then giggled.

"What do you mean? I come here three times a week."

Cara smiled at her pleasantly plump, caramel-skinned friend. Ronnie wore a fuchsia designer jogging suit and pristine white tennis shoes. Her hair, always elaborately coifed, was wrapped in an elegant french-roll with a dramatic bronze streak running through her bangs.

"Ronnie, forgive me, but five minutes on an exercise bike and twenty minutes in the hot tub is *not* my idea of a serious workout."

Veronica tilted her head sassily. "Well, it's as serious as I'm gonna get. Honey, my figure is practically a job requirement. If I lost any weight, people would think my cooking wasn't any good."

As head chef at the Embassy Plaza Hotel, Ronnie took her job seriously. In high school, Cara had the duty of taste testing Ronnie's culinary creations, and Ronnie had the duty of watching Cara's tennis matches. Though the two women seemed like complete opposites, their differences complemented each other.

Ronnie propped her chin on her hand. "Anyway, tell me what has you drinking orange juice like hard liquor?"

Briefly Cara explained the day's events, and true to form, Ronnie's first question was, "What did the guy look like?"

"What?"

"The guy the kid tried to maim. What did he look like?"

Trying to sound blasé, Cara listed the man's attributes as if reciting a grocery list. "Tall, well built, curly black hair, mustache . . . two arms, two legs, the usual." Cara picked up a celery stalk and chewed as if the activity required her full concentration.

Ronnie shook her head. "I'm not buying this nonchalant act. Look at you. You're eating celery. You hate celery! It's been a long time since I've seen you show any kind of reaction to a man. I've got to know more about this guy."

Cara stopped chewing and threw the rest of the celery back on the plate. "Forget it. Guys that good-looking are usually stuck on themselves. He's not my type."

"Sweetheart, it's long past time you got a new type. You don't even give most guys a chance anymore. Those boring losers you *have* been dating don't count."

"The men I date are *not* losers. They're just attractive in a more . . . understated way. Besides, I know what kind of men you're talking about. They don't know how to handle an independent woman."

Ronnie started shaking her head.

Cara leaned forward. "Ronnie, let me put this in terms of food, so you can relate. A man is the icing and *you* are the cake. Cake is just as good with or without icing— sometimes healthier without. Sean wanted me to maintain a steady diet of icing and no cake." Cara leaned back, folding her arms defiantly. "He was giving me cavities."

"Cara, that's cute, but not hardly the point. Not every man is like Sean."

"I know that. I just don't like arrogant men. I like men who respect a woman's opinion."

"You mean men who let you walk all over them. Wimps!" Cara shook her head in resignation. "Never mind. What's going on with you and Andre?"

"Girl, Andre needs money again."

Ronnie filled Cara in on the newest crisis of her on-again, off-again relationship. The man had put Ronnie through so much pain, Cara couldn't understand why Ronnie still had anything to do with him. He was so possessive. He barely let Ronnie breathe on her own, yet *he* didn't know the meaning of the word faithful. The more Ronnie talked, the angrier Cara became.

". . . and then he told me he wants to see other women."

"Again! And he had the nerve to say this after asking you for money! Ronnie!" Cara shot her friend an exasperated look. "You can't let him jerk you around like this. You're giving him too much control over you."

"Look, let's not do this, okay? I know how you feel about Andre, but everything will work out. It always does."

Ronnie always insisted that everything would work out with Andre because she loved him. But Cara knew people sometimes fell in love with the wrong people. She'd learned that the hard way.

"All right, fine. Let's change the subject."

"Well don't think I've forgotten what we were talking about in the first place. I think the fact that your new shift is packed with so many gorgeous men should tell you something. I don't see how you can work in the Garden of Eden and not pick the fruit."

"You know I'm not attracted to the kind of guys that come here." The image of a man's face flashed in her mind as if calling her a liar. She rushed to continue, "They're too hung up on physical beauty—usually their own."

"Cara, that's not fair. You never give them a chance. As soon as one shows any interest in you, you freeze him out."

"That's because they use a lot of pretty words and empty compliments to disguise their true intent. I want a man whose interest in me is more than just physical, and that's not going to happen in a place like this."

"Oh? And you think those computer nerds you date are just interested in your intelligence? Sean—"

"I don't want to talk about *him*. If Andre is off limits, Sean is, too." Cara twisted the end of her braid. "I'm tired of talking about men, anyway. There are more important things we could talk about."

"Speak for yourself." Ronnie retrieved her gym bag from under the table. "I have to go, anyway. I need to change and get to the hotel. See ya later, okay?"

After Ronnie left, Cara spotted the man who'd been randomly popping into her thoughts. Was it her imagination or was he better looking than she'd remembered? She shook her head to clear it. Wendy and Ronnie's infatuations with men were brainwashing her.

Cara frowned, noticing his slight limp. *I'd better go check him out . . . check on him!* She blinked. Where had that come from? she wondered, walking toward him.

A.J. was standing in the lobby, shuffling through his pockets for his keys, when he saw the lady trainer approaching. He felt the corners of his lips curl into a smile.

"Hi. I didn't get a chance to introduce myself earlier. I'm Cara Williams. I wanted to apologize for what happened. How's your foot?"

She was definitely sexier than he'd remembered. He was relieved to see the attraction he felt mirrored in her eyes.

It had been a long day, and a little female appreciation was just what he needed.

"Not too bad. It was just a bruise. No big deal." He held out his hand. "My name's A.J. Gray."

"I'm glad you're okay."

She flashed him a huge smile, but quickly let go of his hand.

"Don't worry. Next time I come to work out, I'll remember to wear steel-toed boots."

She grinned at his joke, then turned serious, pointing at his foot. "I noticed you limping. Will this affect your workout?"

"Not too much. The doc said no jogging or aerobics for a while."

She gave him a pearly smile. "Then I guess that means I won't be seeing you in my step aerobics class."

He hadn't known a woman could look so good without makeup. "You teach aerobics here?"

"Yes. I'm mainly a personal fitness trainer, but I teach two advanced classes."

"Oh? Are you new here? I haven't seen you before. I would have remembered a trainer as pretty as you."

The pearly smile disappeared and was replaced by a cool mask. "No, I'm not new. Just working a new shift," she said, crossing her arms over her chest.

That was a switch. She'd gone from hot to cold in two seconds flat. Was she upset because he'd said she was *pretty*? "Maybe I'll—"

"I'm glad you're not seriously hurt, Mr. Gray." She drew back, indicating the conversation was over.

Mr. Gray? Why was she being so formal? "Please, call me A.J."

She frowned at him but didn't answer. Instead she took another step back.

Had he missed something? Why was she backing off as if he were some street punk yelling catcalls out of a car window? If she reacted this badly to being told she was attractive, what would she do if he laid it on thick? He was just curious enough to find out.

"Cara"—he let her name slide from his lips like molasses—"please call me A.J."

He closed the distance between them, arching his brow wickedly. "I was hoping we could get together for a little *personal* training. You know, I need help *pumping* my iron," he said in his younger brother's best mackdaddy tone. But he couldn't keep the corners of his lips from twitching.

Her eyes widened, and her jaw slackened. She looked as if she wanted to slap him.

A.J. couldn't hold back his laughter. "I'm sorry, Cara, I couldn't resist teasing you. I figured if you were going to give me the deep freeze, I may as well say something to earn it."

If Cara had looked as if she wanted to smack him a minute ago, she looked like she wanted to strangle him now. Her eyes were a burning blaze of hellfire. "Take care of that foot, Mr. Gray," she said in a bitter cold tone. "I wouldn't want you to have any more *accidents.*"

A.J. resisted the urge to shiver as he watched Cara march away. Her attitude could give a man frostbite. He'd been certain she was attracted to him, so where had the ice princess routine come from? His instincts couldn't be that far off.

He'd tried to be on his best behavior—he really had. But she'd gone so cold, he hadn't been able to resist the urge to recapture some of the heat he'd seen in her eyes, even if that heat had burst into fire. Underneath her cool reserve, Cara had passion. He liked that.

Still, he hadn't meant to tick her off that much. Next time he saw her, he'd apologize. Then, maybe he'd figure out what made Cara Williams so uptight.

If he could convince her to speak to him again.

Chapter Two

She'd managed to avoid him for two weeks, A.J. thought, shifting another inch toward the edge of his chair in Capital Consulting's conference room.

Judging by the major attitude Cara was giving him, she'd already made up her mind about him. She wouldn't even give him a chance to explain his behavior on their first meeting. Every time he tried to approach her, she found another excuse to avoid him. That would end today. Since she wasn't responding to the direct approach, he'd just have to sneak up on her. Now he knew her schedule, and when he went to the club that night, he would get her attention.

If his partners ever let him escape from this meeting.

He looked across the long oak conference table to where David Whittaker continued to drone. Ten more minutes and he was out of there, whether Whittaker liked it or not. Three times he'd tried to end the partner meeting, and three times Whittaker had found some reason to prolong it. Just for today, he wished the older man were more like

Jonathan Parker. Anything not directly connected to a computer terminal escaped Parker's notice. Those two took turns trying his patience.

Thank God the partnership worked anyway. *They* handled programming assignments from home, and *he* handled presidential duties from the office. It was the perfect solution for Parker, who wasn't worth a damn around people, and the perfect compromise for Whittaker. After running his own company at a breakneck pace for years, Whittaker's wife had given him an ultimatum—either retire early and spend time with his family, or kiss his marriage goodbye. A.J. knew taking a secondary role at Capital to work at home had been difficult for Whittaker, but that concession had saved his marriage.

The arrangement suited A.J. He needed to have his finger on the pulse of the company. Unlike Parker, he enjoyed working with clients, and unlike Whittaker he didn't have domestic pressures to get in the way.

"Okay, well that sounds fine to me," A.J. said when Whittaker finally paused. "What do you think Parker . . . Parker?"

"What? . . . Oh, yeah, sounds cool." Parker glanced up from his laptop computer as if he'd just awakened from a deep sleep. Throughout the meeting he'd pounded on the keys—oblivious to the meeting going on around him.

"Well, if that's all, I'll see you both, same time, same place, next week." A.J. looked pointedly at Whittaker, silently telling him to let the meeting end.

Whittaker shrugged his shoulders—a surprisingly casual gesture from a man whose crisp, tailored suits never rumpled and whose gray-threaded brown hair never strayed from place.

A.J. smiled. Finally, he could break away.

Parker straightened his frail, birdlike frame, and ran a hand through his shag of sandy-colored hair. "Um, wait.

I almost forgot. Before I came in here today, Chavez told me the Cheverly Bank system crashed this afternoon.''

A.J. let his breath out through his teeth. Sometimes he would swear that guy didn't have an active brain cell in his head. "Parker, why didn't you mention this at the start of the meeting?"

Parker pushed his thick, black-framed glasses higher on his nose. "I forgot. Anyway, it's fine now. It was thrashing so much, they had to bring it down, but tech support got things back up within an hour." He paused to chew on the end of a pen he'd pulled from a wrinkled shirt pocket. "But, I don't know how it could have happened. That system hasn't given us this type of trouble before. Chavez is writing up a report."

"Damn!" A.J. took a deep breath. "Okay. Well, there isn't anything we can do about it right now. I'll discuss this with Chavez tomorrow."

Whittaker raised a skeptical brow. "Don't you think you should follow up on this today?" His eyes were filled with reproach. "You can never be too cautious with these things. When I was running Continental Solutions, I never let a problem slide until the next day."

A.J. shot the older man a quelling look. He didn't have the patience to deal with the older man's compulsive tendencies today. At this point, he needed to work out just to keep his sanity.

"Look, I have somewhere I need to be right now. Trust me. I'll take care of it." With that, A.J. locked his steel briefcase and marched out the door. His pace was so determined, he nearly collided with the marketing director in the hall.

A.J. stopped short in front of her. "Excuse me, Angelique."

"Oh, hi, A.J. Are you on your way out?" When he nodded, she said, "I'm about to leave, too, do you want to—"

"I'm sorry, Angelique, I'm in a hurry." He patted her shoulder and rushed off to catch an open elevator.

Angelique Michaels stared after A.J. *Everyone in this whole freaking company is so uptight.* Tossing her long black hair over her shoulder, she admired her reflection in the mirrored elevator doors. She hoped she wouldn't have to put up with this crap too much longer. She couldn't believe she'd already wasted a year at Capital. A whole year! At least things were finally getting interesting.

She'd thought Brad had been out of his mind, surrounding her with these insipid people, expecting her to *work* for a living. But they had a symbiotic relationship; whenever he asked her to do something unusual, he always made it worth her time.

Turning to view her profile from another angle, Angelique grinned. It wasn't always so bad. Being the director of marketing had its perks. Every now and then Capital got some rich old clients whom she could sweet talk out of little gifts and free meals. She enjoyed lunching with executive fat cats and playing corporate games. Too bad Capital was still pretty small time. They didn't get that kind of clientele too often. Those little baubles didn't come frequently enough to make the job worth it—not for a woman with her talents. She'd learned from the best. Angelique knew how to wring a man for all he was worth. But that was too easy, and incredibly boring. She needed a challenge. And thanks to Capital, this challenge was finally going to bring her the payoff she deserved.

Angelique smile at her reflection. Bringing down Capital was going to be fun.

Cara glanced at her watch. She had forty-five minutes before her aerobics class. Wendy had finally settled into her workout routine and managed to keep her mind on the actual exercises, rather than the male weight lifters. If the free-weight incident had accomplished anything, it had taught Wendy concentration. Cara checked her progress periodically but didn't stand over the girl's shoulder. She wanted Wendy to develop confidence on her own, to know that *she* was in control of her own progress.

Control—something Cara felt she'd finally attained. She'd worked so hard, and now her dreams finally seemed within reach. Everyone had thought she was crazy when she'd quit a promising career in the computer field to become a fitness trainer. Her father had been livid. To this day, he constantly reminded her that he thought she'd made the biggest mistake of her life—next to breaking off her engagement to Sean Ingram. But Cara knew those were the two wisest decisions she'd ever made. Too bad it had taken her so long to realize it.

Actually, she'd enjoyed her job at Monumental Computer Security. After four years of studying computer science in college—at her father's insistence—Cara had grown to love it. Now that things were going well with her job at Tower Vista, Cara could admit she'd started to miss working with computers. She still tinkered with her computer at home, following fitness news groups on the Internet. She became excited every time she thought about the plan that would help her merge her love of fitness and computers.

The idea had come to her during a fitness conference earlier that summer. Most of her peers were showcasing their latest sportswear lines or pushing nutrition cookbooks and exercise videos—the same old stuff she saw every year when she attended those conferences. But this year something new had caught her eye, a display of exercise equipment called Virtual Aerobics that attached to a personal computer. It had been a bit high-tech and cumbersome, but the demo had been intriguing. It sparked an idea that hadn't left her mind since she'd returned from the conference. She'd developed a more practical plan to merge fitness and computers for the everyday user. She'd gathered volumes of information, but she didn't know where to begin. Cara put Valerie, an old friend she'd worked with at Monumental Computer Security, on the case. Valerie had unlimited access to resources that could steer Cara in the right direction.

The sight of A.J. entering the club jolted Cara from her musing. For a couple of weeks, she'd carefully avoided him. She planned to continue, but she was running low on excuses. He'd persistently approached her, claiming he wanted to talk to her, but she'd already had enough of his games. If he thought he was so funny, he could go into stand-up comedy. She didn't intend to be his captive audience. Although that didn't stop her heart from doing jumping jacks every time she saw him.

She couldn't stand feeling like a high school girl with a crush. Alert to his presence. Conscious of her appearance. Aware of every move she made under his watchful eye. She knew better. Yet, she'd caught herself spying on his workout the other day. Sighing, she shrugged it off. She was smart enough to leave men like A.J. alone, but there was no law against enjoying the view, and as far as bodies went, his was one of the best. She'd watched him bench-press the other day, and she'd loved the way the muscles of his arms had—

"There you are, Cara! Just the woman I'm looking for. I need some help with that machine over there."

Startled, Cara turned to find A.J. standing before her. She tried to give him an excuse and ended up stammering gibberish. Feeling her cheeks flame, she fingered her braid, took a deep breath, and started again. "I'm sorry, but my aerobics class is starting soon, and I have to get ready."

A.J. cocked his eyebrow. "Step aerobics, right? The

schedule in the lobby says that class doesn't start for another thirty minutes. Can't you spare a minute to show me how that thing works?"

Cara's gaze followed the direction pointed out by A.J.'s thumb. Silently, she cursed that machine. The Abdominizer was one of Tower Vista's newest additions, and the technology was pretty confusing for first-time users. There had to be some way for her to get out of this. Quickly scanning the gym, she found her salvation lounging against a wall, drinking from a water bottle. "Matt, can you come here a minute?"

Smiling smugly, Cara faced A.J. "I'm sure Matt will be able to help you."

"Hey, Cara, whattaya need?" asked the muscular Italian.

Cara turned to face him. "Matt, could you show this gentleman how to work the Abdominizer?"

Matt paused for a moment, then grinned devilishly. "Uh . . . I'm sorry, Cara . . . but I'm in the middle of something right now."

"What? Matt, I just saw you—" Cara stopped abruptly, immediately becoming suspicious. She whirled around just in time to see A.J. shrug his shoulders in mock innocence, as if moments earlier he *hadn't* been frantically signaling the other man behind her back.

Shaking her head, Cara threw her hands up. "I give up. You men all stick together, don't you?"

Both men quickly shook their heads and feigned ignorance, but as soon as Cara began leading the way toward the exercise machine, from the corner of her eye she saw them engage in one of those complicated, male-bonding handshakes.

Reaching the machine, Cara immediately launched into her instructional spiel. "This is the Abdominizer. It's specially designed to strengthen the leg and stomach muscles, and like most Tower Vista equipment, it's fully automated." She pointed out the electronic panel and the controls that adjusted difficulty and displayed progress status.

"Your hand grips are under the seat, and the back of the chair can be reclined at different angles for more difficult exercises." Cara pointed to the footpads that were similar to the panels of a Stairmaster. "Okay, please sit down and put your feet on the pedals."

A.J. sat on the seat. Cara noticed immediately that the chair needed adjustment to fit his tall frame, which, to her estimate, was about six-feet four-inches.

"How do you adjust this thing?"

Cara smirked at the sight of his large knees awkwardly angling out around the machine as he tried to place his feet on the foot pads. "There should be a release lever under the seat."

A.J. hunted around the seat. "I don't see it."

"I don't know . . . look on the other side."

A.J. peered on the right side of the machine, which was next to the wall of the gym. "There are a couple of levers over here. Which one is it? I don't want to push it the wrong way and, uh . . . hurt myself." He winked at her.

Frowning, she walked to the back of the machine, but it was too close to the wall for her to see under, so she returned to stand over him. "I can't see from there. Get up so I can look under your seat."

"Oh, come on," he challenged. "I don't bite, just look over and tell me which lever to use."

Cara glared at him, but she didn't want to argue. She just wanted to get this over with. She bent over him, careful not to let any part of her body touch his. "I think it's that one." She indicated the lever closest to his hand.

"Which one?"

"That one." She tried to touch the lever, but had to lean over farther to reach it, and lost her balance. She grabbed the side of the machine with her right hand, sprawling over his middle, and clutching his knee with her left.

At that moment, A.J. pulled the lever she'd shown him, and the chair lurched backward, forcing Cara to roll solidly against his chest. He jerked the second lever, and the chair's back reclined under their weight, leaving Cara lying heavily against him, her face only inches from his.

For a stunned moment, neither of them moved. Then Cara struggled to shift her position. She grabbed at his knees for leverage, but her hand slipped between them instead, brushing the most masculine part of him.

"Oh!" Cara gasped. The heat that rushed to her cheeks felt like molten lava. She quickly snatched her hand away, and her gaze met A.J.'s. The blatant desire in his eyes shook her. He boldly returned her stare but made no effort to extricate them from their human pretzel. Flustered, Cara struggled to her feet.

Her head reeled from the desire stirring inside her. Focused on hiding both her desire and embarrassment, she almost missed A.J. deftly adjusting levers to right the machine. Realization washed over her like a bucket of ice water. "You set this up!"

"What?" He seemed to need some recovery time himself.

"You planned this! You already know how this thing works, don't you?"

Swinging his legs over the machine, A.J. swiveled to face Cara. He'd obviously gotten himself together, and his annoying humor had returned. He leveled a crooked grin at her and raised his arms in mock surrender. "Okay, you caught me."

Left speechless by his confession, Cara just stared at him.

"Look, I didn't mean to embarrass you, but what could I do? You keep avoiding me. I don't suppose you'll listen to me now?"

Cara groaned her frustration.

"I didn't think so . . . will you have dinner with me?"

Cara's eyes widened. *There is no end to this man's nerve,* she thought, feeling manipulated and confused. Fury clashed with attraction. She wanted to smack the sexy grin right off his face. Instead she snapped, "Hell, no!" and stalked away.

A.J.'s amused laughter trailed after her. She was startled by her reaction. In an environment like Tower Vista, men often hit on her. She normally replied with the polite rejection line she'd perfected, but with A.J., she hadn't even been able to think of it. Her emotions had taken over. *That* shook Cara the most.

A.J.'s behavior hadn't been the worst come-on she'd experienced. Once a guy had even paid one of her coworkers to slip a naked photo of himself into her gym bag. The attached note had read, "All this could be yours." Even when she'd met him face to face, other than bruising his ego by bursting into laughter, she'd managed to send him away with a polite brush-off. Cara couldn't explain her loss of control with A.J. And to make it worse, the harder she tried to avoid him, the more he was in her face.

The exercise machine incident set the tone for their relationship over the next month. A.J. invented creative ways to ask her out, and Cara curtly refused. She wasn't ready to admit it yet, but it was becoming more difficult to resist his warm sense of humor. A.J.'s crazy antics had even managed to win over Wendy.

One evening, Cara stood before Wendy's treadmill in complete frustration. Even though they'd chosen a goal speed that Cara knew Wendy could handle, she continually fell below it.

"Come on, Wendy. You aren't concentrating. You did almost twice this speed last week. What's wrong?"

As before, Wendy shrugged her shoulders and picked up the pace, temporarily.

Then, to make Cara's evening more difficult, A.J. Gray climbed aboard the treadmill directly opposite Wendy. Cara rolled her eyes and positioned her back to him, hoping he wouldn't cause any trouble.

A few minutes later, Cara noticed Wendy picking up speed. "Good job, Wendy! You must have gotten your second wind."

Wendy maintained her speed, and Cara's eyes began to glaze over as her mind wandered. She was startled back to reality when Wendy let out a high-pitched giggle. Cara's head jerked up. She couldn't remember ever hearing Wendy laugh.

She looked over her shoulder to see what Wendy was laughing at. A.J., slicing his arms back and forth, taking tiny steps, was pretending to run at top speed on his treadmill, then he slowed down and pretended to run in slow motion like an action shot from a movie.

Cara cut her eyes at A.J.'s spectacle. He was distracting Wendy from her workout—or was he? She glanced at the monitor and found that, not only had Wendy exceeded her goal speed, but was maintaining the higher speed comfortably.

She glanced back at A.J., and watched him kick his feet up in front of him as he attempted to run on the treadmill backward. She turned back to Wendy who was still running steadily, entertained by A.J., oblivious to the fact that she should rest. "Wendy, you've done great today. You can stop now."

Wendy seemed reluctant to slow down until a voice from behind Cara announced, "Whew! I think that's it for me, too." Cara turned in time to see A.J. stop dead on the treadmill and make a show of nearly crashing into the wall behind him.

Wendy continued to giggle until A.J. approached them.

He offered her his hand. "You must be Wendy. I don't believe we've been formally introduced." He stared pointedly at Cara. "I'm A.J. Gray."

Wendy's face reddened. "I know. I'm sorry! I mean for what happened before, not because you're . . . I meant to apol—"

"Hey, don't worry about it," he said, waving away her apology. "You actually did me a favor. I'm paying an arm and a leg for this place, and I want to take advantage of everything this club offers. Now that I've visited the first aid center, I can finally say I've gotten my money's worth."

Wendy, who seemed desperate to maintain her solemn expression, couldn't hide the twitching of her lips.

"So, what's Cara teaching you anyway? Kamikaze weight lifting?"

"Oh, no. It wasn't Cara's fault. I wasn't paying attention."

A.J. smiled knowingly. "Oh, I see. Checking out the eligible bachelors, huh?"

Wendy turned three shades of crimson. "Well, I go to an all-girls school, and—"

A.J. grinned and held up a hand. "No need to explain. No harm done."

Wendy frowned. "I'd feel much better if you'd let me make it up to you. Is there anything I can do?"

"Don't worry about it," A.J. said, but clearly Wendy would not be placated until he thought of a worthy penance for her crime. "Okay. There *is* one favor you can do for me. You seem to know this place well. Could you show me how to work this machine over here?"

Before Cara realized what was happening, A.J. had led them to the Abdominizer which she'd come to think of as the "Instrument of Torture."

"Oh no!" Cara glared at A.J., but he ignored her.

"Sure, it's simple," Wendy answered eagerly.

"Oh, no!" Cara said again, shaking her head.

"I'm sorry, Cara," A.J. teased, "I know *you'd* prefer to help me, but I think Wendy might do a better job. *You* get too distracted by other things when you try to instruct me."

A.J. sat on the Abdominizer, and Wendy had him working the machine like a pro within a matter of minutes.

At that moment Cara began to realize that A.J. may have had a point. Why hadn't *she* been able to teach A.J. to use the machine without sprawling all over him? Why had it been so easy for him to manipulate her? Was it possible that she'd been so distracted by his presence that she'd *let* herself fall into his trap?

Cara wasn't ready for the answers to those questions— she had a feeling she wouldn't like them one bit.

After that evening, Cara had resigned herself to the fact that Wendy was firmly stationed in A.J.'s camp. During their sessions, she constantly brought up his name. Although Cara was grateful that he'd helped boost Wendy's self-esteem, she couldn't help resenting his rapport with her. He'd gotten Wendy to speak more in five minutes than *she* had in as many weeks.

Days later at The Big Squeeze, Cara was still trying to sort out her feelings for A.J. when he joined her.

"Where's your sidekick?" he asked, glancing at his watch. "Aren't you normally with her now?"

"Not that it's any of your business, but Wendy's home sick today."

"Aw, poor thing. She's a sweet kid."

"You have that role down pat, don't you?"

"What?"

"You know, pretending that you care. You charmed the socks off her."

"What? You don't think I care? You think I was nice to Wendy just to impress *you?*"

"Well, if you were, I'm not impressed."

"Good. Because I genuinely like Wendy. She's cute and she's sharp."

Cara raised her brows at him. "Yes, she is, but most people don't see that right away."

"True, but I'm not most people. All Wendy needs is to believe in herself a little."

Cara smiled, leaning forward. "Exactly. I've been trying to help her with that by forcing her to do things on her own. That way, when she accomplishes something, she knows it came from her and not me. She's made incredible progress in such a short time. Unfortunately, I'm afraid when she goes home, her parents undo all my hard work."

"What do you mean?"

"They push her too hard. I think she feels inadequate because she can't live up to their high standards. They need to ease up and let Wendy figure out who she is for herself."

"I don't know about that. It's important for parents to take an active role in their children's lives. Too many kids today are left to raise themselves, and the results aren't always pretty. A parent is directly responsible for what a child becomes, and most don't own up to that responsibility."

"I'm not saying they should abandon Wendy. I just think they give her too many standards to live up to."

"A child needs structure and guidance."

"Yes, a *child* does, but Wendy's not a child. She's sixteen years old. After a certain point, parents need to loosen the reins and let a kid develop independence. It's not right to control every nuance of someone's life."

A.J. snorted. "Once Wendy goes out into the real world, she'll have *plenty* of time for independence. Look around. Do you know how much this place costs? Many of the teenagers you see in here have too much freedom as it is. Parents don't bother teaching their kids any values. They just hand them whatever they want. Here's a new car. Oh, you wrecked it? Here's another one. And they don't have to work for a damned thing. At least it sounds like Wendy's parents care enough to pay attention to what she's doing.''

"Oh, give me a break.'' Cara folded her arms on the table, thinking about her own upbringing. "I bet you'd feel differently about it if she were a guy.''

A.J. frowned. "Why would you say that?''

"Because your attitude reminds me of my father's. I'm seven years older than my brother, and he was a lot less sheltered than I was.''

"That's probably because boys and girls need different things growing up.''

Cara rolled her eyes. "That's chauvinism.''

"It's not chauvinism. It's reality. More things can happen to girls, so you have to be more careful with them.''

"That's ridiculous. Why do girls need more protection?''

"Because they're more vulnerable to rape or assault.''

"And who is going to rape and assault them? Other women?''

"Of course not, but—''

"That's right. It's men who put women in danger. So, how much sense does it make to keep a tighter rein on women because *men* can't control themselves? It seems to me that if we forced the same moral codes on boys that we do on girls, maybe the *girls* wouldn't be in danger in the first place!'' She tilted her head, waiting for his reply.

"What? Nothing to say?'' Cara asked, ready for another male chauvinistic retort. She and Sean had had a full-blown argument over this issue. She couldn't wait to hear what kind of comment A.J. would make.

A.J. shook his head. "There's nothing I *can* say. I'd never thought about it that way before. I think it's a shame that more fathers don't live up to the responsibility of teaching their sons what it *really* means to be a man. But it also proves my point that parents need to be *more* active in their children's lives, not less. As you just said, boys and girls *both* need guidance and control.''

Cara had been truly surprised by A.J.'s adjustment to a new perspective, and she'd thought about that discussion for days afterward. Now, before her advanced step aerobics class, Cara shook her head in wonder, remembering the look on A.J.'s face when he'd talked about a parent's responsibility. His words had stunned her to silence. She'd never suspected that A.J. had a serious side. With his perpetually upbeat and joking manner, she'd pegged him as a frivolous playboy. Had she misjudged him? Cara suspected that his intensity on the issue of parental responsibility stemmed from something very personal. For a brief moment, she'd thought she'd seen a vulnerable side of him, but she couldn't be sure because, a moment later, he'd changed the subject and resorted to flirting outrageously with her again.

Cara shook her head as if to physically jar thoughts of A.J. out of her head. She entered the aerobics room and selected the pieces of her step from the stacks on one side of the room. She peered through the glass wall, to the juice bar on the other side. Then she walked across the hardwood floors to the front of the room and, while setting up her step, she looked out the glass wall on the left—not out the window beyond at the beautiful view of the Tower Vista lake—but to the lower level below where the Nautilus equipment was located.

Cara turned away and went to stand before the large stereo system in the center of the mirrored wall. But even as she sorted through her collection of tapes, searching for music to use for class, Cara found herself looking in the mirror, scanning the room for . . . what? What was she looking for? The answer hit her with the force of a medicine ball. *A.J.* She was looking for A.J.

She looked across the room to the rows of cardiovascular machines under a line of television screens. He wasn't there.

Normally, he would've made an appearance by now. A.J. always made his presence known soon after he arrived. Realizing that today was the first day he'd failed to show up, Cara was appalled that she not only noticed his absence, but worse, missed him. While she'd thought his presence annoying, she'd obviously become accustomed to his ridiculous pranks and irritating flirtations.

"I'm losing it," she said aloud.

Cara went back to her step and began warming up as people arrived for her class. Two teen-age girls came in and set up their steps right in front of Cara, as usual. Cara said hello to the girls and then, with her back to the class, stretched her legs out in front of her, grasped the toes of each foot and brought her head down to her knees. She grinned when she heard the two teenagers playing their favorite before-class game.

"Eew! Monica look, a two."

"Yuck. Potbellies should be outlawed. What do you think of that guy over there? A seven?"

"Mmm, maybe a six and a half—he's too skinny. Oh, look at that guy on the Stairmaster, definitely a ten-plus."

"Where? Oh, for those legs alone, he gets two tens."

Cara couldn't resist taking a peek at the guy who was receiving such high marks. She always got a chuckle over their game. Trying to look casual, Cara sat up and looked into the mirror in the direction of the Stairmasters. Her heart skipped a beat. Even from across the room, Cara knew that A.J. was looking right at her. For a moment, their eyes met in the mirror, and Cara felt the same euphoric high she felt after she'd been jogging. Then she forced herself to look away. Thank goodness most of her class had arrived, and she could begin. But her body was tingling. He was watching her. She didn't need any exercise; one look from A.J. had the same effects as running a marathon. *I'm in big trouble.*

From across the room, A.J. watched Cara intently. He was getting to her. For a brief moment, he'd seen her vulnerability. Her eyes had lit when she saw him, and he'd caught a hint of a smile on her lips before she looked away. If he'd been uncertain of her feelings before, he was certain now. His feelings for her were deepening, too.

Pressure was high at the office. Both the Bernhardt Transportation and Creswell Architects systems were down, and he hadn't been able to get away at his usual time. Normally, with things so hectic, he would skip his workout, but he wanted to see Cara. At first he'd pursued her out of curiosity, but the more he saw, the more he liked. The first day he'd learned she was passionate, and their encounters since then showed she was feisty. She was sensitive in her dealings with Wendy, and she proved her intelligence when they argued.

He felt his groin tighten as he watched Cara peel off the jacket to her tracksuit, revealing the top of a red striped leotard. He could see the full outline of her breasts and her incredibly tiny waist. He wanted her so badly, he ached. His movement on the Stairmaster slowed. He felt as if someone punched him in the gut as he watched her slide her pants down each leg. In his mind, he saw Cara undressing for him. Then he stopped exercising altogether, trying to control his body's reaction to the images dancing in his head.

He watched her attach a battery pack to a belt around her waist and adjust a microphone headset. She took her place in front of her step and began to give the class instructions as she moved fluidly over it. He watched her legs keep time with the beat and the seductive sway of her hips outlined in the bright leotard.

The class mimicked her moves. Cara laughed and joked with a carefree air he'd never seen before—and the class loved it. Hell, from her, he'd love it, too. But it had been a long time since she'd looked at him with anything but reproach. Suddenly, he felt envious of the easy rapport she shared with her students. He wished she would—

A.J.'s lip curled into a devilish grin. He'd finally thought of a place where Cara couldn't ignore him.

Chapter Three

I'm late, Cara thought as she dashed across the aerobics room floor. She'd been frantically searching for a battery pack for her headset, and by the time she'd finally found one, most of her class had already arrived. Quickly she got herself together, but before she was ready to begin, a new arrival parted the crowd. With a succession of "excuse me's" and "pardon me's," A.J. created a position for himself directly in front of Cara. Then he stacked his step three levels high. Cara rolled her eyes and took a deep breath before marching up to him.

She lowered her voice so the rest of the class wouldn't hear. "What are you doing here?"

"What does it look like?"

She crossed her arms over her chest. "Have you ever taken step aerobics before?"

"Nope," he answered cheerfully.

"Well then, I suggest you start with a beginner's class. This is advanced step."

A.J. shook his head. "Nah, I'm a quick learner."

Cara was beginning to hate his crooked grin. "Your step is stacked too high. Beginners shouldn't start with more than one level."

"I've got long legs."

With a frustrated sigh, Cara returned to her step. Fine. If he wanted to kill himself in front of the whole class, there was nothing she could do about it.

She started the music, and a pulsing beat filled the room. "Okay class, are you ready?"

"Yes!"

"Whoop!"

"Yeah!"

She loved her advanced class. They had so much energy and spirit. Their high level of participation kept her motivated. "All right then, let's go!"

Cara led them through the beginning warmup, and to her surprise, A.J. was able to keep up. She caught his eye, and he winked at her with a smug expression on his face. But their expressions reversed a few minutes later when Cara brought the class up to pace. Since most of the class was already familiar with the complicated routines, A.J. fell out of sync. Disoriented, he faced front when the class faced back and continuously tripped over his large feet trying to maneuver them on top of the step.

"Okay now, bring it up . . . kick . . . down and cross. Now to the left . . . and turn."

Before long, A.J. had given up trying to keep up with the class, and he began performing his own comical antics. Spurred by the class's attention, he lifted his legs higher than necessary and waved his arms more vigorously than he should have. Cara nearly gave in to her laughter when A.J. stood atop the step and began doing his own version of The Running Man. She hadn't seen anyone do that move since she'd gone dancing with her younger brother years ago.

Cara continued with the class while trying to ignore A.J.'s

outrageous performance. He was making it difficult for
her and the class to concentrate, but Cara was genuinely
impressed with his flexibility. Few men of his build and
height could lift their legs as high or stretch as far as A.J.
could. His overenthusiastic movements almost landed him
on his rump a few times, but to his credit, he eventually
got the hang of it.

When A.J. finally followed the class through a complicated string of movements, he won over the crowd. They
began to encourage him with a soft chant of *"Go! Go! Go!"*
in time with the music. After that, Cara gave up trying not
to laugh and actually felt a grudging respect for his ability
to keep up.

After class, a few of the students approached A.J. to
let him know how much he'd livened up the class or to
congratulate him on catching up, but when Cara gathered
her things and headed out of the room, A.J. left his admir-
ers and followed her.

"Hey, that was fun. Maybe I should join your class regu-
larly."

"Oh, no!" Cara pretended to ward him off with her
hands, but for the first time, she gave him a genuine smile.

"So, how about having dinner with me?"

Cara, still in a good mood from class, actually considered
her answer. "I don't think that's a good idea. You're really
not my type, and I doubt that I'm yours either."

"How do you know? You never take the time to get to
know me. If you're so sure I'm not your type, go out with
me once and prove it."

"Mmm . . . I don't think so." The laughter in her voice
took the edge off her answer.

Just then, a regal, silver-haired woman from Cara's class
passed them. To Cara's horror, A.J. stopped the woman
with a hand on her arm and asked, "Ma'am, don't you
think this beautiful lady should go out with me?"

Cara felt the familiar burning of her cheeks that had

become commonplace around A.J. The woman appeared to be around sixty-five and looked every bit the conservative aristocrat. A violent urge to kick A.J. passed through Cara.

The woman looked him up and down, then leveled a wicked grin in Cara's direction. "Of course you should go out with him, dear. Hell, if I were a few years younger . . ." With a tilt of her head, she spun on her heel, swinging her towel in a circle as she sashayed away.

Cara and A.J. burst out laughing.

"Well, there you go! Surely, you can't argue with a recommendation like that?"

Still laughing, Cara said, "I don't know. I'll have to think about it."

And she intended to.

Cara woke the next morning and began to dress for her consulting appointment. But even as she picked out her clothes and braided her hair into her customary French braid, A.J. lingered on her mind.

Yesterday's episode replayed in her head. Grinning over the memory, Cara had to admit that A.J. had finally managed to trampoline over the walls of her reserve. Now, she had to admit she was attracted to more than just his incredible body. She couldn't casually dismiss her feelings for him any longer. She'd discovered that behind his endless flirtations, A.J. had a sensitive side. Not to mention an irresistible sense of humor. Trying to escape her feelings for A.J. was like running on a treadmill; no matter how fast she ran, she never really got away.

She'd almost accepted A.J.'s last invitation. She really *hadn't* given him a chance. He might not be anything like Sean. She didn't want to judge him unfairly, but she didn't want to repeat past mistakes either. She'd watched many friends date the same man in a different body time and again. On the other hand, she didn't want to miss an opportunity for something special. A.J. *could* be sincere.

Cara laughed at herself. Why was she making such a big deal out of this? The bottom line was she *wanted* to go out with A.J. It was just a date, not a lifetime commitment. For once, she deserved to indulge herself. She had her eyes wide open. Why couldn't she enjoy his company and keep control of her heart?

Cara sat on her rose-colored bedspread as she pulled on her nylons. Now that she had that decision out of the way, she could concentrate on more important things. Valerie had finally come through with a lead for her health-fitness project. She'd called a few days ago with the good news.

When she'd picked up the receiver, Cara had heard, "Hi Cara, I've got some info for your proj." She'd known instantly that it was her old friend from Monumental Computer Securities. Besides her distinctive New York accent, Valerie had a unique way of phrasing things. She did everything at the speed of light, which included talking. Full words or sentences slowed her down.

"Okay, Val, what did you find?"

"A name—Capital Computer Consulting. It's totally perf for you. Small company. Steadily growing. Excellent rep for its integrity. Believe me, Cara, that's rare in this biz."

Cara heard a rapid clicking in the background and knew that the sprightly redhead was probably typing away at 150 words a minute as they spoke. "Rare? What do you mean?"

"Hon, I've known some small companies to offer unnecessary services to pad the bill. Bigger companies are either out of your price range or only handle large accounts, like gov jobs. Capital specializes in the little guy."

Valerie had gone on to assure Cara that Capital could help her discover whether or not her project had a future. Cara knew she could rely on her old friend. Valerie was the chief investigator at Monumental Computer Securities, and they were one of the best of their type in the area. During the year Cara had worked there, Valerie had been her mentor. She could trust Valerie's advice because nothing came out of her mouth unless it had been double-checked first.

Now, as Cara stood in front of the mirror dressed in a stylish burgundy suit, she was ready for her appointment at Capital Consulting.

When she arrived, she was escorted to an empty office to wait. A few minutes later a door opened and a beautiful raven-haired woman with golden skin entered the office. The woman had striking features, the most prominent of which were her almond-shaped eyes that slightly tipped up at the corners, hinting an Asian influence in her bloodlines. She was dressed in a green silk designer suit and wore emerald accessories that appeared genuine. Cara thought the woman seemed a little overdressed for an employee of a small consulting company. Maybe she was a client who'd wandered into the wrong room.

"Ms. Williams?" The woman fixed her with a cool smile and raised an inquiring eyebrow. Cara nodded and stood, extending her hand in greeting. The woman ignored her hand and picked up a clipboard from her desk, which she appeared to study. "I'm Angelique Michaels. I'll be conducting the initial interview." Without raising her eyes from the clipboard she said, "Please have a seat."

Cara sat down, fighting to hold her temper. She'd been under the impression that, as the client, it was *her* decision whether or not to hire Capital. Why did she suddenly feel like *she* was on a job interview?

Angelique sat behind the desk, taking her time to cross her legs at the perfect angle and arrange her hair, almost as if she were trying to create the perfect cover photo pose. Then she picked up her notes and began to tap her long crimson nails on the back of the clipboard. "I have an overview of your ideas, but why don't you tell me about your little project in your own words?''

Cara tried not to gnash her teeth. "Basically, the result would be an on-line resource for people to get health-fitness information on things like nutrition, exercise, weight control, muscle building, etc. All they would have to do is log in to a database and choose their topic of interest. Then they could either send E-mail or interact directly with a professional to help them with their particular situation. Since it would be dedicated only to health-fitness, the client wouldn't have to wade through or pay for any extraneous information.''

Cara shifted her gaze to Angelique, who was intently examining the lacquer enamel of her manicure. Cara pressed her hands together tightly, forcing herself to smile without baring her teeth.

Placing the portfolio she'd compiled on Angelique's desk, she said, "Maybe you'd like to look at the information I've gathered for the project. I've covered a range of topics. Each one is itemized in the table of contents.''

Angelique ignored the portfolio, placing her clipboard on top of it. She leaned back in her chair and heaved an exasperated sigh. "I get the idea, and frankly, it's been done.''

Cara leaned forward. "I've checked around, and I didn't find any networks dedicated specifically to health-fitness. Any similar computer networks are associated with other services and don't offer the same intensity—''

"Yes, well,'' Angelique cut her off, "can I ask you one thing? How do you propose to compete with the established on-line systems that offer more diverse services for the money? I mean, really, how many health-fitness computer jocks are out there? Have you done a survey of your target population?''

"Uh, well . . . I haven't . . . I mean—''

"That's what I thought, but that's immaterial really. Let me see your financial plan."

Cara stared blankly. "Um . . ."

"You don't have one, I see. Well, how many people are on your staff?"

"Well, I really just wanted to—"

"Ms. Williams, do you really think you've thought this through?"

"I . . ." All Cara could do was point at her portfolio.

"To compete with similar services your project would require a minimum of . . ."

Cara didn't bother listening as Angelique ticked off, on each finger of both hands, all the things Cara's project needed and didn't have. Her hopes had already sunk into the depths. Oh, she knew what the other woman was trying to do. Cara had never been easily intimidated. She'd known women like Angelique Michaels before. Her type cozied up to men in order to get what they wanted, but other women were competition. The first order of business with her kind was eliminating the competition. Cara knew how to hold her own, and normally she wouldn't let a woman like Angelique get to her, except for one simple fact: Everything Angelique said was true.

Granted, Cara had come to Capital for help, and she couldn't imagine why they let this woman treat potential clients so rudely, but that didn't change anything. Cara knew when to admit she was in over her head. She hadn't expected miracles overnight. She'd only wanted to find out if her project had a chance. Now she had her answer. She didn't have the money, staff, or experience to pull it off.

She'd been out of the computer field for a long time. Maybe she'd been fooling herself when she'd thought she could make this work.

* * *

A.J. hung up the phone in his office. Everything was going according to plan. The business was doing well. Capital had just signed a new contract. Unfortunately, that was going to tighten things up in terms of staff. He needed to focus all his attention on the Ross, Locke & Malloy account, which meant he would have to add to Angelique's workload. He hated to do it, but he had no other choice. Everybody was working overloads, but once the law firm project was solid, they could expand the staff and branch out. Until then, everyone had to help out wherever they were needed. He had to make sure Angelique could fit Brookland Temps into her schedule.

Anxious to get everything settled, A.J. sped down the hall to Angelique's office. If she could get this client squared away, he would be free to do preliminary work on the Malloy systems. A.J. was so engrossed in his thoughts that he didn't bother knocking on Angelique's door. Bursting into the office, he said, "Angelique, I need to—"

A.J. stopped cold when he saw Cara sitting across from Angelique. What was she doing here? Recovering his manners, he said, "Excuse me for interrupting, ladies." He nodded toward Cara. "It's a pleasure to see you, Ms. Williams. What brings you to Capital Consulting?"

Angelique rushed to answer first. "Actually, we were just finishing up. Ms. Williams was about to leave." She picked up a folder and began to hand it across the desk. "Did you want to speak to me, A.J.?"

Cara stood and reached for the folder, but A.J. motioned for her to sit down. "Please wait here a moment, Cara. Angelique?" He held the door open indicating that she should meet him in the hallway.

Angelique preceded him through the door, still holding

the folder. A.J. made his point quickly. "I need to know if you can squeeze another client into your schedule?"

Angelique frowned. "Another one? A.J., my schedule's pretty tight as it is."

"I know, and I promise this is the last one. I'm turning down work from now on, at least until the first phase of the Malloy project is complete. After that goes through, we'll be able to increase staff and talk about relocating. Brookland Temps won't require much work. I just need you to follow up with their people."

Angelique smiled brilliantly. "Anything for you, A.J."

"Great. Now tell me what Cara Williams is doing here."

Angelique smirked. "Oh her." She rolled her eyes. "She wanted to start a health-fitness on-line service."

"Oh yeah? What did you tell her?"

"Considering she didn't have financial backing, employees, or any real knowledge of what she was getting into, I told her to come back when she'd thought everything through."

"What?"

"Of course, I was nothing but polite. I told her that we'll be here to help her when she's ready."

"I know Cara. She strikes me as a together kind of woman." He pointed at the folder Angelique held. "What's that?"

"Oh this?" She clutched it to her chest. "It's just some information she put together. I don't think—"

A.J. plucked the folder from her hands and started flipping through it. "This is good stuff. Very well thought out. Look, she even has an index for the area where each piece of information would be most useful. Did you look at this?"

"I didn't have to, she clearly—"

"Why don't you get started on the paperwork for the Brookland account? I'll finish with Cara."

Angelique gave him a puzzled look, but she didn't question him.

* * *

Cara shifted positions in her chair again and then began playing with her braid, smoothing and twirling it. She even unbraided the bottom and braided it again. *I can't believe he works here. Just my luck. The guy is everywhere. Of course, he has to appear when I'm having a bad day.*

Cara threw her braid over her shoulder, tapping her fingers on the desk. Then she jumped to her feet and began pacing. Why had he told her to wait? Who was he to this company anyway? The way he'd barged in, he must be important. Not to mention the expensive suit he was wearing.

She'd known A.J. must have been doing well to afford the club's membership fees, but she hadn't thought about it before. It didn't matter, anyway. She wanted to leave. She didn't feel like explaining her reasons for being there. She'd been humiliated enough, and now she just wanted to go home and lick her wounds. If he dared to ask her out, she'd die.

Cara went back to her seat to gather her things, and just as she was ready to bolt, A.J. and Angelique reentered the room. Angelique shot her a look full of venom and curiosity but said nothing as A.J. motioned for Cara to follow him.

When they were in the hallway Cara said, "Um, I was just leaving. I'll see you at the gym." She reached for the portfolio he held.

He held it out of her reach and shook his head. "Ah-ah-ah. Come to my office. I want to talk to you."

"A.J., I really don't—"

"Just ten minutes. I really want to talk to you. Besides, I'm not giving this back until you come with me." He tucked her folder under his arm and headed down the hall. With an exasperated sigh, Cara followed.

When she was seated in front of him, she maintained a rigid posture, determined to escape as soon as possible.

"Angelique gave me a brief overview of your situation, but why don't you tell me about your project in your own words."

Cara let out a weary sigh. "Why? I've already been through this."

"I was under the impression that you came here for help. Why don't you let me help you?"

"Ms. Michaels already gave it to me straight. I don't see what you can do that she couldn't."

"Since I'm the president of the company and have access to resources Angelique does not, why don't you let me be the judge of that."

Cara's face grew hot. *He's president? This just gets worse.* After a few moments of embarrassed silence, Cara gave him a grudging apology and explained her situation.

A.J. listened quietly, then took time to browse through her portfolio. "I think I can help you."

Cara stared at him skeptically.

"Don't misunderstand. Everything Angelique told you was true. If you have your heart set on making this work as an independent on-line service, you'll have your work cut out for you. But, if you're willing to tailor your research for a different kind of project, maybe I can help."

He gave her a moment to absorb what he'd said, and when she nodded, he continued. "I think your health-fitness project would work out well for DataVision Multimedia. The president, Mitchell Crofton, has been a friend and client to Capital, and they're branching into more family-oriented products. If you think you'd be interested in rearranging some of your information, I think we could pitch your idea to him for a sizable consulting fee. What do you think?"

Cara was speechless. Just a moment ago, she'd seen her dreams go down in flames, and now, like a phoenix, new hope was rising from the ashes. Suddenly she was suspicious. "Why would you do this for me? What do you get out of this? Is this your way of convincing me to go out with you?"

Instantly, she regretted her impulsive words.

"Contrary to what you may believe, I'm not so desperate that I use my business to manipulate women. Capital is important to me, and I wouldn't sacrifice its integrity for anything. I know what it's like starting out in a business. When I can cut someone else a break, I do. Capital wouldn't be where it is today if someone hadn't given us a break when we needed one. You do what you can to get your foot in the door, and once you're in, only hard work can keep you there. All I'm doing is offering the service that I assumed you came for. This arrangement could be beneficial to you and DataVision. And as for what I get out of this—that should be obvious. I expect to get paid for the consulting services that I provide. Now, if you're not interested in pursuing this venture, let me know."

Cara bit her lip and twirled her braid between her fingers. "I apologize," she said sincerely. "What I said was out of line. You've been more than generous with your time, and I appreciate your offer. I know it was genuine."

Still, she hesitated. Accepting his offer would change everything. She had no problem reevaluating her project goals. Her problem was with A.J. Just this morning she'd decided to go out with him, and now, only a few hours later, she found herself in a business proposition with him. There was no way she could have both. She'd already discovered what a strong effect he had on her. A dual relationship with him would leave her too vulnerable. Before she knew it, her relationship with him could end like the one she'd had with Sean. She couldn't risk losing control again.

But, she couldn't pass up the opportunity A.J. had presented her. It wasn't likely that she'd find one like it anywhere else. Maybe it would work if she only allowed a business relationship.

On the other hand, she'd decided to give in to his advances once. What made her think she could continue to resist him? It was too hard to fight his desires and her own. Maybe, just a personal relationship.

No, she couldn't give up her dreams in favor of a man.

Cara looked at A.J. He was leaning back in his leather chair, watching her patiently. He looked so sexy in his tailored navy suit. Just her luck, he was one of the few men who looked great in either a suit or athletic wear. She could see the outline of his broad shoulders under the jacket, and she remembered how his muscles looked in those skimpy tank tops he wore at the club. And his arms—

A.J.'s voice interrupted her thoughts. "So, what's it going to be, Cara? Do you want my help or not?"

Chapter Four

Cara blinked at A.J.'s question. She opened her mouth, but nothing came out. Rubbing a hand over her throat, she tried to swallow the dryness in her mouth. Her skin burned under his expectant gaze. How could she make such an important decision in her current state?

"I need time to think about this."

A.J. leaned back, steepling his index fingers. He looked every bit the savvy business man, and Cara felt like a twelve-year-old. This man made a startling contrast with the wise-cracking, practical joker she knew from the club. The man who sat before her meant serious business.

"I understand you need time to absorb this, Cara, but Mitchell Crofton is a busy man. He may not be able to fit us into his schedule, which would bring us back to square one. Do you want me to talk to him? You'd still have an option to decline if DataVision is interested, and if they're not . . ." He shrugged his shoulders.

It wouldn't hurt to find out if they were interested. "Okay, I'd appreciate it if you'd talk to him."

Money seemed the next natural topic. Capital was providing a service by making contact with DataVision. "What's your normal fee for a service like this?"

A.J. told her, and her face must have reflected her panic because he immediately tried to reassure her. "Don't worry. Capital works with a lot of small businesses and individual clients. We can always work something out."

Cara remained silent.

"Since I consider you a friend"—A.J. flashed his charming smile—"and Mitch is a friend, I'll talk to him as a favor to you. If he's interested in buying your information, Capital will accept a reasonable percentage of your profit as payment. If they're not, we'll call it even."

Cara's first instinct was to tell him that she didn't expect any favors, but that would have been foolish. She couldn't afford to turn down his offer. She wouldn't find an opportunity like this anywhere else, so she agreed, praying she'd done the right thing.

She'd walked into Capital Consulting with a firm grip on her life, and now that had changed. But A.J. didn't have to know. With feigned confidence, she concluded the business meeting as if she'd planned for it to end this way all along. A.J. said he'd get back to her as soon as possible.

As she left his office, Cara realized this was the first time they'd ended a conversation without A.J. asking for a date.

Angelique stood in the doorway of her office and watched Cara walk to the elevators. What could A.J. have wanted with *her*? She snorted. He probably wanted to rescue the damsel in distress. He liked to play that knight in shining armor role to the hilt.

What a waste. She rolled her eyes and ran a hand through her hair, enjoying the feel of the silky strands between her fingers.

When she'd first arrived at Capital, her instinct had been

to find an ally—someone who might prove useful if things didn't go according to plan. Out of the mix of misfits, she'd chosen A.J. He was aggressive. A risk taker. He exuded raw power. Too bad his boy scout attitude spoiled the whole package.

Oh well, she thought. He sure as hell wouldn't get rich that way, but that wasn't her problem. She turned and walked back into her office, fingering the emerald necklace hanging from her throat. *She* was already on her way to becoming a wealthy woman. And she didn't give a damn if it was at A.J.'s expense.

A.J. chuckled into the telephone receiver. "You never change, Mitch."

"Well, either you have, or there's a woman involved in the equation somewhere. You never accept favors, no matter how often I offer them. I think you like knowing I owe you."

"Man, I keep telling you. You don't owe me anything. I didn't mind giving your daughter lessons."

"Well, I rest easier now that Melissa knows some self-defense moves when she walks across campus at night. You know I'd do anything for you. There's no price too high for a father's peace of mind. Just make sure you get me that proposal by Monday. My schedule's pretty tight, but I'll try to get back to you later in the week. I'm flying out to the New York offices Monday evening."

"Thanks, Mitch. I really appreciate this."

"So, tell me about this woman you can't bear to let down."

"Cara?" When he thought of her, so many things rushed to his mind. What could he say?

"Is she anything like that woman who used to live in your apartment building? She conned you into setting her VCR every time she wanted to tape a T.V. show."

A.J. laughed. "No, Cara is definitely nothing like Mrs. Churchill. She's young."

"And knowing you, gorgeous. Is this the old damsel in distress routine? I know you love rescuing beautiful women."

"No way. Cara's beautiful but independent."

A.J. didn't know what had provoked his sudden urge to help her. At first he'd just wanted to soften the blow of what Angelique had already told her, but the hard work she'd already invested impressed him.

"I think that's why I found myself involved with this project. She was so determined. I knew she wasn't going to give up." He remembered the strength and pride he'd seen in her eyes.

"And you wanted to make it easier for her. So, tell me. What's going on with you two?"

"There's nothing to tell." A.J. couldn't deny his own selfish reasons for wanting to help her. She was softening toward him, and if working together would give him an edge with her, he wasn't above using it.

"Yet," Mitch finished for him.

The next morning Cara's alarm clock jolted her out of a restless sleep. Anxieties and wisps of conversation, locked in her head, had swirled into a series of murky dreams. Each dream had faded into another, all of them hazy and disorienting, and none of them fully remembered. But A.J. was the first thing on her mind when she opened her eyes.

He remained on her mind as she went through her morning routine, and before she left for the club that afternoon, Cara had made a decision. Around A.J., she lost her grip on situations. Having a personal relationship with him was impossible. It didn't matter that she was attracted to him or that she'd genuinely begun to like him. She knew better than to let her heart rule her head.

Cara hung around the house until the last minute, just in case A.J. called. Part of her was relieved when he didn't. Now that she'd made a firm decision, she'd expected her heart to feel lighter, but for some reason, she still felt dissatisfied.

By the time she met Ronnie at The Big Squeeze that evening, Cara was a nervous wreck.

Ronnie reached across the table and grabbed Cara's hand.

"If you touch that braid one more time, I swear I'm gonna get some scissors and cut it off." She eyed Cara's braid wickedly.

Today Ronnie's hair was arranged around her head in a mass of Shirley Temple ringlets, held back by a headband that matched her turquoise jogging suit.

Cara threw her braid over her shoulder and began tapping her fingers on the table.

"Okay, why are you so fidgety?" Ronnie asked. "Are you nervous about going out with A.J.?"

"What?" Cara stared blankly.

"Last time we talked, you said you'd finally decided to date him. Is that why you're so hyper? Have you told him yet?"

"There's nothing to tell him. I'm not going to go out with him . . . ever. The situation has changed." Cara told Ronnie about her visit to Capital Consulting.

"You mean you're going to kick this guy to the curb because there might be some wild chance you two will work together?"

Cara nodded.

"So what if this business thing doesn't click? Then you'd go out with him?"

"No."

"Why not?"

Cara started to reach for her braid, and after a warning

look from Ronnie, clasped her hands in her lap. "It's safer this way. If I go out with him, I'd have too much to lose."

Ronnie gave Cara her "what-planet-are-you-from?" look.

"Look, Ronnie. If I went out with A.J., I would be too vulnerable. I can't—"

"I think you're being selfish," Ronnie cut in.

"What? How can you say that? I'm the one who's—"

"You're the one who hasn't got a *damn* thing to lose. *You* are the one with the advantage."

"What are you talking about?"

"It's not like you to be so self-centered."

"Ron-nie!"

"Look, this guy has been honest about his feelings for you from jump street. He's pursued you despite your bad attitude. He helped your client—what's her name? Wendy? He has even—"

"Ronnie—" Cara tried to interrupt, but it was too late. Her friend was on a roll.

"He has even gone out on a limb to help you with your project, even though any place else would have laughed in your face. And you're telling me that *you* are too vulnerable? Tell me what you have to lose? He opened himself up to you with both his feelings and his business. What have you put on the line? Nothing. He doesn't even know you had considered going out with him. As far as he's concerned, he could strike out with you personally, *and* end up with nothing in this business deal. Seems to me, you're the one with nothing to lose and *everything* to gain." With a swivel of her neck, Ronnie sat back in her chair and folded her arms across her chest.

Cara was silent as a stinging heat spread over her face. Ronnie was right. Cara had given nothing of herself, whereas A.J. constantly put himself on the line.

Ronnie leaned across the table and patted her hand. "Cara, I don't mean to be hard on you. I just wanted you to see that you're not the only person with a stake in this."

"I know, Ronnie. Thanks. You've given me something to think about."

"You know, playing it safe won't get you anywhere in life. To get anything worthwhile, you have to take a risk every now and then. Shoot, who am I telling? You're the woman who ignored everybody and quit your computer job to become a fitness trainer. You know all about risks, and you also know that when they work out, they're well worth the trouble."

Cara still felt wary.

"Just tell me one thing. Do you want to go out with him? Be honest."

Cara took a deep breath to clear her head. Honestly? "Yes."

"Well, then, what's stopping you? You made that decision before the business thing came up, and he'll still be there, whether it works out or not. You're only cheating yourself if you don't give it a try."

Ronnie had a way of breaking things down for Cara. The way she put it, Cara suddenly felt like she'd made a big deal over nothing. She was still in control, and she could decide what she wanted to happen. She just needed to be up-front with A.J. about her feelings.

"You're right, Ronnie. I guess it's easier for you to see the whole picture." Cara grinned. "Now if only I could get you to look at your own situation from the same perspective," she couldn't resist adding.

"Touché. But Andre and I have worked things out. He's changed. You'll see."

After Ronnie left, Cara took a moment to clear her head. She wasn't indecisive by nature, yet whenever A.J. Gray was involved, she lost her objectivity. Thanks to Ronnie, she realized that she wasn't being fair to A.J., or herself. She wanted to go out with him, so she would. Now *that* was the first decision she'd made all day that felt right. Suddenly, instead of laying in her chest like a sunken rock, her heart floated.

Despite Cara's lighter mood, the evening passed painfully slowly. She wanted to talk to A.J., but she couldn't find him anywhere. By the time her advanced aerobics class was over, and he still hadn't shown, Cara began to worry.

She needed to take her mind off him, so she decided to look in on the water aerobics classes that Tower Vista had just added to the fall schedule. On her way to the main pool, she passed the auxiliary gym and saw her coworker, Matt, peeking in the window of the door. Then he stepped back and began pantomiming martial arts moves.

"Matt? What are you doing?" She couldn't hide the laughter in her voice.

Matt stopped and turned to her, his cheeks reddening slightly. "Cara, hi. I was just watching your friend in there." He pointed at the window.

"My *friend*?"

"A.J. Um, the guy your client dropped the weight on."

Cara stepped forward. "A.J.? What's he doing in there?"

Matt smiled. "It's so cool. He's teaching tae kwon do to these kids . . . from like, the ghetto or something. I talked to him before class, and he said I could stay, but I felt stupid with all those little kids in there, so I've been watching from out here. I thought maybe he could show me a few moves after class."

Cara grinned at Matt's eagerness. It was funny to see him excited like a little boy on Christmas. Cara peeked through the window. "I didn't know A.J. taught tae kwon do here."

"He said when he started the program last spring, he taught all the classes himself, but he got too busy, so he got some other guy to take over. Today, the guy was sick, so he's doin' it."

Cara looked at Matt. "He started *what* program?"

"It's so cool. He said he went to some boys' big brother type thing in D.C. and volunteered to teach the kids some moves, but they didn't have anywhere for him to do it. So, he got special buses to pick the kids up and bring them here after school. But the kids can't participate unless they go to school every day. Their teachers have to sign some paper or something."

Cara raised her eyebrows. "Well, just when you think you know somebody," she said under her breath.

"What?" Matt asked, looking in the window. "Oh, they're packin' up. I'm gonna see if A.J. can show me some stuff."

"Okay, see you later," Cara said and Matt disappeared through the door. A.J. was full of surprises, she thought as she went upstairs to wait for him.

She was leaning against the front desk in the lobby, talking to the check-in clerk when A.J. came from the men's locker rooms. He headed straight for her.

"There you are," Cara said.

He stood still for a moment, just looking at her as if he were trying to memorize her features. Cara shifted her weight uncomfortably and lowered her eyes to avoid meeting his hot stare. That was a mistake. Her gaze dropped to his chest, and he looked incredible. The jacket of his navy tracksuit hung open, revealing a white tank top that made a striking contrast against his mahogany skin. The tank dipped low enough for Cara to see a nice portion of his pectoral muscles. She hadn't realized male cleavage could be so enticing.

"Wow." *Did I just say that out loud?*

"I was just about to say the same thing."

"I wasn't . . . um, what I meant was . . ." Cara felt a familiar burning in her cheeks.

He just winked at her.

Cara opened her mouth to say something and then

closed it again. It was unbearably hot, and her skin was tingling all over. It took a moment for her to realize that he was speaking to her.

". . . didn't call earlier, things got busy, and I thought I'd wait and talk to you here. Then I had to take over the tae kwon do class. The instructor is out sick today, and he asked me to fill in. Were you looking for me?"

Cara nodded.

A.J. grabbed her shoulder and began steering her toward the door. "Walk me to my car so we can talk in private."

When they stepped out to the parking lot, the cool night air was a comfort to her burning skin. Cara took a long breath to calm her riotous nerves. Her heart seemed to pound so hard, she wondered if A.J. could hear it. He was looking ahead, searching for his car. She felt too vulnerable to bring up their personal relationship first, so she plunged right into the second topic pressing on her mind. "So . . . did you talk to your friend?"

He stopped walking and turned to her. "Yeah. As a matter of fact, I did. Based on what I told him, Mitch thinks the project has promise. The good news is that he wants to see a proposal."

"A proposal? You mean one of those. . . ?" she waved her hand, trying to think of the right words.

"It's just a summary stating what you plan to deliver and what you would expect to receive in return. It's not too complicated."

"I wouldn't know where to begin."

"Don't worry. I can help you flesh out the details and put it together. But the bad news is that he needs the proposal by Monday morning."

"Monday! You mean this coming Monday?"

"Yeah. He's getting on a plane for New York that night, and he's doing us a favor by looking it over on the flight. His schedule is pretty hectic. He'll get back to us later in the week. Don't worry. If we work on it all day Saturday and maybe part of Sunday, we should be able to get it done. You do want to go ahead with this, don't you?"

"Yes, I do. I really appreciate you helping me like this." She smiled at him.

"Okay, then why don't we plan to get started tomorrow afternoon. I need to finish a few things in the morning, but I could come over around noon."

"Why don't I just meet you at your office?" There was no sense in tempting fate.

He moved toward her. "We can do it that way."

She backed up against the stone wall bordering the parking lot. "I think it would be best."

He took another step, blocking her view of everything other than his broad chest. She inhaled his fresh masculine scent. He must have just showered.

"Look, Cara, if we're going to work together, I think there are a few things we ought to get straight." He leaned forward, caging her with his arms. "From the beginning, I've made no secret of how I feel about you. You, on the other hand, haven't once been straight with me about your feelings."

A.J. leaned down to her five-foot eight-inch level so that they were nose to nose. "You're just as attracted to me as I am to you, but this is your last chance to admit it. If you insist on running away from what's between us, I can't stop you. But frankly, I don't think you can ignore this." He bent his head until their lips touched.

The kiss began as a light brushing, as if he were waiting for her to pull away. But when she responded by leaning into the kiss, A.J. slid his hands around her waist and fit her body to his. At first, Cara clutched his upper arms, bracing herself against the sensations that rolled over her like ocean currents. Then she relaxed against him, wrapping her arms around his neck.

He held her closer, slipping his tongue between her lips. Cara welcomed his tongue into her mouth with a few tender strokes of her own. She could feel his excited response, which sent a rush of heat straight to the core of her body.

With a groan against her lips, A.J. broke the kiss, slowly tapering off with a string of smaller kisses placed on and around her mouth. Cara released her grip from his neck and tried to regain her balance.

Taking a deep breath A.J. straightened. "I'll assume that means you've decided to stop running."

Chapter Five

Cara's eyes widened. "Can I touch it?"

A.J. smiled encouragingly. "Please."

Cara ran her hand over the smooth surface. "Oh," she gasped.

"What do you think?" he asked.

"I'm impressed, but it's so small."

"Yes, in this case, the smaller the better."

Cara gently placed the miniature glass statue back on the bookshelf in A.J.'s office. She'd arrived twenty minutes earlier, and A.J. had insisted on giving her a complete tour of Capital Consulting. The tour had finally ended in his office. Though Cara had been there before, her mind had been otherwise occupied, and she'd failed to notice its modern elegance. It in no way reflected the disorder that Cara had come to associate with computer companies.

In the center of the room sat a black lacquer table which served as A.J.'s desk. And on top was a large black computer monitor accompanied by a black keyboard and mouse. Black bookshelves and file cabinets lined the right side of the room, and on the left, a long smoke-colored glass table sat before a black leather couch. The pearl-gray carpet and walls offset the dark furniture, and light filtering through the ivory curtains covering the floor-to-ceiling window behind A.J.'s desk gave the office a quiet ambiance.

Cara had studied each ornament or fixture, trying to distract her mind from A.J.'s presence. At the most inconvenient times their kiss intruded on her thoughts. Especially now, with A.J. standing close behind her. How could she focus on business when all she wanted to do was kiss him again?

"Well, I guess we should get started." Cara searched for the folders she'd prepared for the project.

"I'm ready when you are." A.J. led Cara to the sofa. "We'll probably be more comfortable working here."

Cara situated herself at what she judged a safe distance from A.J. and opened her note pad.

"Okay," he began, "Mitch will expect to see a marketable idea for a fitness CD-ROM. Do you have any ideas on how you'd like to organize this information? If you don't, I can make some suggestions."

Cara tugged on her braid, which had gotten caught inside the neck of her purple sweatshirt. "Actually, I do have some ideas." She began to outline her thoughts, hesitantly at first, occasionally looking at A.J. for a reaction. But, as she spoke, her natural confidence returned. Her ideas were good ones.

"So I figure everything would be cross-referenced— nutrition, specific workout routines, and general fitness precautions. Overall, we would focus on building a personal health plan that includes diet and exercise. With one major ingredient—repetitive warnings to seek a physician's approval of the final plan. One thing I hate to see in this field is a diet or workout schedule that claims it's right for everyone."

A.J. nodded approvingly as she continued. "It should

be user-friendly, too. He or she could simply type their personal information into a database installed on the hard drive, indicating the areas they want to focus on, then the system can make recommendations. If a woman is interested in toning her thighs, the program can provide a list of moves that work on that area. And since we're talking CD-ROM, it can come complete with video clips that demonstrate the movement.''

When Cara finished, she was out of breath. "I'm sorry. Did I get a little carried away? Last night, when I was working on this, I got excited about the advantages the CD-ROM medium provides. Sound clips, video clips, massive text storage, photographs . . . the possibilities are endless."

A.J.'s smile was encouraging. "Actually, I'm really impressed. I hadn't expected you to have things so well thought out. I thought we'd have to sweat this out from scratch, but as it turns out, we should have this proposal drafted by dinner time. All we have to do now is work out the details . . . what role you expect to play in the project and what role you propose DataVision will play. If the proposal is accepted, we can get more into the technical stuff." A.J. pulled out a legal pad and began jotting notes.

Twenty minutes later, he handed her a spreadsheet. "To speed things up, I had Angelique print out a market survey for fitness computer software. It seems to be a growing trend that hasn't been overrun yet. Now is a good time to hit with this kind of product."

Cara frowned at the mention of Angelique. "Speaking of Angelique, she really stands out, doesn't she? . . . I mean—"

A.J. held up a hand. "I know what you mean. Angelique is a character—she has her own unique style of business. By the way, I told her to apologize for the way she treated you."

"How did you know?" Cara was surprised. Often, men were blind to the true nature of women like Angelique.

"I've noticed that Angelique lacks . . . *finesse* when dealing with other women. Fortunately, most of our clients are male, so it hasn't been a problem, but I won't let her personal whims affect Capital's customer service reputation."

"I'm kind of surprised to see someone like her working for a computer company."

A.J. chuckled. "Yeah, I was surprised myself when she answered our ad for a marketing director almost a year ago. What she doesn't know about computers, she makes up for in market savvy. We were pushing for a huge law firm account and the bidding went on for nearly a year. Angelique helped us pull in a steady stream of clients to keep us going. She really knows her stuff."

Cara snorted. She was no longer in a conversational mood. Angelique rubbed her the wrong way.

A.J. and Cara continued to work until the telephone interrupted them.

"Hello . . . Eddie." A.J. turned to face Cara and mouthed the words *my brother*, holding up a finger to indicate he'd only be a minute. He turned around to resume the conversation.

Cara tried not to eavesdrop, but she couldn't help it when A.J.'s voice went cold, lowering an octave.

"There's no way in hell I'm giving you money . . . No. I don't care if you need to buy her a birthday present. You should have thought of that before . . . That's right, but that doesn't give *you* a right to any of it . . . Well in that case I'll pick it up for you and send it to her myself."

Cara frowned.

"Of course, it's fair. That cuts out the middle man, and I know exactly how the money's been spent."

At that point Cara stopped listening. A drum beat of anger pounded in her ears. How could A.J. be so cold with his own brother? Making him beg for money so he could buy some poor girl a birthday present? And what right did A.J. have to dictate how the boy spent it? His money or not, he wouldn't even let the boy pick out his own gift? Cara shook her head in frustration. What went on between A.J. and his brother was none of her business, but she couldn't help wondering—was he going to try to run *her* life, too?

Cara heard A.J. slam down the phone. She didn't trust herself to look at him, but she could feel him watching her.

"I'm going downstairs for a soda. Do you want anything?"

Cara shook her head, still not meeting his eyes.

"Okay, I'll be back in a minute." The door clicked shut behind him.

A.J. lifted the cold soda can to his forehead. He wished his brother would get his life together. Eddie had no sense of responsibility, just like their father.

His father had disappeared when he was twelve and Eddie still a baby, leaving their mother to raise two children on her own, taking multiple jobs just to keep food on the table. Alma Gray had played with her children, never complaining or showing the strain. But A.J. had known how hard it had been. He'd done odd jobs to bring in as much money as he could to help his mother. He refused to run away from his responsibilities—the way his father had.

Unfortunately, Eddie was a different story. He'd always been content to let A.J. look out for their mother while he partied and played. These days, A.J. had to beg Eddie to visit or even call their mother.

Her birthday had been *two months ago,* and *now* Eddie wanted to buy her a gift? A.J. knew better. He'd never hidden his disapproval of Eddie's expensive stereo system, collection of basketball shoes, and the other luxuries Eddie spent money on in lieu of paying his rent. The last time Eddie had talked A.J. into giving him money, Eddie had promised to buy their mother a new VCR for Mother's Day. Later A.J. discovered that Eddie had used the money toward spring break in Florida.

A.J. thought over their telephone conversation. He had no intention of giving Eddie another dime. A.J. would pick out a gift and send it himself rather than give Eddie the opportunity to blow more money on clothes or a new speaker system.

When A.J. returned to the office, he could feel the change in the atmosphere. He sat next to Cara, setting a can of fruit punch in front of her. "I know you said you didn't want anything, but I thought you might get thirsty later."

Cara mumbled a thank you but didn't touch the drink. Several times A.J. tried to engage her in conversation and received nothing but one word answers in return. Somehow he'd managed to get her mad at him again. He should have known their truce wasn't permanent. He'd been waiting for her to back away from him ever since their kiss yesterday. He hadn't been able to stop thinking about it, but obviously Cara hadn't given it a second thought. Maybe he ought to refresh her memory? He studied Cara's profile. Her eyebrows were furrowed, and her lips were pressed tightly together. Uh uh, he didn't feel like getting slapped at the moment. He'd have to find another way to loosen her up.

"Cara, why don't we take a little break?"

She looked at him from the corner of her eye. "Didn't you just take one?"

A.J. grinned. "Yes, but you haven't had one. Besides, I want your opinion on something."

"What?"

"Come here." A.J. walked to his desk and pulled a second chair around to the front of his computer. "Come on."

Cara stared at him from her place on the couch. Finally, she joined him.

Heaving an exasperated sigh, she said, "Okay, what are you up to?"

A.J. reached in a drawer and pulled out a square envelope. "Mitch sent me this game a while ago and asked me to tell him what I thought of it. I haven't really had a chance to play—it's a two-player game—so I thought now would be the perfect time."

"We don't have time to play games! This proposal is due Monday!"

"Like I said, you need a break." A.J. pulled a silver disk out of the envelope and placed it into the CD-ROM drive of his computer. He installed the software and movie quality graphics took over the screen.

Cara crossed her arms. "I'm not playing."

A.J. suspected Cara had a competitive streak and decided to bait her. "Sorry. I forgot girls are no good at games like this."

As expected, Cara's eyes flared. "I didn't say I *couldn't*, I said I *wouldn't!* Actually, I beat my younger brother at video games all the time!"

A.J. gave her an evil grin. "This isn't one of your brother's little Sega or Nintendo games. This is a man's game. It takes skill."

Cara pushed up her sleeves. "Just tell me how to play."

A.J. explained the rules and within minutes they were deeply embroiled in intense warfare. Not that the game itself was warlike. It was actually more of a mystical game in which unicorns and fairies roamed an enchanted glade. It was a game of strategy and skill where each player attempted to solve a series of puzzles before the other to save the glade from an evil wizard.

A.J. watched Cara trying to suppress her smiles when she saw how *manly* his "man's game" turned out to be. He'd known he was pushing it, but at least he'd gotten her into the game. Already the mood was beginning to lighten. A.J. and Cara spent the next hour trading quips and matching wits while they played the game's multiple rounds. They had turned it into a tournament of sorts, and there was only one winner per round. So far, Cara was ahead by three rounds.

"Okay it's my turn!" Cara reached for the mouse as A.J. pulled his hand away. Her fingers brushed his, and he made no move to hide his reaction to her touch. Cara quickly turned to focus on the screen, but A.J. knew she'd experienced the electricity that had passed between them.

Cara stared pensively at the large black monitor, and A.J. stared at Cara. He'd known many beautiful women in his lifetime, but none of them had Cara's fresh, natural loveliness. Her smooth, brown skin would taste sweeter than any honey. Just like her lips. Her face was so pure. She wore no makeup except for some eyeliner under her perfect, almond-shaped eyes. And her hair, pulled back in a French braid, left a light wisp of bangs on her forehead and exposed her long, graceful neck. A neck that, even now, invited him to bury his lips in its hollows. A.J. leaned forward as if compelled by a higher power.

"I did it!" Cara exclaimed.

A.J. snapped straight in his chair. He blinked rapidly to refocus his attention. Cara had finished the game. She faced him with a triumphant smile on her face that she quickly suppressed.

"Well, congratulations. You really kicked my butt on that one. You have a talent for solving those puzzles. Half the time I didn't have a clue."

Cara just stared at him.

"What's wrong?" he asked.

"You mean that, don't you?" She continued to stare at him as if she were trying to see into his soul.

"What? That I didn't have a clue? I think that's obvious, but you don't have to rub it in."

"No, not that. You aren't upset about losing?"

A.J. shrugged. He didn't know where she was going with this, but he sensed it was important. "Um, I guess these problem-solving games aren't my strong suit, but apparently they're yours. If we ever go on a game show, I want you on my team."

Cara just shook her head as if deep in thought.

"Are you okay? You certainly are the sorriest winner I've ever met. Shouldn't you be jumping around and yelling or something?"

Cara flashed him a smile. "That was fun. Thanks for making me play. Is there a ladies room around here?"

"Down the hall and around the corner. It's past the elevators."

"Okay, I'll be right back."

Cara left A.J. to puzzle over her reaction. Oh well, he thought. At least he'd managed to ease the tension between them. Maybe when she got back, he could talk her into having dinner with him.

Cara rested her back against the counter in the bathroom. A.J. was hard to figure out. One minute he was driving her up the wall, the next minute he had her rolling on the floor laughing. She knew why he'd coaxed her into that game. It didn't take a mind reader to know that she'd been upset with him. His little plan had worked. It was impossible for her to stay mad.

She hadn't realized how much she judged other men by her father and her former fiancé. After winning the game, she'd waited for the inevitable explosion. Whenever she'd played innocent games with Sean or competitive sports with her father, they'd both reacted badly if she won. Things had gotten so bad with Sean, she'd avoided doing *anything* competitive with him. A couple of times she'd even let him win to avoid the sulky behavior and yelling that followed whenever she'd beaten him at something.

It had been a long time since she'd jumped around a room, proclaiming victory at the top of her lungs. Sean had taken more from her than she'd realized. But A.J. seemed genuinely impressed by her strengths rather than threatened by them.

Maybe he wasn't like Sean at all. He certainly didn't seem to share Sean's poor sportsmanship, but that didn't explain everything. She still didn't understand why A.J. had acted like an overbearing jerk with his own brother. She needed to be more sure of him before she let herself get too involved.

Yet just being around A.J. was becoming difficult. She couldn't escape the physical attraction between them. When their hands had brushed moments before, she'd made the mistake of looking into his eyes. The raw passion she'd seen had nearly melted her. Combined with the private explosions that were taking place inside her body, she'd nearly gone up in flames. She'd been tempted to turn around and throw herself into his arms, especially when she'd imagined she'd felt his breath on her neck.

Thank goodness she'd been blessed with a talent for focusing under pressure. It was the only thing that saved her from doing something reckless with A.J. She'd forced herself to focus her energy on solving the game's final puzzle.

Cara took a deep breath and headed back to A.J.'s office. Somehow she'd find a way to solve the puzzle of A.J.

Chapter Six

Just as Cara was becoming restless, A.J. held out his watch. "It's six o'clock. We've made good progress today. We'll only need to work a couple of hours tomorrow afternoon. Why don't you let me take you out for dinner? One, for beating me at the game this afternoon, and two, because we've been cooped up in this office all day." He leaned forward on the sofa and watched her closely.

Cara smiled. He seemed to brace himself for rejection. "That sounds good to me." She swallowed a laugh at his raised eyebrows. "In fact, I have a suggestion. A friend of mine is a chef at the Embassy Plaza. Great food guaranteed. Why don't we have dinner there?"

A.J. flashed his crooked grin. "Sounds good."

"Why don't I go home and change, and I can meet you there in say . . ." she checked her watch, "an hour and a half?"

"No!"

"Huh?"

"I insist on picking you up."

"A.J., that's really not necess—"

"Please?"

It wasn't worth an argument. "Okay, but I have to run now if I'm going to be ready in time." She quickly collected her things and rushed out the door.

Thirty minutes later, as Cara searched for her favorite red pumps, she remembered to call Ronnie. She dialed the private number which rang in the kitchen.

"Hi, Cara. What's up?"

"Ronnie, I hope you have room for two more in the dining room tonight because A.J. and I will be there in . . . oh, less than an hour."

"On a date? I finally get to meet this man?"

"Yeah, you'll meet him. Just don't embarrass me." Cara juggled the phone as she put a gold earring in each ear.

"No problem. Now, what are you wearing?"

"My red dress."

"Which one? I hope it's not the dark one with the high collar?"

"No, it's the clingy one with long sleeves and a full skirt."

"Good! That one shows off your legs. Now for the really important question: what *have* you done with that hair?"

"Don't start on me, Ronnie. I don't have time—"

"Not that braid! You need a sexy hair style to go with that dress. Too bad I'm not there to hook you up."

"Uh-uh. The last thing I need is one of your fancy hairdos. Trust me. My hair is fine the way it is."

Ronnie merely grunted.

"Anyway, I just wanted you to know that we'd be there soon."

"Great! Now I'll have something to look forward to. A Senator rented a private dining room tonight, and you know how I hate those politicians."

After Cara hung up the phone, Ronnie's comment nagged at her. Should she have tried to fix her hair differently? She touched her braid, then glanced at her watch. A.J. was due any minute, but maybe she still had time to—

The sound of the doorbell eliminated all hope of any last minute hairstyle changes. Shyly, Cara approached the door. Would he like her dress? She smoothed the soft fabric, wishing for a chance to check her appearance. The bell chimed again.

Taking a breath, she pulled open the door . . . and her breath quickly fled.

A.J. looked fantastic. Impeccable. Under a light trench coat, he wore a charcoal-gray suit with a dark shirt and a blue and gray tie. And a sexy five-o'clock shadow veiled his jaw. The image was both sophisticated and reckless. Its effect on her pulse was . . . dangerous.

"Hi, come in. You look . . . great." Cara stepped aside so he could enter the room.

"I was just about to tell you the same thing. You look beautiful in red."

All worries over her appearance faded. His words were pleasing, but the real compliment came from his eyes. His gaze stroked over her hair, then slid down her body in a light caress that lingered at her waist before traveling upward to rest on her face.

As he helped her into her coat, she felt his breath on her neck and smelled the familiar scent of his cologne. What would happen if he lowered her collar and kissed her neck? What if she turned around to stroke his bristled jaw? Would he kiss her? What if she didn't get control of herself? They'd never make it to the restaurant.

On the way to the hotel, their sexual tension eased into the friendly rapport they'd shared earlier. By the time they were seated at their table, Cara was in control again.

A waiter approached the table. "Cara! What a pleasure. Ronnie didn't mention you'd be dining with us this evening."

"It's my fault, Phillip. It was a last minute decision."

Cara gave the waiter a charming smile. "A.J., this is Phillip, my *favorite* waiter."

Phillip winked at A.J. "Don't you believe it. Cara says that to every one of us, but she's still our favorite customer." He turned back to her. "You *will* be Ronnie's guests, of course?"

She nodded. "Of course."

"Does the gentleman need time to look over the menu?"

She didn't give A.J. a chance to answer. "Yes, he does, but I'll have the usual."

When the waiter left, A.J. leaned across the table. "Who's Ronnie?"

Cara took a sip of her water before she answered. "My friend, the chef. I hope you don't mind. I know you wanted to reward me for my *impressive* win this afternoon," she said, grinning mischievously, "but as Ronnie's guests, the meal is complimentary."

"That's okay." A.J. returned her mischievous grin. "I'll find some other way to make it up to you." He picked up his menu. "So, what *is* the usual?"

"My favorite dish. It's not on the menu. Ronnie makes it especially for me."

A.J. wrinkled his nose. "What is it, some vegetarian-health-food-tofu something?"

Cara giggled. "You'll see when they bring it out. You might even want to try some."

"No thanks!" A.J. shook his head. "Working out is as far as I'll go for healthy living. When it comes to eating, I'm completely indulgent. As a matter of fact, I'm going to have the shrimp scampi, loaded with calories, just the way I like it."

After Phillip had taken their orders, A.J. leaned back in his chair and looked at Cara intently. "So . . . how long have you known Ronnie?"

At that moment, it dawned on her. A.J. thought Ronnie was a *man*. She started to correct the misunderstanding, then hesitated. Sean had turned three shades of green if she even *mentioned* a male friend. He would have had a fit if she'd brought him to a fancy restaurant, then let another man pay the bill. A.J. wasn't Sean, but how would he react if she let him know just how close she and Ronnie were—*before* letting on that Ronnie wasn't a man.

"Ronnie and I go way back, since high school. We're as close as two people can be." She watched his reaction.

A.J. sat stiffly for a moment, his face an unreadable mask. She waited for jealousy, suspicion, or pointed questions. Instead, A.J.'s shoulders relaxed, and a slow smile spread over his face. "Great. Then I can't wait to meet the chef who's treating me to a free meal."

Mentally, she raised her eyebrows. He'd obviously been uncomfortable, maybe even jealous, but he hadn't acted on those feelings. "I'll make sure you meet Ronnie before we leave." She couldn't wait to see his face.

As they waited for their meal, Cara turned the conversation toward business. "So, you mentioned having a big account in the works."

A.J.'s eyes lit up. "The Ross, Locke & Malloy contract is our *biggest* account. We're designing a full system for their D.C. law offices, and if that goes well, we'll work on all their firms across the country and even internationally."

"I'm impressed. Is this the account that took almost a year to land?"

"Yes," he said, obviously pleased by her interest. "Just over ten months."

"Why so long?" Cara took a sip of her wine.

"While their D.C. offices were being remodeled, they were accepting bids from every consulting firm in the area. We had some steep competition, and frankly, Capital went after the account on a long shot. We didn't actually expect to get it."

Cara raised her eyebrows. "Oh yeah?"

"Yeah. We were surprised when they narrowed it down

to Capital and RSI—Resource Systems International. It was a close call. RSI is a bigger organization with strong international connections. A few years ago, I'd even worked with their CEO, Bradley Kincaid, as an independent contractor. I thought we'd lose the job because Kincaid is a real butt-kisser. He'd do anything to reel in a client."

Cara leaned forward. "So how did you beat him out?"

"Ross, Locke & Malloy decided to go with us *because* we're a smaller firm. We can give them almost exclusive attention."

"Great. All your hard work paid off."

A.J. leaned back. "Well, yes and no."

"What do you mean?"

"Capital can still lose the account to RSI."

Cara frowned. "Why?"

"One of the stipulations in our contract states that we have to bring in the first phase of the project, the D.C. offices, on time and under budget. If there are any problems or delays, RSI gets the contract by default."

"That doesn't seem fair," Cara said, wrinkling her nose.

"Actually, it's not that unusual. Ross, Locke & Malloy are taking a big risk using a smaller company like Capital. They need a guarantee that we can do the job. If we hadn't agreed to that stipulation, we wouldn't have gotten the contract at all."

"Wow. I'd hate to have to work under that kind of pressure."

Phillip arrived with their dinner on a serving cart, both dishes covered with silver domes. Cara smiled with anticipation.

A.J. rubbed his hands together. "Finally! I don't know how much longer I could have made it with just bread sticks." He nodded at Cara's covered platter. "What's the special dish?"

Cara held up a finger for Phillip to pause before lifting the dome on her platter. "I told you. It's my favorite dish.

It's an ... *international* combination that Ronnie makes just for me."

A.J. leaned in to watch Phillip remove the cover. Cara watched his eyes widen as he took in the thick, juicy, hamburger with a healthy side order of fries arranged artfully on the silver platter.

Cara picked up a fry. "A good old *American* hamburger with *French* fries." She couldn't resist giggling at A.J.'s expression.

He shook his head, chuckling. "Okay, you got me. That'll teach me to make assumptions about you." Then he paused. "Wait a minute. I thought you said it wasn't on the menu. There isn't a hotel in the world that doesn't have hamburgers and french fries on the menu."

She lifted her bun. "Not with Thousand Island dressing, cheddar cheese, and romaine lettuce."

The atmosphere became relaxed, and A.J. directed the conversation toward Cara.

"Now, tell me how a fitness trainer got so involved with computers."

Cara dabbed her lips with her napkin. "Well, actually it's the other way around. I went to college and got my degree in computer science. I had a minor in health-fitness, but my first job was for a computer security firm, Monumental Computer Securities. MCS."

A.J. leaned forward, eyes bright with curiosity. "Computer securities—that's a good field."

"Yeah, I really enjoyed it. I started with an entry-level position, but they'd begun to train me as an investigator before I left. I kind of had a knack for problem solving and troubleshooting. You know, that sort of thing."

He reached over and took a fry from her plate. "That explains why I got my butt kicked on that game today. You should've warned me you were a trained professional."

Cara smiled. "I wouldn't say that, but if I'd stayed at MCS, I probably could have done pretty well. I'd started going out on assignment to observe the senior investigators. It was fascinating work, computer viruses, encryption codes, all that stuff.''

A.J.'s brow furrowed. "If you enjoyed it so much, why did you leave? Couldn't you have worked as an aerobics instructor part time or something?"

"Actually, that's exactly what I was doing before I quit MCS to work at Tower full time. I know it sounds strange, but it's just something I had to do for myself. I don't expect it to make sense to anyone else."

"You might be surprised. Try me."

Cara looked into his eyes. They were clear and sincere. When she'd started making major life changes, all her friends had treated her like she belonged in a mental institution. Ronnie was the only person who hadn't acted like she'd quit her job to join the circus. Her father had nearly disowned her.

She took a deep, fortifying breath. "The only reason I studied computer science in the first place was because my father insisted. He was a high school P.E. teacher, and I grew up playing every sport you could name. When it was time for me to go away to college, I told him I wanted to major in health-fitness. He had a fit. He said I was too smart to waste my life that way and that I should study something academic, like computers. Well, as soon as the words were out of his mouth, he latched onto the idea. We argued about it for weeks. I'd had no interest in computers. Finally, I got tired of arguing. Unfortunately, I'm headstrong, just like my father. If I hadn't given in, we'd have gone on about it forever.

"So I majored in Computer Science and minored in Health-fitness. As it turns out, I found that I not only like computers, but I'm pretty good with them, too. And for a while, I didn't mind pursuing them as a career."

Cara felt him watching her closely, then he asked, "What changed?"

She looked down at her nearly empty plate. "What changed?" she repeated, twirling the end of her braid. Should she tell him about Sean? "Well, a lot of things changed."

Cara studied A.J.'s face. His eyes, which at times seemed to mock her with their humor, frustrate her with their determination, and stir her with their sensuality, now soothed her with their warmth. Yes, she decided. She wanted A.J. to understand everything about her. She wanted to give their relationship a chance.

"While I was working at MCS, I met Sean." Cara looked at A.J.; his posture seemed more rigid, but his eyes remained warm, inviting her to continue. "We were together for almost a year, and we were engaged."

A.J. sat straighter but said nothing.

"Sean had always been caught up in those traditional male/female roles. When we went out to dinner, he had to pay. He couldn't stand the idea of me treating him. When we stayed in, I was supposed to cook. I should have known then that we were doomed because I never did like cooking." Cara tried to crack a smile but wasn't sure it was successful. Some of the memories were bitter ones.

"At first I thought it was something we could work through together. You know, eventually he would learn to respect my independence, and we would find a happy medium. That's what happens when you love someone, right? But instead the opposite happened. For a while, even *I* stopped respecting my independence."

Cara smiled derisively. "I fell into his routine. Letting him take care of me. It was so easy to do that I didn't even see it coming. At first, I felt safe and protected, but I woke up one day and realized I was Sean's fiancée and nothing more. I had no identity. I didn't even recognize myself anymore. I needed to stand on my own and assert myself. So then I started trying to take care of Sean. Doing the kinds of things for him that he'd been doing for me. He couldn't stand it. It wasn't masculine to lean on a woman for anything in his opinion. A man always has to be in control."

A.J. listened quietly, his face deceptively calm, but Cara saw the vicelike grip he had on his napkin.

"Anyway, I stopped trying to look out for him and started concentrating on myself. I needed to do something just for me. So I quit computer security and became a fitness trainer. That's when my relationship with Sean really fell apart. Number one, he couldn't stand not being the only thing in my life, and number two, he couldn't respect my decision any more than my father could. That's when I realized that he didn't respect me. It was a messy breakup, but I'm happier without him. The rest as they say, is history."

A.J. let out a long breath. "So, what made you decide to get back into computers?"

"Well, I really do enjoy computers. I still play with the one I have at home every chance I get. Now that some time has passed, I can admit that I miss the field. I love the idea of doing something with both of my interests. Now, I can go back because I want to, not because of anyone else."

"Well, that makes sense to me." His eyes were full of gentle understanding.

Cara smiled but noticed that A.J. was still strangling his napkin. She reached over and touched his hand lightly. "Hey, you're suffocating the poor thing."

A.J. looked down at his hand as if it belonged to someone else. "Oh, sorry." He released the napkin, then pointed to the last, lonely, shrimp on his plate. "You want a taste?"

Cara shook her head.

"Come on, I've been stealing your french fries all night. Have a taste." He grabbed the shrimp by its tail, rolled it in the buttery sauce, then held it out to her.

"Okay." She reached out to take the shrimp, but A.J. pushed her hand away.

"Uh-uh. Come on, the sauce is dripping."

Cara leaned forward and bit the shrimp A.J. held to her mouth. She couldn't prevent her lips from grazing the tips of his fingers. "Mmm, delicious! I've never tried shrimp scampi before. It's wonderful." Cara licked her lips.

"Yes, delicious." A.J. murmured. His eyes focused on her lips. A.J. straightened, taking a breath. "The food was excellent. Ronnie really knows his stuff. When am I going to meet this guy?"

"Oh," Cara tried to suppress a giggle. "I have to tell you something."

"What?" A.J. asked, but then Phillip returned to check on them.

"Phillip, could you tell Ronnie that we'd like to pay our respects to the chef?" Cara asked.

Phillip nodded eagerly and disappeared into the kitchen.

A.J. leaned back in his chair. "Good. I'm anxious to meet him."

Cara leaned forward. "Well, that's what I wanted to tell you—" but before she could finish, Ronnie bounced out of the kitchen wearing a white uniform and a tall chef's hat.

Ronnie stood beside the table and folded her hands serenely. "Okay, I'm ready for praise. Tell me how much you loved my cooking." Ronnie waited patiently and received a burst of laughter instead.

The indignant chef placed her hands on her hips. "What's so funny?"

A.J.'s natural charm took over. "Ronnie? It's a pleasure to meet you. I'm A.J., and dinner was excellent. The best scampi I've ever tasted. I apologize for the laughter. It's nothing personal." A.J. shot Cara a stern look. "I think Cara was playing a little joke on me."

Cara gripped her stomach trying to stop laughing. "Ronnie, I don't know why, but somehow, A.J. got the impression that you were a *man*."

"You *didn't*," Ronnie screamed, joining them in the laughter.

A.J. eyed Ronnie's chef hat. "I didn't know chefs really wore those hats."

Ronnie grinned at A.J. It was obvious they would be fast friends.

"Some still do. I wear mine because I can't *stand* those awful hairnets. Ugh!"

Ten minutes later, A.J. sat alone at the table, waiting for Cara to return from the kitchen. Ronnie was showing her a wedding cake she'd designed for a ceremony taking place the next day. He was grateful to have a moment to himself. Dining with Cara had been an experience.

She'd really had him going, letting him think Ronnie was a man. His gut had twisted when she'd told him she and Ronnie were "as close as two people could be." He'd almost lost his cool, until he remembered the look in Cara's eyes when he'd picked her up at the apartment. She may have spent weeks running from him, but she'd never been able to disguise her attraction to him. She wasn't the type to play one man against another. Still, he'd felt a rush of relief seeing that Ronnie was female.

When she'd told him about her ex-fiancé, he'd nearly lost it again, but that time he'd known he had to keep it together. She'd taken a giant step by confiding in him. She was beginning to trust him, and now he knew why she'd resisted him for so long.

He *had* come on strong. He winced, remembering some of his more aggressive antics of the past. He would take it easy with her from now on. It didn't take a psychologist to see that Cara feared letting a man control her life again.

It would take some time to convince her that he was different, but he could pass any test she threw his way. The little game with Ronnie's name had been the first one.

A.J. savored a private smile. He didn't mind jumping through a few hoops to ease Cara's mind. She was worth the effort. She was the kind of woman he could fall in love with.

He looked at his watch. Almost ten o'clock. He didn't want the date to end so soon. Then again, he had the goodnight kiss to look forward to. He'd waited all day for an opportunity to kiss her again. They'd gotten so comfortable with each other, he couldn't face her backing off again. He had to ease her into a more romantic mood.

A few minutes later Cara returned to their table, and they left the hotel. On the drive home, their relaxed atmosphere began to fade. Cara became quieter the closer they got to her apartment. A.J. sensed that the sexual electricity crackling between them caused the strain. Maybe he could distract her into loosening up.

"Ya know, Cara. I've been thinking about your project. You came up with some great ideas this afternoon."

From the corner of his eye, he saw her turn away from the window to face him. "Thanks."

"I think if we focus on the interactive quality of the software, we could end up with a unique product."

"Really? In what way?" she asked eagerly.

"Well, do you have a CD-ROM drive on your computer at home?"

"Yes."

"Great. When we get to your house, I'll show you what I mean." A.J. smiled to himself when she readily agreed. Now that he had his foot in the door, Cara would be in his arms before she knew it.

Chapter Seven

He needed to touch her. Sitting close to Cara in the tiny bedroom she used as an office, A.J. could literally feel the heat radiating from her body. The spicy scent of her perfume, the rise and fall of her breasts, and even the sight of her long, delicate fingers flying over the keyboard, kept him constantly aroused. He wanted to feel those hands running over his body. In his mind, he could see her hands deftly unknotting his tie. He saw a pink-tipped nail pushing his shirt button through its hole. Honey-toned hands reached for his belt buckle.

"You were right. This demo disk is giving me a lot of ideas. Could we include a spreadsheet like this one?" Cara pointed at the screen.

"Yeah," A.J. answered, glaring at her profile.

He'd only pulled out the stupid disk to distract her from what was happening between them long enough to get him through the front door. Now he wished she hadn't been so easily distracted. She eagerly tapped away on her keyboard, while he sat beside her, suffering an exquisite torture.

He looked at his watch. It was getting late, and he'd wasted enough time. He moved to stand behind Cara's chair while she jotted notes for the proposal.

"You've been bent over that computer for nearly an hour." He wrapped his fingers around the tightly corded muscles of her shoulders and began to knead gently.

"Mmm," Cara sighed with pleasure.

He sucked in his breath as if he'd been punched in the gut. For the second time that day, her graceful neck drew his attention. Trying to subdue his lascivious thoughts, he continued to work the muscles from the slope of her shoulders to the sensitive area just behind her ears.

Cara made another satisfied murmur, letting her head fall back against his chest. "Where did you learn to do this?" she asked in a husky voice.

The sensuality of her tone made A.J. bite his lip, hoping the pain would chasten his libido. He wanted to go slower. She needed to know she could trust him. "You should know," he said in a quiet voice. "Tower Vista gives the best stress-relieving massages I've ever had."

"Ooh. Remind me to check into that. If it feels half as good as this, I'm there."

That was it. He couldn't take anymore. He had to taste her lips. Slowly he swiveled her chair around until she faced him, then he bent to his knees until their faces were level. The soft, heavy lidded expression on her face sent electric currents racing through his groin. He brought his face to Cara's, and she leaned into his kiss.

Their lips touched, and his control started slipping again. It had been a lifetime since their first kiss. The sweet acquiescence of her mouth hastened his thoughts beyond just kissing. Making love to Cara would be hotter than anything he'd experienced with another woman. He'd known that after their first kiss. Cara guarded her heart well, and he was glad. Passion like hers shouldn't be squandered on just any man.

Suddenly he was dissatisfied with their position. With her sitting in the chair, he couldn't feel the length of her body. And he wanted her firm, feminine form pressed against him. Without breaking contact with her lips, A.J. put his hands around Cara's slender waist, lifting her against him as he stood.

When he set her on her feet, Cara's body curved heavily into him, and he deepened their kiss. He slid his tongue gently into her mouth, and she accepted him willingly. Running his hands from her waist to her back, he enjoyed the soft warmth of the clingy fabric beneath his fingers. His hand slid to her firm, round derriere and traced the outline of her underwear with his finger.

Cara sighed deeply against his mouth, making a soft whimpering sound. He'd discarded his suit jacket long ago, and now Cara was rubbing her hands all over the outside of his shirt. He could feel the impatient raking of her nails through the thin material. He knew she wanted to touch the bare skin of his chest. He'd also become impatient with the cloth that blocked her skin from his.

Excitement shot through his body, making it hard for him to continue standing. Various parts of his body had become unbearably heavy. Swiftly, he sank onto the chair, curling Cara on his lap. With one hand, he helped Cara free him from his tie and open the buttons of his shirt, while he used his tongue to paint intricate designs on the side of her neck. Gently, he flicked at her earlobe, before he sucked it completely into his mouth.

Cara's hands found their way inside his shirt. Her fingers stroked the muscles of his body so lightly, her nails barely grazing the surface of his skin, that he trembled violently. An ache grew inside him so intense he didn't trust himself to continue.

Just as A.J. was summoning all of his strength to set

Cara away from him, she shifted on his lap, straddling the hardest part of him. Cara moved her mouth over his, parting her full lips, and A.J. forgot all of his good intentions. He hadn't planned to make love to her yet, but she didn't seem as wary as he'd expected.

A.J. pressed her into his erection. Damn, she tasted so good. One of his hands found the hem of her skirt, and began sliding up the length of her nyloned thigh. He couldn't wait any longer to undress her. When his fingers reached the waist of her nylons and began to tug at the flimsy material, he felt her body still.

The way Cara slowly slid from his lap, A.J. thought she meant to speed up the process. He waited for her to pull off the nylons herself, but instead she turned away from him.

She put some distance between them, then looked at him over her shoulder. The shy expression on her face made him want to wrap her up in his arms all over again. He knew what she was about to say, and he could tell she wasn't anxious to say it.

He held up a hand to stop her from speaking. "You know what? It's getting late, so I'm gonna get going."

The relief in her eyes told him he'd done the right thing, but she surprised him with a long hug, a sweet kiss on the lips.

He felt like a wreck with his tie hanging loose around his neck and his shirt half pulled out of his pants, while Cara looked perfect. No mussed hair or wrinkled clothing. The only sign of their romance was the deepened color and extra fullness of her lips.

Pulling on his jacket and tucking his shirt in his pants, A.J. headed for the door. He leaned down to brush his lips over Cara's in goodbye but made the contact quick because he was still fully aroused.

He tilted her face up to his. "I hope I didn't rush things

tonight, but I enjoyed your company. Thanks for having dinner with me, Cara. It was worth the wait.''

Walking to his car, A.J. couldn't help grinning. His date with Cara had gone better than he'd hoped. After tonight, she couldn't deny what was happening between them.

Sunday evening, entranced by fatigue, Cara poured bubble bath into a cascade of steaming water. When the tub was full, and a thick white layer of foamy bubbles covered the surface, Cara sank into it. With her hair braided into a coil on top of her head, she lay back and let the water lap up to her chin. The warm water caressed her neck, and Cara realized how sore she'd let herself become from bending over a computer all day. She reached up with a wet hand to massage the aching muscles and was reminded of strong masculine hands that had performed that very service the evening before.

The memory caused a tiny wave of heat to break inside her. So much for taking things slow. She'd been one step away from letting him make love to her. That wasn't like her. Sean was the only man she'd been intimate with, and then only after a year of dating. Now she was ready to give in to A.J. after only one date. She was worse off than she'd thought.

That afternoon, at his office, she'd tried to slow things down. She'd kept things strictly business while they worked, and thank God he hadn't pressured her. They finished the proposal, and tomorrow morning A.J. would have it couriered to DataVision. But before she left for the evening, she had allowed A.J. to kiss her goodbye. And he'd made that kiss count.

He'd been great about not pushing her, but that wasn't the problem. *She* was the problem. Already she cared about him more than she'd expected to. What would happen if she fell in love with him?

Cara sat up so quickly a wave of water splashed over the side of the tub. *Whoa! Where had that come from? It was too soon to worry about that.* She was letting her hormones take over. As Ronnie was quick to point out, *it had been a long time.* Too long. She was making too much out of a few kisses. Besides, she had their business relationship to think about.

Actually, she didn't have too much to worry about in the business department. First of all, the proposal might not be accepted. Second, if it were, she probably wouldn't deal with Capital too often. After the initial introductions, she could deal with DataVision directly. The extent of her working relationship with A.J. couldn't last more than a few weeks. That would give her plenty of time to adjust to their personal relationship and set up boundaries. They just needed to take things slower.

There were still so many things she didn't know about A.J. He was different from Sean in several ways—he wasn't threatened by female competition or jealous of male friends. Those things were important, but she still had to resolve the issue of how he'd treated his brother on the telephone. She'd wanted to ask him about it, but didn't want to hear that it was none of her business. A.J. was obviously a generous and caring person. His participation in the martial arts program for the kids showed that. She just needed more time to figure out how she felt about him.

Friday afternoon, A.J. sat in his office thinking about Cara. He'd seen her twice at the gym, but they'd talked only briefly each time. He had a feeling she was trying to slow things down. He could accept that. She could take all the time she needed. Now that she'd finally stopped running from him, he could afford to be patient. He'd come on too strong in the beginning, and now he didn't want to scare her off.

Things were still hectic at the office. Everyone had a full workload, but that wasn't an excuse for the technicians to get sloppy. Three more systems had crashed over the past few weeks. He'd had a serious discussion with each technician, and they all swore they weren't slacking off. But no one could explain what was bringing the systems down, and Capital couldn't afford to have these kinds of problems now. Ross, Locke & Malloy would be watching them closely.

He worked damned hard to maintain Capital's reputation, and he wasn't about to blow it now. He'd checked into each incident carefully and individually. They were unremarkable. A petty virus here, a faulty circuit there. Each problem apparently random and unrelated. But together they spelled trouble. Either someone was lazy, or . . .

Before he could complete that thought, the telephone rang. "This is Gray."

"A.J. It's Mitch. I just got back to D.C. this afternoon."

"Hi, Mitch. How did it go in New York?"

"Great. Got a chance to catch a play on Broadway. Anyway, I wanted to let you know about your friend's proposal."

He leaned on the corner of his desk. "What's the word?"

"Well, it's a saleable product . . . but I think I may have to pass on this one."

A.J. picked up a pen and began to twirl it. "Pass? Why? I thought DataVision was trying to broaden its market?"

"We are, but we're focusing on bigger, long-term projects. Cara's fitness CD-ROM isn't in our league. We'd end up sinking more money into it than we'd get out of it."

A.J. frowned, jamming his pen like a dive-bomber into the blotter on his desk. "I see. Cara understood there were no guarantees. But thanks anyway, Mitch." Damn!

He hadn't expected to feel so disappointed. And he hated to disappoint Cara.

"I'm sorry, A.J."

He bounced the pen on its point. "That's okay, you don't—"

"Unless . . ."

A.J. stilled the pen. "Unless, what?"

"Well, I was just thinking. DataVision wouldn't be able to do the data gathering and a lot of the initial preparation for the CD-ROM. But packaging and distribution would be no problem. If someone else took care of those steps, we could give it our brand name and market it."

"Somebody else like who?"

"Capital. You could help Cara gather and prepare the data."

A.J. blinked in surprise. "Capital?" He sucked in his breath, frowning at the phone. "I don't think we can do it. We're tied up until the first Malloy project wraps in December. But you might be on to something. I could give Cara some names. I'm sure Data Pros or The PCS Group could do it. Maybe even Fargo Systems. Not that I like sending business to the competition." A.J. had gotten so carried away, it took him a minute to realize that Mitch was trying to get his attention.

"A.J. . . . A.J.!"

"Yeah?"

"We're getting a little complicated here. We'd take this on as a favor to you, but I'm really not interested in getting involved with other companies. It was just a thought. If Capital can't handle it, maybe we should shelve the idea."

"Damn! I don't know. We've got too much on our plate already. Even if I could spare the manpower, I don't know when we'd find the time." There was no way they could do it. The Malloy systems. Cara. God, he hated the thought of telling her the project died because of him.

"Well, I just thought I'd throw the idea out to you. I'm

sorry, man, that's the best deal I can offer. But if you can't do it, maybe farther down the ro—"

"Wait," A.J. broke in. *There had to be a way to make this work.* "Maybe we can work something out."

"Yeah? What do you have in mind?"

"I don't know. Let me think a minute."

There was no way. They couldn't do it.

Cara was counting on him.

They didn't have enough manpower.

He could handle the extra load himself.

They couldn't spare the time.

He could come in an hour or two early every morning.

He spent too much time at the office already.

He couldn't let Cara down.

"Look, A.J.—"

"We'll do it. If we shift things a bit, Capital can handle the project."

There was a long silence on the other end. "Are you sure? Maybe you want to think about it for a while."

"I'm sure."

"Well . . . Cara must be *some* lady."

"Yeah, she is."

Cara hung up the phone. They were going to do it! Her health-fitness CD-ROM was going into production! DataVision wouldn't merely pay her for her ideas, she was going to work on the project from start to finish. She was getting everything she'd wanted. She had her job, she was getting back into computers, and she had . . . A.J.?

Cara thought back to the telephone conversation she and A.J. had just had. She'd been so excited when he'd told her the deal was going to go through, her mind had raced ahead a mile a minute. What had he said? Something about working with Capital directly. She couldn't remember the details, but DataVision wasn't going to get involved until the final stages of the project. That meant she'd be working with A.J. throughout the process.

So much for her hope that Capital would only play a small role in the business arrangement. And hadn't A.J. said he'd be handling her account personally? They'd be working . . . together. A fog fell over Cara's brain. How was she going to make both relationships work?

She needed to clear her head. Cara looked at the clock. She had an hour and a half before she had to be at the club. Maybe if she went for a walk—

The doorbell rang. When Cara answered it, Ronnie nearly knocked her down as she rushed past her into the apartment. Laughing, Cara shut the door and turned to face her friend. "Ronnie, what's your—"

Cara stopped short. Tears were running down Ronnie's face and she clutched a magazine in her hands.

"You'll never believe this! I still can't believe it! He said he loved me. How could he do this to me, Cara?" Then Ronnie sank to her knees as a violent wave of sobs wracked her body.

Cara immediately helped Ronnie onto the sofa. Ronnie wasn't the teary-eyed type. Whatever bothered her had to be serious. When her friend had calmed a bit, Cara said, "Tell me what happened."

Still sniffling, Ronnie held out the magazine that was crumpled between her fingers. "Page fifty-seven," Ronnie said in a dull voice.

After careful prying, Cara freed the magazine from Ronnie's grip. She found the correct page, "It's a review!" She scanned down the page. "I didn't know Andre was reviewing for *The Washingtonian* now." Cara looked warily at Ronnie.

"Halfway down on the second page—read it."

Cara did as she was told, then gasped. "That sonofa—"

"I'm ruined. He ruined my career," Ronnie said in a deadpan voice as she stared into space.

Cara couldn't believe her eyes. She'd never liked Andre, but she'd had no idea he was capable of such underhandedness. Andre was a food critic for a small local paper and occasionally reviewed Ronnie's restaurant. Apparently he'd moved up the ladder to review for *The Washingtonian* magazine and for his debut column he'd chosen to give a scathing assessment of Embassy Plaza dining—and one of Ronnie's signature dishes in particular.

Cara shook her head and stared at Ronnie's bleak expression. "Why would he do something like this?"

"That's what I wanted to know. So after I saw this, I went to his apartment." Ronnie focused her red-rimmed eyes on Cara. "He was moving some hoochie into the apartment, but he was *kind* enough to take five minutes to give me an explanation. He said he knew it would be hard for me to accept that he was moving on with his life—with someone else. So he thought if I hated him, it would be easier for me to get over him. He said he knew I wouldn't want anything more to do with him after this." Her tone became self-derisive. "He was right about that!"

Cara's jaw dropped. "He tried to sabotage your career, your reputation as a chef, just so you would get over him easier! That's a crock of—"

"He said he wasn't trying to hurt my career. He had the nerve to tell me that it would blow over, that every chef gets a bad review eventually, and no one would hold it against me!" Ronnie's voice turned cold. "Six years! I wasted six years with him. If he didn't love me anymore, he could have just said so. He didn't have to go after my job! Of course, people will hold it against me! It was in the damn *Washingtonian!* I'll be lucky if the Plaza doesn't fire me when I go in to work tonight!"

"Oh, Ronnie!" Cara pulled her friend into her arms and hugged her while she cried. They spent the rest of the afternoon talking, and Cara was almost late for work. She felt Ronnie's pain. Cara knew that kind of pain. The kind of pain that came when someone you loved hurt you, and you knew you could have prevented it. She only prayed that Ronnie would get Andre out of her life for good this time. She'd thought the things that man had put Ronnie through over the years were awful, but interfering with her livelihood was lower than anything he'd done before. Now, Ronnie not only had to cope with a broken relationship, she had to work damage control on her professional reputation as well. How could one man wreak so much havoc on a woman's life?

By the time Cara got to work, the realization slowly came over her. Just like Ronnie had given Andre the power to hurt her career, A.J. held Cara's future in computers in the palm of his hand. Business and romance were a dangerous mix.

Angelique glanced at her watch. She had fifteen minutes left on her lunch break. Brad should have called by now. She sank into the bucket seat of her Jaguar and crossed her arms. This had better be important because she felt like an idiot sitting around in her car waiting for him to call.

Five minutes later, she heard the high-pitched trill of her cellular phone. Angelique snatched up the receiver. "Finally, damn it! I've been waiting for nearly an hour!"

"Testy, aren't you? I know you've missed me. Don't worry, sweetheart. We'll get together real soon." His voice was warm with sensual promise, but she knew manipulating people was the only thing that truly turned him on.

And the only thing Angelique "missed" about Brad was the jewelry he left on her pillow after they'd been together. Nevertheless, they played their roles. "I've been a good girl, Brad. I think it's time for a bonus. I saw a jade brooch at Saks this afternoon," she said, admiring her lipstick in the rearview mirror.

"I'm not so sure. It seems to me that you've been amusing yourself instead of attending to the matter at hand."

The fool. He didn't know how to work the game like she did. "Bradley," she purred. "It would be too obvious if I went straight for the Malloy systems. I've already told you, this way the problems seem to be random. They won't be able to link it to us when the contract reverts to RSI."

"How do I know you're not stalling? It's time to go in for the kill. I don't think I can . . . reward you, until I see the kind of results we agreed on."

"Give me some incentive, Brad. I don't work for free." She licked her lips.

"Don't play games with me, Angelique. If you can't deliver, and I mean immediately, I'll cut you off and find someone who can." His voice returned to his smooth sensual tone. "But just to prove that I'm a nice guy, meet me tonight, and I'll give you all the incentive you need."

Angelique gritted her teeth as she softened her voice. "Whatever you—"

"Good." The line went dead.

When A.J. got out of his car that night, he looked at his watch. Twenty after ten. Maybe he could catch her. He ran up to the building and yanked on the doors. Locked. Peeking through the glass he saw a few Tower Vista employees walking around inside. Maybe she was still there. He turned and scanned the parking lot, wishing he knew what her car looked like. He waited under a streetlight to see if she would come out. Sure enough, five minutes later, Cara came out of the building. He waved, then started walking toward her.

"Oh, hi, A.J.," she said when he got close enough for her to recognize him.

He smiled at her. She looked beautiful as always. "Hi Cara," he said softly, then leaned forward to kiss her hello.

Cara ducked her head and began searching through her purse, talking quickly. "I'm glad you dropped by. We need to talk about a few things."

A.J. grinned at the top of her head. He must make her nervous. He'd take things slow. "Yes, we have a lot to talk about. I had a meeting this evening, so I couldn't make it for my workout. I decided to drop by on my way home to see if you wanted to go for a cup of coffee." He decided not to tell her that he'd worked all evening at the office to make room in his schedule for her project. He couldn't wait to tell her he'd set up a meeting for her Monday morning with Mitch.

"That sounds fine. There's a little cafe down the street." Cara pulled her keys from her purse and swung them on her finger as if she'd unearthed a buried treasure. "Finally! I found them!" Her eagerness sounded forced.

"Do you want to drive or should I?"

"Um, why don't we take two cars. There's no need for you to come all the way back here afterward."

"Oh, it's no problem, I could just—"

"No, really. I think this way is easier." Cara was already walking toward her car. "You can follow me," she called over her shoulder.

He had no choice. Ten minutes later, they were seated in a booth at Michael's Cafe. They'd ordered two Cappuccinos, but Cara asked to keep her menu. She continued to study it intently.

A.J. felt a surge of tenderness toward her. She was *really* nervous. A smile crept to his lips. He understood. Their relationship was still too new. She needed more time to get used to it. He studied her lovely features. Holding back would be difficult, but she'd be worth the wait.

He grinned, watching her twist the end of her braid around her finger. What could he do to ease her tension? Resting his chin on his hand he said, "Do you know you play with your hair when you're nervous?"

Cara started, looked at her hand, and then giggled. "Yeah, I know. It drives Ronnie up the wall. She hates my braid in the first place. For as long as I've known her, she's been trying to get me to try a new hair style . . ."

A.J. lost track of the conversation as she continued to ramble. "Cara . . . Cara?" A.J. interrupted. "Why don't you tell me why you're so anxious?"

Cara's words halted, and she stared at him blankly.

Maybe he'd better get the less personal stuff out of the way first. "If it's about the project, don't worry. DataVision is very interested." He tried to reassure her. "I've taken care of everything. Monday morning we have a meeting with Mitch. We'll go over—what's wrong?" he asked when he saw her expression.

She was frowning at him and sitting arrow-straight in her seat. "Monday morning?"

He nodded.

"Is the meeting already set up?"

He cocked his head. "Yeah."

"Why didn't you consult with me before you set up this meeting? How could you be sure that I was free?"

"I'm sorry. You work afternoons so I just thought—"

"I hope you don't plan to make this a habit," she said sternly. "If we're going to work together, I expect you to treat me with respect. That means consulting with me *before* you arrange any business meetings."

"I apologize, Cara. I didn't mean to upset you." So much for nervousness. She definitely wasn't feeling shy now.

"Yes, well that's what we need to talk about—how our business relationship will work from now on. Now that I've officially hired Capital, I expect to be treated just like any other client. I want to be included in any major decisions. I also expect you to treat me as an equal and respect my creative input. I'm no novice to computers, so I hope you don't expect to take over this entire project. Remember, it was my idea."

A.J. sighed deeply. "Cara, that's not a problem, but I need to—"

"Wait, I haven't told you the most important ground rule."

There she goes again with the braid! After what he'd just heard, A.J. wasn't sure he could handle any more rules.

"Um, this is hard, so I'm just going to say it." She took a breath. "I only want a business relationship with you. There can't be anything personal between us anymore."

He was right. She'd said the last thing he wanted to hear. "What's going on? I thought we'd agree to take things slow. Look, if you're worried about me rushing you—"

"No, that's not it. I just think—no, I know this is for the best. I need to focus on my career goals right now, and I can't let anything jeopardize that. Trying to balance two relationships will just complicate things. One of us will regret it in the end."

"Cara! I thought we'd been through this already. Don't back out on me just because you're a little scared. We're good together. You know that."

"Please don't try to pressure me. I've had enough of that from you."

A.J. laid his head in his hands. How had he gotten back to square one so quickly? "Okay. Fine. Let's go." He stood.

"You didn't touch your Cappuccino."

"I don't want it." He threw enough money on the table to cover both drinks and tried not to flinch when Cara placed her own money beside it then handed him change. Silently, he took the money and walked her to her car.

"If you find you have a problem with the meeting, call my secretary. Otherwise I'll see you at ten Monday morning. My office."

She nodded, and then he watched as she got into her

car and drove off. Once she was gone, he walked to his car, staring as if he didn't recognize it.

"Damn!" He smacked the flat of his palm against the car window. Then, after taking a few deep breaths, he silently got into his car.

A.J. rested his head on his steering wheel. What had he gotten himself into?

Chapter Eight

He's jealous, Cara thought looking across the table at A.J. Throughout the morning's business meeting, Mitchell Crofton had lavished attention on Cara, and A.J. was *not* pleased. Then Crofton had announced he was treating them to lunch at the Red Sage.

Feeling uncomfortable, Cara rubbed the back of her neck, remembering too late that her braid wasn't there. She'd let Ronnie talk her into a more "corporate" hairstyle. Soft curls were piled atop her head and accented with a light fringe of bangs and two long curling tendrils on either side of her head. The effect was both sophisticated and feminine. To accompany the hairstyle, Cara wore her red "power" suit. She always wore her favorite color when she needed an extra dose of confidence.

Today she'd needed plenty of confidence to face A.J. Delivering the strictly business policy had been more difficult than she'd expected. She hadn't anticipated the genuine look of rejection on his face. And she hadn't counted on feeling so guilty for causing it. She'd worried all weekend about this meeting, fearing that A.J. would hold a grudge and make things difficult for her. But she'd worried over nothing. A.J. had handled himself with cool professionalism all morning, apart from the jealousy.

Crofton directed a brilliant smile at her, draping an arm across the back of her chair. "How was your pasta, Cara?"

"It was delicious. Thank you, Mr. Crofton."

"For the last time, call me Mitch." The gleam in his eyes bordered on flirtatious. "Your respect for formality shows that you're a true lady, but we're all friends here."

Cara's cheeks warmed. Mitchell Crofton, somewhere in his early fifties, was still an attractive man. Now Cara understood why he and A.J. got along so well. They were both shameless charmers. Crofton had catered to her every comfort, solicitous and complimentary of her opinions. It was difficult not to like the older man, and she knew she would enjoy working with him.

A.J., on the other hand, was sulking. He only spoke to her when she addressed him directly, and she hadn't seen his crooked grin all morning. She couldn't complain. It wasn't fair to ask him to keep their relationship on a business level, then become upset when he wasn't as friendly as usual. She wished things could be different, but, after seeing what had happened to Ronnie, things could be no other way. They would *both* have to accept that.

After lunch, Crofton offered to have his driver take them back to Capital, but A.J. politely declined, saying that since Capital was only two blocks from the restaurant, he would walk. Without thinking twice, Cara offered to go with him.

"Why don't you stay and wait for Mitch's driver?" A.J. eyed her high heels. "There's no need for you to walk."

"Don't be silly. I'm not going to sit here and wait when I can walk back with you and be on my way home by the time the driver would get here. Besides, these shoes are very comfortable, and it's a nice day. I think I'd enjoy the walk."

"Suit yourself."

"Thank you. I will. Do you mind waiting a minute while I go to the ladies room?"

"I'll meet you outside."

Five minutes later, Cara joined him outside and A.J. headed for the crosswalk. He was disappointed that she'd decided to walk back with him. He needed some time alone. Being in her presence all morning, knowing there would be nothing more than business between them, had been torture. Mitch's flirtations hadn't helped either.

"Hey slow down!" Cara did a little skip to catch up.

"Oh! Sorry," he said, slowing his pace.

"I think the meeting went well, don't you?"

She really looked delicious with her hair up like that. Soft, sexy . . . and so aloof. "What?"

"The meeting with Crofton. It went well. I think he was open to my ideas."

"Yeah, I guess."

They lapsed into a long stretch of silence as they began walking toward A.J.'s building. He was still brooding over the meeting when he heard someone call his name.

"Hi, Thomas," A.J. called when he saw the bum leaning against a street light, holding a styrofoam cup. He walked up to the old man.

"How's it going, A.J.?" The man held out a dirty hand.

A.J. shook it. "Just fine, Thomas. I heard a storm is coming. Take care okay?" He pulled a bill and two slips of paper out of his pocket and dropped them into the cup.

He took a couple of quick steps to catch up to Cara. When he reached her, he kept walking, expecting her to fall into step next to him.

Instead she grabbed his arm. "Hey. You and that homeless man are pretty friendly."

He kept walking. "Yeah? Well, I pass him every day."

"So what did you put in the cup? I recognized the money, but what was on the paper?"

"Nothing special." He said, hoping she'd let the subject drop.

She stepped in front of him, halting his stride. "Come on, tell me."

He let out a long sigh. "It was just a coupon." He started to walk around her.

She stepped in front of him again. "*Coupon?* A coupon for what?"

A.J. felt heat creeping up his neck. What was the big deal? "Look, the man who owns the convenience store down the street is a friend of mine. He lets me buy coupons that are good for a cup of coffee or a sandwich or something. I carry them to give to people like Thomas. Okay? Are you satisfied?"

She moved out of his way and fell into step beside him with a puzzled look on her face. "Yeah. That's really nice. Most people who live in D.C. walk by the homeless like they're a part of the landscape."

"Yeah," A.J. muttered halfheartedly. He wanted to change the subject. He decided to bring up the topic that had been on his mind all morning. "You know, Cara, I noticed that Mitch was flirting with you a lot today. He doesn't mean anything by it. He's always been a lady's man, but if it makes you uncomfortable, I'll talk to him for you."

Cara seemed distracted. "No, he doesn't bother me. He's a nice man. I like him."

A.J. scowled and fell silent.

"What's wrong?"

"Nothing." He didn't feel like arguing.

"Come on, I know something's bothering you. What did I say?"

"You mean what did you say *today?*" he said bitterly.

"A.J., please don't play games with me. We're going to be working together. Tell me what's on your mind."

Once again, she insisted on forcing the issue. Well, she asked for it. This time he stepped in front of her, forcing her to stop walking. "Do you really want to know what's bothering me? I want to know why one week you agree to date me, and the next you make me feel like the scum on the bottom of your shoes?"

"That's not true—"

He continued as if she hadn't spoken. "You tell me things have to be strictly business. Okay, I have to accept that, but today Mitch starts drooling all over you and suddenly that's fine!"

Cara looked anxiously around at the people who were giving them odd looks as they passed. She tried to pull him along. "A.J., let's go."

He stopped her. "No. You insisted on pursuing this, and I want an answer."

Cara shifted her weight from foot to foot. "Um . . . what was the question?"

"Why is it okay for Mitch to flirt with you, but you can't stand anything remotely personal from me?"

She didn't answer.

"Come on."

"Um . . . I don't know." She averted her eyes.

"Yes, you do," he pressed.

She was beginning to squirm. "Crofton's flirting doesn't bother me like yours does."

"I know that. Why?" he asked impatiently.

"Because I'm not attracted to him like I am to you, that's why," Cara shouted, placing her hands on her hips.

A.J. blinked at her. He hadn't expected her to admit it.

Then it seemed to dawn on her exactly what she'd said. "I mean . . . it's different. I mean—"

He held up his hand, unable to control the smug smile he felt curving his lips. "It's too late! You can't take it back. That's all I needed to hear." He turned to walk the rest of the way to the building, leaving Cara to trail after him.

Parker flipped open his laptop. Another partner meeting. Ever since they'd landed the Malloy account, they'd had twice as much paperwork to sift through. He didn't care much about that stuff, but at least he'd have some new programs to work on. He began to pound on his keyboard, half listening as Gray and Whittaker went over the agenda.

A few minutes later, he stopped. They were at it again. Most of the time they went through the motions of trying to make him feel included, but at moments like this, he was invisible. He didn't care. He preferred to stay in the background anyway.

Reluctantly, Parker looked up from the screen. Whittaker was on Gray's case again. It sounded like the same old crap, so he refocused on the monitor. He tried to concentrate, but bits of the conversation kept filtering in.

Whittaker was raising his voice. ". . . on the line for some woman you want to impress!"

Gray's jaw tightened. He was angry. Parker decided he'd better pay attention.

"Whittaker, this has nothing to do with impressing a woman. Cara Williams is our client, nothing more."

Whittaker straightened, looking smug. "We agreed not to take on any more clients until the first division of the Malloy project was complete. Staff is tight as it is. We don't have time for a paltry little job like this."

"It's a simple data preparation project for DataVision. They're going to handle marketing and distribution. I'm not asking anyone else to work extra hours. I can fit it into my schedule. Now let's get back to the *real* issue. When I met with Stanton—"

"I think this *is* the real issue. We have everything riding on Malloy, and you're taking on nickel and dime jobs we don't need. Besides, if you hadn't agreed to that conditional contract, we wouldn't have to worry—"

"If I hadn't agreed to that contract, we wouldn't have the job at all, and you know it."

"Gray, the risks you're taking with this company are going to get us into hot water. When I was running Continental Solutions . . ."

Parker tuned out. The old man always brought it back to that. Whittaker thought Gray was a reckless risk-taker, and he never missed an opportunity to tell him so. He was right about one thing. Gray was aggressive. He *did* take a lot of risks, but they always seemed to work out for him. He was like a cat who always landed on his feet. Everything Gray touched turned to gold. Parker could see why the old man would resent that. Whittaker was just waiting for Gray to slip up so he could jump in and save the day. Prove that his "time-honored traditions" were better than Gray's "newfangled" business tactics.

Parker's attention returned to the two opponents. They'd finally calmed down and moved on to the next item on the agenda. Another system went down.

Another system went down!

Parker straightened. "Why didn't someone tell me the Radburn Electronics system cra-ashed?" Parker swallowed hard. Damn it! Why did his voice always have to crack when he got angry?

Whittaker waved him off. "Oh, Parker, I'm sure we told you. You probably forgot."

Gray met his eyes. "Parker, Radburn went down late Sunday night. The service call happened to come in while I was still here, so I went ahead and took care of it."

"But I'm in charge of tech support. Why wasn't *I* called?"

"Well, Parker—" Gray started.

Whittaker cut in. "What difference does it make, Parker?

You know now. What I want to know is what do you have those fools in tech support doing? This is the fifth system to crash in two months. We've got a reputation to uphold . . ."

Parker felt his anger draining away as Whittaker droned on. It wasn't such a big deal that Gray took care of the call. But the only way he was going to get Whittaker off his case was if he figured out what was bringing these systems down once and for all.

This was his chance to prove himself.

"What could you *possibly* be thinking?" Cara entered A.J.'s office, announcing her presence by slamming the door.

A.J. pointed at the telephone receiver and motioned for her to be quiet. "I'm sorry, John, go ahead."

He tried not to let her distract him as she cleared off a corner of his desk and perched on the edge, facing him. He tried to continue the conversation, but Cara hummed, tapped her fingers, and swung her legs until he finally ended the call.

"I'm sorry, John. I'm going to have to call you back. An unexpected *problem* has come up." He looked pointedly at Cara as he hung up the phone. "Didn't Leslie tell you I was on the phone?"

"She was away from her desk, so I came in."

He frowned. "Well, what can I do for you?"

"You can treat me with respect, first of all." She got off his desk and stood.

"What are you talking about?"

"I'm talking about the message your secretary left on my answering machine. You expect us to work on the CD-ROM after I get home at night? At ten-o'clock?"

"Well, I figured we could—"

Cara placed her hands on her hips. "I sincerely doubt

you meet with any of your other clients at that hour, now do you?"

"No, but—"

"Exactly, but you expect to meet with *me* after hours? Why? Did you think during non-business hours you could coax me into some non-business-like behavior?"

A.J. resisted the urge to roll his eyes. He needed business hours to work on the Malloy project. He'd hoped they could work on her project a few hours after work, and weekends. "Not at all—"

"Good, because unless we can arrange to meet during more suitable hours, I may have to talk to DataVision about using another consulting firm," Cara said haughtily, crossing her arms over her chest.

A.J. massaged his temples. She was giving him a headache. "How do you feel about meeting first thing in the morning—eight?"

"That's more like it. I hope we don't have to have any more discussions like this one."

And before he could say another word, she was gone. But unfortunately, he felt that was just the beginning of his problems with Cara.

Cara leaned back at A.J.'s conference table and surveyed the layout for the CD-ROM. A.J. had been pacing the floor behind her, leaving most of the decisions up to her, occasionally offering suggestions. She felt him stop to look over her shoulder.

"The warning about consulting a physician would fit in well with the weight-loss section over here."

She looked back at him, grinning. "Great, and I was thinking about something else, too." For an instant she held her breath. He was closer than she'd realized, and she could smell his cologne. She had to focus hard not to lose her train of thought. "The . . . weight-loss information would have more impact if we included statistics on the success rate of the plans and—"

A.J. sat next to her and shook his head. "I don't think we can do that."

Cara instantly became indignant. He'd vetoed her last idea, too, suggesting that including a calorie conversion chart might place too much emphasis on weight-loss rather than overall fitness. She wasn't going to let him shoot her down twice.

"Why not? This is important information. And don't try to tell me it's unnecessary because I *know*—"

"I didn't say it was unnecessary—"

"Great! Then we'll include statistics," she said, hoping that if she stood firm, the issue would be settled.

"We can *not* include statistics. By the time the software is released, that information would probably be outdated. We should only use information that will be useful for a few years."

Cara clenched her jaw. She knew he was right . . . and that really ticked her off. For some reason she wasn't ready to give up on the idea yet. "All software needs to be upgraded. We'll just send out upgrades with current statistics."

"That's not practical, Cara. As soon as the software hit the stores, upgrades would have to be shipped. You'd never make any money."

She cut her eyes at him. She knew she was being childish, but she couldn't help it. A.J. knew his business well. She'd just wanted to impress him with how well she knew *her* business.

"There is no need to treat me like a five-year-old. It was just a suggestion." She flipped her braid over her shoulder. "Statistics would have made the product stronger, but since money is more important to you than quality . . ."

She saw him gaze heavenward and take a deep breath. "How about this? Why don't you include a reference list of phone numbers where up-to-date statistics can be obtained? That way, if people are really interested, the information is there."

Cara smiled. She'd held her ground and forced him to see things her way. "That'll work. Now, when are we going to look at the video clips?"

A.J. tried to focus on the screen in front of him, but his vision began to blur. He looked at his watch. It was 7:30 A.M. His employees would be in soon, and he'd been in the office all night. Working through the night, then catching a few winks on the sofa before starting all over had become routine since he'd been working with Cara for the last three weeks.

Squeezing her into his schedule had been more difficult than he'd planned. He needed those precious night hours to catch up on the Malloy account since he spent most mornings working with Cara.

A.J. shook his head and closed his bleary eyes. He didn't know why he kept giving in to her. The more he tried to help her, the more difficult she became.

He leaned forward and rested his head on his desk. It was time to face it. He was a fool for love. The constant pain in his chest every time he thought about Cara *was* love, wasn't it? He thought so . . . but he'd never been in love before.

In the past, there hadn't been time. Women had been an accessory. A.J. had spent too much time reaching for success to let them get too close. Now, suddenly, he was ready for a house and a family. He was ready for a woman like Cara. But was Cara ready for him?

After he'd gotten her to admit she was still interested in him after lunch with Crofton, he'd hoped she'd eventually come to her senses. It had been three weeks. Torture for him, but she didn't seem dissatisfied with their relationship in the least. He was starting to believe she'd never change her mind about him.

Where did that leave him? With a giant workload and a never-ending state of arousal that had no hope of relief.

The cool desk felt good against his forehead. Maybe if he just dozed for a minute. Just as he felt himself drifting off, he heard his office door swing open and then slam loudly. Wearily, he lifted his head.

Cara leaned over him. "Sleeping? Don't you have a bed for that?"

He groaned. "It was a long night. I was just resting."

She studied his face. "Long night painting the town red?"

"I wish," he muttered, then began shuffling papers on his desk. "I wasn't expecting you today. Did we schedule a meeting?"

Cara ignored his question. "You look terrible. Your eyes are all red. Didn't you get any sleep last night?"

A.J. ignored Cara's question. "Did you come to get started on the midi clips? I listened to the music samples you picked out. I think they'll work out well. Now we need to—"

"Answer me, A.J.! You look like hell." She scanned the office. "Where did you sleep last night?"

"Isn't that a little personal?"

She glared at him.

"Okay, I was working late last night, so I stayed here. It's no big deal."

Cara propped herself on the edge of his desk and leaned forward. "You should take better care of yourself. You're president of this company. Why don't you give yourself some time off?"

A.J. snorted. "Yeah, right! Why didn't I think of that? I'll just take some time off. And while I'm gone the company will just run itself, right?"

"Boy, aren't you cranky. That's what you have partners

for. Can't the two of them fill in for you while you rest for a few days?"

"No! This is my responsibility," he snapped. "I think I know a little bit more about running this company than you do, okay? Now why don't you tell me what you're doing here?"

"Sorry! I wasn't trying to tell you how to run your company. It was just a friendly suggestion. It's not my problem if you want to work yourself to death."

"Cara!" A.J. had lost his patience.

"Okay. I've been thinking. I know you said I didn't need to sign the DataVision contracts until we got to that phase of the project, but since I've already signed the agreement with Capital, I figured it would make sense to get all the paperwork out of the way all at once. So I just thought I'd drop by and pick them up."

A.J. stifled the urge to curse out loud. He wasn't up for this. "You could have called. I need to have the other partners sign them first. I'll have my secretary mail them to you when they're ready."

"Or you can call me, and I'll come pick them up."

A.J. closed his eyes. His head was pounding. "Whatever."

"Okay then, that's all. Don't let me keep you from your nap."

Her sarcasm made him wince.

Once she'd left, A.J. sank into the interior of his leather chair. There was no chance things would improve between them. As matter of fact, she was becoming harder to work with by the day. She challenged any advice and every suggestion he offered. Even when she knew he was right! It was almost like she was constantly reminding him who was in charge.

A.J. groaned. Of course she wanted to remind him she was in charge. She'd said as much herself. She would never let another man control her. Obviously she feared he'd try to take over her project. Maybe even push her to the background and try to take all the credit.

If Cara knew what was in his heart, she'd never believe that was possible. His feelings were strong and too real to deny. They hadn't developed slowly or gently, creeping into his awareness subtly. His feelings had burst from his heart and clubbed him over the head, making his head reel from the force of the blow.

He should have been happy. He wanted to enjoy the freedom of finding the person he wanted to spend his life with. But first he had to hack through Cara's fears.

A.J. rested his head in his hands. One thing was clear. He had to prove to her that he wasn't interested in controlling her. And he couldn't tell Cara he loved her until he had.

Chapter Nine

Angelique twisted in the bucket seat, watching the parking garage for passersby.

"I have no choice. Only the partners have access to that account."

"And why is that?" Brad said in a goading tone.

Angelique made an obscene gesture at the phone. "I already told you—"

"Because," he interrupted, "they've tightened security as a result of those useless computer pranks you've been playing." His voice became harsher. "You're wasting my time. You insisted on doing this your way, and now you're going to pay for it."

Angelique rolled her eyes and sweetened her tone. "Bradley—"

"Each week Capital moves closer to completing this project without mishap, the price goes down."

"Brad! you can't—" Angelique caught her reflection in the rearview mirror. She cursed the fear she saw in her eyes.

"You've got two weeks to get results. After that, I knock off ten thousand dollars. And another ten each week after."

Angelique licked her lips and then swallowed. She had to play this from another angle.

"That won't be necessary. I know more than one way to break down a system. You know that. I'll have something for you by the end of the week, I promise."

"Don't bother promising—just deliver." The line went dead.

She slammed down the phone. That pompous, ivy-league jerk. She sat and cursed him for a few more minutes, then got out of the car and slammed the door. Bringing down the Malloy system was harder than she'd expected, but she wasn't about to lose so much as a penny.

Cara leaned back on the sofa in A.J.'s office. "I'm hungry."

A.J. looked over at her from where he worked at his desk. "Do you want to order something? There's a Chinese restaurant down the street that delivers."

She held her stomach and groaned. "That sounds wonderful. I didn't get a chance to have breakfast this morning."

A.J. dug through his desk, then tossed Cara a menu for the Chinese restaurant. It was Saturday and they'd been working for hours without a break.

Cara frowned as she scanned the menu. A.J.'s attitude had changed lately. When they'd first started working together, he was laid back and lively. He would crack jokes and take breaks just to challenge her to a rematch at whatever computer game she'd last beat him at. But this morning when she came in to work, he'd gotten down to business immediately. No jokes. No breaks. As soon as they settled one issue, he moved right on to the next without taking a breath. It was almost as if he were trying to rush her along.

Cara pulled on the end of her braid. She had no right to complain. He was just doing what she'd said she wanted, keeping their relationship *strictly* business. But he was working too hard. She remembered finding him asleep at his desk earlier that week.

He needed to relax, and there wasn't any reason why they shouldn't at least be friendly. If she lightened the atmosphere, maybe he'd loosen up again.

They continued to work until the delivery man brought their order. Then when A.J. tried to take his food back to his desk, Cara patted a spot beside her on the couch.

"Why don't you eat over here? There's more room, and you won't get your desk all messy."

"I eat at my desk all the time. It's no big deal."

"Oh, I see. You just don't want me stealing any of your Kung Pao Shrimp."

He hesitated for a moment, and then joined her on the couch.

They cleared her paperwork away and spread the food out on the table. For several minutes they ate in silence. Cara felt him looking at her as she pushed her pepper-steak and rice around on her plate.

He held out his carton. "Do you want to try some of this?"

"No. I was just kidding about stealing your shrimp."

He nodded, then dug into his food. Less than a minute later he stopped. "Look, Cara, I owe you an apology."

She sat up and faced him. "For what?"

"I snapped at you the last time we talked. You know, when you mentioned me needing some time off?"

Cara turned back to her food. "Oh, that. No problem. Obviously, I'd caught you at a bad time."

"Yeah, that was part of it, but I didn't mean to bite your head off."

She peered over her shoulder at him and bit her lip. "Well since you brought it up, what's the big deal about delegating some of your responsibility to your partners? They can't possibly be working as hard as you are."

He gave her an incredulous look. "Why do you say that?"

"Because I don't think you'd let them."

"We all carry our own weight. I only—"

"Wait. I'm not finished. Don't forget I've been hanging around this place for a few weeks. I've seen how you do things. You act like you're responsible for every little problem that comes up."

"I *am*. I—"

"What? You run this company by yourself? Aren't your partners responsible, too?"

"They—"

"Do you remember what happened when we had that meeting with the Alpha group, and you were clearing your schedule with Leslie? She got that call from a client who needed some papers faxed immediately."

"Yeah. I faxed them. So what?"

"That's the point. Leslie is your secretary. That's what she's for, but instead you insisted on faxing the papers yourself. Not many company presidents would bother."

"He was an important client, and Leslie had to copy spreadsheets. I just wanted to make sure—"

"What about that time one of the guys got sick, and Chavez needed a hand manning the phones in tech support? You skipped lunch so you could finish up with me and help him, too."

"Well what was I supposed to do? Leave him hanging?"

"Why didn't you call Parker? Isn't he in charge of technical support?"

"Yes, but I was here, so—"

"Well then what about—"

A.J. held up his hand. "Stop! I know what you're getting

at. But Cara, I'm not some control freak who needs to run things all the time. I just don't want to let anyone down.''

"I'm not saying you are. I've had my share of experience with control freaks, and believe me, you're not one." As soon as the words were out of her mouth, Cara realized what she'd said. A.J. *wasn't* controlling. Somewhere along the line she'd made up her mind about him, and she hadn't even realized it. She didn't have time to mull that thought over because A.J. was still talking.

". . . few more things Parker and Whittaker could handle, but I'm not sure if I can get used to the idea of delegating responsibility. It's hard to think about asking someone else to do something that I'm perfectly able to do myself."

"What good will you be to the company if you wear yourself out trying to take care of everything?"

He was quiet for a few minutes. "Yeah, that's something to think about."

"Good," Cara said, feeling satisfied. Then she began to eye the remains of A.J.'s Kung Pao Shrimp. "Um, I changed my mind. May I?"

He tilted the carton toward her. "Help yourself."

By the time the last of the food was gone, Cara was comfortably sprawled on the floor in front of the coffee table, patting her stomach. "Mmm. I'm full."

Beside her, A.J. pulled open a package. "Not too full for fortune cookies, I hope."

Cara perked up. "Never. Fortune cookies are the best part of Chinese food."

He gave her a cookie, but when she started to break it open, he stopped her. "Wait. When you read your fortune, you have to add the words 'in bed' to the end."

"You're kidding. I'm *not* doing that," she said, shaking her head.

"Come on. Don't be such a prude." He gave her a sharp look. "It's just for fun."

Cara sighed as she broke the cookie. "Okay. Here goes: New adventures are on their way," she raised her eyes to A.J.'s, and he nodded for her to continue, *"in bed."*

A.J. arched his brows wickedly, and Cara's cheeks heated. She giggled. "Okay. Okay. Let's hear yours."

He unwrapped his fortune cookie, and then looked over at her. "You don't want to hear this."

"Yes, I do. Come on, this is *your* game."

He grinned. "All right. You are going to have a very comfortable old age—*in bed,"* he said, shaking his head. "Told you it wasn't a good one."

"Sounds like your golden years will be very . . . *restful,"* Cara said, laughing.

"Yeah well, let's get back to yours. I want to hear about these new advent—"

"I think it's time to get back to work, don't you?" She looked pointedly at her watch. Her skin tingled from the look he was giving her. She knew he was only playing, but she hadn't forgotten their kisses the night they'd gone to dinner.

"Darn!" A.J. snapped his fingers. "Just as things were starting to get interesting."

They hadn't been back to work for ten minutes when the phone rang. A.J. looked up, startled. "Who'd call me at the office on a Saturday?"

Cara stiffened. *Please, don't let him have another confrontation with his brother.*

"Mamma! Hi!" His voice warmed with obvious affection. "Did you get my package . . . good. I'm glad you liked it."

Cara grinned. She never would have pegged A.J. as a mamma's boy. One of her papers slid to the floor, and when she bent to pick it up, she banged her knee on the coffee table. "Ouch!"

A.J. looked in her direction. "That was Cara. Yes, she's here. No, Mamma, I'm not fooling around at the office . . ."

He winked at her. "Okay, hold on." He held the phone out to her. "My mother wants to talk to you."

Cara blinked, pointing to herself. "Me?" She went to him then mouthed, "What do I say?" but A.J. just shrugged his shoulders, giving her the phone.

"Hello, Mrs. Gray?"

"Cara? Please call me Alma. I just wanted to say hello," she said cheerfully. "My son has mentioned you so often. You two aren't fooling around over there, are you?"

Cara's heart skipped a beat. A.J. had mentioned her to his mother?

"Mrs. Gray, uh, Alma . . . I can safely say my relationship with your son is nothing but business." Heat prickled on the back of her neck where she could feel A.J.'s gaze boring into her.

"What a shame. It's long past time that boy got married."

Cara remained silent. What could she say?

"I'm just joking with you, Cara. I hope you don't mind," she said with a sprightly laugh. "But it *has* been a long time since he brought a woman home to meet me. When I heard your voice in the background, I got excited. I hope I haven't embarrassed you."

Cara giggled. "No, not at all."

"Good . . . so *are* you married?"

"Married? Uh—"

A.J. took the phone out of her hand. "Okay, that's enough, Mamma."

When A.J. got off the phone a few minutes later, he sat beside Cara on the sofa. "I hope my mother didn't put you on the spot."

"No. She's cute. Sounds like you and your mom are very close."

A.J.'s eyes softened with a look Cara had never seen before. "Yep. She's the best. She wanted to make sure I didn't forget that we're supposed to see a play tonight."

Cara leaned forward, cradling her chin on her palm. "Do you two spend a lot of time together?"

"As much as I can."

She smiled wistfully. "That's great. My mother and I have never been very close."

A.J. raised an eyebrow. "Really? Why not?"

Cara sighed. "I was always closer to my father, at least until recently. You know, 'Daddy's little girl.' I love my mom, but I guess I used to resent the fact that she always let my father have the last word. It didn't make sense. She was a strong woman in her own right, but when it came to my dad, she let *him* make the important decisions."

A.J. nodded.

"What about you? Are you close to your dad, too?"

A shadow fell over his features. "No." He turned away from her, picking up a folder. "By the way, I asked Parker to help you transcribe text files next week. I have an early meeting that might run long, so he volunteered to take my place."

Cara blinked. "Oh . . . okay." Guess he was trying to tell her that subject was closed. Darn! Just as things were starting to get interesting.

Cara knocked on Parker's apartment door. She had to ring the bell several times before the door finally opened. When it did, Parker stared at her as if he didn't recognize her.

"Parker?"

He blinked, straightening his glasses. "Cara!" He looked down at his wrist only to discover he didn't have on a watch. "I was expecting you."

Clearly he hadn't been. "Great." Cara smiled. "Can I come in?"

Hurriedly, he stepped aside, and Cara moved into the

apartment, gingerly stepping over cables and computer parts.

Parker ran a hand through his shaggy hair, then tried to smooth his wrinkled clothing. "I'm sorry about the mess."

Cara gazed around the room. The apartment had very little furniture, and every flat surface of what he did have was covered with an assortment of monitors, computer cards, cables, and millions of tiny screws.

"Oh, don't mind me. This is fine." She smiled weakly.

"Well, we won't be working out here anyway. The equipment we need is in my bedroom." He started leading her down the hall.

"I don't know—shouldn't you at least buy me dinner before we head for the bedroom?" Cara teased.

Parker stopped so suddenly, she almost ran into his back. "Oh!" she gasped.

He whirled, a startled look in his eyes. "If you're uncomfortable, I could bring everything out here. I didn't mean to—"

"Parker! I was just kidding. It's okay. The bedroom is fine."

He flushed. "Oh, yeah. Sorry." He continued down the hall. When he reached his bedroom, he pulled out a keyring and unlocked the door.

"You keep your bedroom door locked?"

"Yeah, all the expensive stuff is in here."

When the door swung open, Cara understood what he meant. Straight ahead, on a large wraparound desk, sat a row of three seventeen-inch monitors, four PC terminals, and two printers. On the side was a lineup of machines that Cara couldn't even identify. Contrary to the clutter in the outer room, this room was exceptionally neat and defied being called a bedroom except for the small twin bed wedged in the far corner of the room.

"This is some setup. I'm impressed."

Parker looked genuinely pleased. "Thank you. Let me show you around."

He went on to show her his hardware, then began helping her transcribe documents for her CD-ROM. As they worked, Cara witnessed a transformation taking place. Parker's awkwardly hunched shoulders squared, and his normally flustered demeanor relaxed into one of confidence. Gone was the gawky and distracted computer nerd who'd greeted her at the door.

Later, when they took a break, Parker put a disk in the machine. "This is my favorite video game."

Cara had expected the typical shoot-em-up kind of game her brother liked to play, but instead a complex puzzle in an array of colors and shapes appeared on the screen.

He grinned at her surprised reaction. "I like brain games. People are so mindless these days because everything's automated. No one takes the time to think things through. Go ahead, try it."

Cara struggled with the puzzle for several minutes. Then she gave Parker a frustrated look.

"Here's a hint. I call this one myopia."

She frowned. "Nearsighted?" She focused closely on the puzzle and suddenly the solution became clear. After that she solved the next two puzzles quickly. Each was different, requiring an uncommon method of reasoning. Occasionally, she looked to Parker for hints.

After solving five or six puzzles, Cara realized she was having fun. Computers were Parker's world, and in his world he took on an almost scholarly persona.

"Parker, you're really great with . . ." She paused when he wrinkled his nose. "What's wrong?"

He shrugged. "Would you call me Jonathan?"

"Sure, no problem. You don't like to be called Parker?"

"It's not that, well . . ." He blushed. "It's sort of a partner thing. Ya know? We all call each other by our last names."

Cara hid her smile. He'd said that with such pride. As

if he were discussing code names for a secret club. "I understand, Jonathan. How did the three of you get together anyway?"

Parker's eyes glowed, and his voice took on an animated tone. "Gray and Whittaker met first, and they were looking for a third person to help with programming. They looked for a long time, but no one could do the kind of stuff I can do. So when they finally found me, they offered me a piece of the partnership."

"Sounds like they were lucky to get you."

Parker looked up. "Don't get me wrong, I was lucky to hook up with them, too. Before I joined Capital, I was doing a lot of freelance stuff and working on my own projects, but I didn't really fit in anywhere." He smiled. "But now I'm with Capital, and we fit. We're a team."

"That's great. I guess the partnership works out well for all of you."

His eyes clouded for a minute. "Yeah. Whittaker and Gray go at it sometimes." He looked up quickly. "But it's no big deal."

Cara leaned forward. "They go at it? Why?"

He shrugged. "Whittaker used to own his own company, but his wife forced him to give it up because he didn't spend enough time with the family. I think he resents that Gray is president. He thinks he should run the company. He's older and has more experience. At least that's what he keeps saying."

"Do you think he's right?"

Parker shook his head vigorously. "Nah. Gray's awesome. He knows what he's doing. Sure, he takes risks sometimes, but they always work out for him. He really knows how to make things happen. I wish I could . . ." He stopped and shrugged his shoulders, looking away.

Cara was surprised at the warmth bursting in her heart at Parker's praise and obvious admiration for A.J. "Then I guess A.J. really—"

"Man, he really knows how to handle pressure. I mean, I'd freak out with everybody on my back all the time, but Gray doesn't even break a sweat. It's enough that the Malloy people and Whittaker keep pushin' deadlines, but now with your project he never leaves the office. I'd probably start fu—uh, messing up, but he just rolls with it."

Cara's back went rigid. "What are you talking about?"

"You know, the Malloy project has heinous deadlines. We weren't supposed to take on any more clients until December when the deal was solid." Parker shook his head in awe. "But Gray's got it together. I guess 'cause you're a friend, he's doing all the work for you himself. No one else was gonna work on this CD-ROM, but I asked him to let me help out. I think he sleeps in his office some nights."

Cara's whole body suddenly went cold. "Why didn't someone tell me? He shouldn't be working on my project if he's got deadlines to meet. I'm sure I could have found another—"

"Oh, he had to. If Capital didn't agree to do the data preparation, DataVision was gonna pass on the project. It wouldn't generate enough revenue or something. But don't worry. A.J.'s been getting everything done. But boy is Whittaker pissed!"

Cara thought back to the way she'd been treating A.J., sauntering around his office like a prima donna, acting as if by giving him her business she were doing him a *favor*. All the while she'd been making his life more difficult. Guilty heat stung her face, and her heartbeat roared in her ears.

"Cara!" Parker shouted in her ear. "Are you okay?"

Cara blinked. "Actually, Jonathan, I'm not feeling well. Can we finish up another day?"

He shrugged. "Sure, no problem. Do you need some aspirin or something?"

Cara shook her head. "No thanks." There was only one person who could make her feel better now.

* * *

Thirty minutes later, Cara followed A.J. into his office and shut the door behind her.

A.J. sat on the corner of his desk. "What do you need, Cara?"

She rolled the end of her braid between her fingers, eyeing his sofa. "Could we sit down for a minute? I want to talk to you about something important."

A.J. sighed heavily with a what-did-I-do-now? look on his face. "Sure, have a seat."

She swiveled to face him. His face was unshaven, and his clothes were a bit wrinkled, as if he'd been sleeping in them. Remorse stabbed at her heart. "A.J., I came here to apologize to you."

His head jerked up. "What for?"

"I just came from Jonathan's. He told me about the . . . 'heinous' deadlines you've been under, and that you practically live here so you can meet them *and* help me with my CD-ROM."

"He never did know when to keep his mouth shut," A.J. muttered.

Cara put her hands on his knees, forcing him to look at her. "No! I'm glad he told me. You obviously weren't going to. Instead, you've been killing yourself trying to keep everyone happy."

"Look, Cara, I'm sure he made it sound worse than it really is. It hasn't been that bad."

"*Didn't* Capital agree not to take on any more clients until December?"

"Yes, but—"

"*Haven't* you been sleeping at the office lately?"

"Not always. I only—"

"Okay, then don't tell me it's not as bad as I think it is. On top of everything else, I've gone out of my way to make your life more difficult, and that's why I want to apologize."

She leaned forward to stroke the stubble on his jaw and watched his eyes darken with desire. "Since I first met you, you've been nothing but good to me, and all I've done is think of myself. *My* fears, *my* worries. You're nothing like the men I've known in the past, and I'm sorry for treating you like you were."

For a minute, A.J. closed his eyes, and when he opened them, Cara felt herself being pulled into his arms. The minute his lips touched hers, her heart felt as if it had been sprung from a trap. Why had she denied herself this incredible pleasure?

Cara lifted herself onto his lap so she could be closer to him, and after the kiss ended, he held her. Nothing had felt this good in a long time. She'd been punishing them both, and it was liberating to finally admit how much she cared about him.

"Wait a minute," A.J. said, pulling away so he could see her face. "What about your 'strictly business' policy?"

Cara leaned forward and brushed her lips over his before she kissed the tip of his nose. Then she moved down to nip his earlobe and whispered in his ear, "Don't you think I mean business?"

Chapter Ten

A.J.'s office door cracked open and Angelique peered in. "Can I talk to you for a minute?"

He arched an eyebrow. "Sure. What's on your mind?" Usually when Angelique wanted to talk, she barreled ahead.

"Well," she said, shutting his door behind her. "Do you need any help with the Malloy project this weekend? I've caught up on my accounts, and I know things have been hectic around here lately."

"No thanks. This is one weekend I *won't* be in the office." He smiled to himself. Cara had lived in the area all her life and hadn't seen most of D.C.'s tourist attractions. He'd promised to show her the highlights Saturday.

Angelique's eyes brightened. "Any special plans?"

"Not really," he said evasively. What he did and with whom was none of her business.

"You deserve a weekend off. Enjoy it," she said politely, twisting her ring and shifting her weight.

"Thanks. I will." When she just stared back, he gave her a questioning look. "What's wrong?"

"Well, I don't know how to approach this. I hope *nothing's* wrong, but I thought I'd better tell you anyway."

"Go on." He hoped another system wasn't down. Things had finally started to calm down.

"I just got a phone call from David. He wants me to ask the Brigmans, Mr. Keely, and Schuster Inc. to go through him instead of you from now on."

A.J. raised an eyebrow. *"Did* he?" Whittaker. That backstabber. Those were their top clients next to Ross, Locke & Malloy. What was he up to?

"Yes," Angelique said, wringing her hands. "He said you had your plate full these days, so responsibilities were being more evenly distributed."

A.J. carefully kept his expression blank. He'd taken Cara's advice and started delegating *some* of his responsibilities, but he'd never let it go *that* far.

She wet her lips. "If these were your orders, forgive me for double-checking, but it just sounded kind of strange."

"No. You did the right thing, Angelique. I'll take care of this with Whittaker myself."

"Should I talk to the clients?"

"No." His answer was sharp and clipped.

Angelique left without another word, but A.J. hardly noticed. He was focused on how he would deal with Whittaker.

Angelique shut her office door and grinned. Perfect. David Whittaker's call provided her with the ideal setup. Now that she'd clued A.J. in on what his partner was up to, he'd have someone to blame when things really got out of hand. She'd cast herself as the concerned employee, and she'd be long gone before anyone knew different.

* * *

Cara flopped onto an empty bench in front of the National Gallery of Art. The October air was cooler but still pleasant, as the sun's warmth lingered on her skin. "I'm tired. Let's sit down for a few minutes."

"I thought you wanted to go inside?" A.J. sat next to her.

Cara gave him a sheepish look as she kicked at the crunchy brown leaves at her feet. "Actually, I'm really worn out. I know I insisted on dragging you all over the city, but I'd rather sit here and rest."

As soon as A.J. had told her that they were touring D.C., Cara had made a detailed list of all the places she'd wanted to visit. He'd suggested that they didn't tie themselves down to an itinerary, but she'd insisted on mapping out the entire day anyway.

She looked up at the darkening sky as clouds moved to partially block the sun. "Besides, the storm clouds are getting closer. We may as well enjoy it outside while we still can."

He leaned back. "Whatever you want. This is your day."

They'd rushed through their tour, not wanting to get caught in the inevitable thunderstorm. They'd only managed to visit three spots on her list: The National Air & Space Museum, The Washington Monument, and Planet Hollywood. And despite the storm clouds that had followed them, people were everywhere, feeding the pigeons, jogging, and playing on the mall.

Cara took a breath of fresh air and again looked up at the sky. "You know, we can visit the Lincoln Memorial and some other museums another day." She glanced over at him. "I think I'd rather . . . A.J.?"

He was staring off into a crowd, looking as if someone had just knocked the wind out of him.

She nudged his shoulder. "What's wrong?"

A.J. slowly turned to face her, but it was another moment before he blinked into reality. "Nothing," he finally said.

"What were you staring at?"

"That man looked just like my father," he answered casually.

"Where?" Cara squinted at the crowd. This was the first time A.J. had mentioned his father. "Was it him?"

"Probably," he said matter-of-factly.

She moved forward on the bench. "Do you want to try to catch him? We can still get his attention."

"His attention is the last thing I need now."

Cara remained silent. They'd gotten closer over the last two weeks, but their relationship was still held together by a fragile thread that might not yet be strong enough for such a weighty issue. As silence stretched that fragile thread taut, she wracked her mind for a new topic of conversation.

A.J. shifted toward her but continued to look straight ahead. "I was twelve when he left, and I didn't see him again until I was thirty." His voice was even, stripped of emotion.

Cara held her breath. She felt the gossamer bond between them fortify itself with the steely strength of trust.

"He showed up at my office out of nowhere. He said he'd made a lot of mistakes in his life, but now he was ready to face up to them. He'd fallen on some hard times, and if I could just 'throw him a bone,' he could make everything right."

"What did you do?" she asked, her voice almost a whisper.

"I knew he just wanted the money," he said bitterly. "I knew I'd never see him again anyway."

He turned to look at her, and Cara saw the pain behind the cold determination in his eyes.

"So I gave him five hundred dollars and told him to stay the hell out of my life."

Cara reached over and touched his hand.

"That was five years ago. I know he's lived in D.C. all that time, but so far, he kept his end of the deal. Probably the only deal in his life he could live up to."

As A.J. spoke, Cara began to understand him in a way she never had before.

"My mother always used to call me Anthony-James, like my father. When I turned thirteen, I told her I wouldn't answer to that name anymore, so she started calling me A.J."

"I guess she understood." Cara squeezed his hand.

"I didn't want anything to do with the man. But my brother was a different story."

"He doesn't feel the same way?"

"I don't know. He's just like my father. Can't keep a job. Blows all his money as soon as he gets it. He's always trying to find a way to get more out of me." His cold tone became heated. "Do you know he called me about a month ago saying he wanted to buy Mamma a gift for her birthday? Her birthday was in July!"

Suddenly, Cara was feeling stifled. No wonder he'd been so angry with his brother. And here she'd had A.J. tried and convicted without knowing the whole story. She'd drawn all the wrong conclusions about him.

A.J. shook his head stiffly. "He's just like Dad, always trying to get one over on somebody." His jawline tensed.

Cara leaned over and kissed him on the cheek. He gave her a smile that said, *Thanks, I needed that.*

He squeezed her hand, then stood. "Come on."

As they walked, Cara studied A.J.'s face, feeling closer to him than she'd ever felt to anyone. Her heart began to pound faster as her chest filled with emotion. She almost came to a dead stop when she realized what the emotion was. Stumbling, she matched her pace to his.

What she felt for A.J. was more intense and satisfying that anything she'd felt for Sean. The emotion crept up on her, spreading over her heart the way dawn spread over the dark night sky. Cara felt light, elated, free.

Here was the man she'd thought was controlling. In reality, he needed so desperately to prove he wasn't like his father, he felt responsible for the world. Here was a man who was unselfish and strong, humorous and sexy. Here was the man that she loved.

A.J. unlocked his office door. "I'll only be five minutes. I just want to find some papers for the Malloy account, then we can go to dinner."

Cara stood patiently by the door as five minutes stretched to ten. "A.J.," she warned, and when he didn't respond, she wadded up a flyer someone had handed her on the street and threw it at his head.

The neon-blue missile narrowly missed his right ear, but he didn't seem to notice. "I know, sweetheart, just let me make one quick phone call, then we can go."

She rolled her eyes. "Well, I'm getting a soda. What floor is the machine on?"

"Fourth. Get me one, too," he said, punching numbers on the phone.

When she returned, the office was empty. She heard rustling in one of the rooms down the hall and assumed he'd become so engrossed in his work, he'd forgotten they were supposed to go out for dinner. The day had been too special to end by ordering takeout while A.J. worked all evening, so she went to find him.

She stepped into a room filled with rows of computer workstations. Angelique was fussing on a cellular phone while punching keys at one of the terminals.

"I don't care, this *is* progress, and I expect . . . because they don't trust each other. It's bound to split . . . Oh, don't worry about him, he's an idiot. I have my own plan for him."

Cara felt awkward for eavesdropping and quickly turned to leave.

"What are you doing here?" Angelique fired at her back.

Cara turned around. "I could ask you the same thing. A.J. said everyone was off this weekend."

"Call you back." Angelique slapped the phone shut. "I'm working, and you have your nerve eavesdropping on me."

Cara's blood began to boil. She nodded at the phone. "Oh? Do you always talk to your clients in that tone of voice?" She paused, cutting her eyes at the other woman. "Now that I think about it, you probably do."

Angelique took a step forward. "Look, you—"

"And if you're working, why aren't you using the telephone on the wall? That can't be . . ." Cara stopped talking when she noticed Angelique staring behind her. She turned just as A.J. put his hand on her shoulder.

"What's going on?"

Angelique shrugged innocently. "I stopped by to download a file from the Internet. This is my boyfriend's phone. I'm sorry, but *she* walked in while he and I were having an argument. *She* got upset and started making a fuss—"

"Wait a minute—" Cara interrupted.

A.J. stood between them. "Hey, hey. Calm down." He turned to Angelique. "Lock up when you're done, okay?"

She turned and flipped off the computer. "All done! See you Monday," she said, slinking out of the room as if she expected male eyes to follow every movement.

"Are you ready? It's raining outside so we might want to—" he started.

"A.J., I did *not* start making a fuss. She may have been talking to her boyfriend, but you should have heard her tone. I don't like this. I think she's up to something."

He put his arm around her. "I know you don't like her—"

"She—"

"Don't worry. I'll take care of it." He steered her out the door. "As I was saying, it's raining outside, so instead of going to a restaurant in this weather, we might want to go back to my apartment and eat there. It's only ten minutes away."

Cara gave him a skeptical look. "Who's cooking?"

He grinned. "I am."

"Okay, then let's go."

Angelique stared out the window.

So it's like that, is it?

She watched as A.J. and Cara ran hand-in-hand through the rain to the car. A satisfied smile curled her lips at the sight of the happy couple. She wondered how much Cara would like her boyfriend when he was broke.

Chapter Eleven

By the time they reached A.J.'s apartment, the rain had stopped.

When Cara entered his living room, she was struck by the same feel of cool elegance that she'd found in his office. The furniture was tastefully chosen and thoughtfully accessorized in the same color scheme of black, pearl-gray, and white.

"You know what, A.J.?" she asked as he showed her around the apartment. "You have a flare for decorating."

A.J. grinned sheepishly. "Not really. My mother insisted on decorating my apartment *and* my office."

"Ah-ha!" She gave him a self-satisfied smile. "Mamma's boy!"

"What?"

"I never would have guessed, but you're a mamma's boy," she teased.

A.J. pulled her into his arms. "Yep! And proud of it! You got a problem with that?"

Cara giggled. "What if I do?"

"Then I'd do what any self-respecting mamma's boy would." He gave her a squeeze. "I'd tell you to take it up with my mother."

Cara laughed, hugging him back. "You're silly." She looked over his shoulder. "Ooh, you have a balcony."

She let go of him to look through the sliding glass doors. A.J. opened them, and they went outside. The evening air was damp from the rain but unexpectedly pleasant.

"I can't believe how warm it is for this late in the fall. I didn't know we were going to have an Indian summer."

"More likely it's global warming."

"Ugh! That's not a very romantic thought." She leaned over the wood-slatted railing that overlooked a park. The balcony was so high, all she could see were the tops of brown and gold trees, blurred by the mist like an impressionistic painting.

A.J. came up behind her, slipping his arms around her waist. "Forgive me," he whispered into her neck. "You didn't tell me you wanted romance. Let me see if I can do better."

He turned her around in his arms and brought her hand to his lips, kissing the inside of her palm. "I'll be right back."

When he returned, a romantic Brian McKnight song was playing, and he held two glasses of wine. Placing both glasses on the patio table, he held his arms out for her. "Dance?"

Cara walked into his arms. "I'd be delighted."

They swayed slowly to the music, and the warm mist draped them, insulating them in their watercolor dream.

After a few turns around the balcony, the dancing stopped. She looked up to see what had happened and found her lips brushing A.J.'s.

The unexpected kiss sent a warm, liquid thrill through her body, and she moved closer to press herself against him. He continued to sip at her lips, but Cara's heart pounded an impatient beat. Now that she had him in her arms, she didn't want to let go. It had taken them so long to get to this point, and her own insecurities were responsible. She didn't want to waste another minute.

A.J. pulled his mouth from hers to whisper in her ear. "How am I doing?"

Cara blinked, taking a moment to realize he was referring to his efforts to be more romantic. She brought her lips to his ear. "Too good," she whispered back.

He gave her a playful squeeze. "Ah, there's no such thing as 'too good,'" he answered softly, but when he lifted his head to look into her eyes, she knew he saw exactly what she'd meant. She wanted him. Now.

She watched his eyes darken with the realization and couldn't suppress her rising feminine pleasure at what the knowledge was doing to him. All intent for sweet romance disappeared. Now his eyes were focused on seduction.

A.J. tightened his arms around her, moving forward until she felt the wooden balcony rail at her back. Again she found his lips on hers, but this time there was no gentle sipping or sweet teasing. His mouth melted over hers, parting her lips immediately for his tongue to find its mark.

Anticipation trickled over her skin, almost in a tangible form, heightening the sensation of A.J.'s hands moving over her body. Their clothes seemed to cling between them, as Cara impatiently tugged his shirt from his waistband. She allowed their bodies to separate only long enough for her to pull the shirt over his head. And as she ran her hands over his bare torso, her fingers seemed to glide over the slick, shining muscles.

By the time Cara realized it was raining again, she was past caring. The sky had darkened, cloaking them in the quiet night. She couldn't hear anything but the uneven rhythm of the rain dropping around them and the soft music floating from the living room.

"A.J.," she whispered. "Can anyone see . . ."

"Shh. Don't worry. There's nothing but trees down there."

His hands were under her blouse, exciting her nipples with the flats of his palms. The rain had molded the cotton shirt over his hands as he cupped her breasts, and the intimate sight stirred the liquid heat at the core of her body.

She moaned her impatience, and he removed her shirt and bra, flattening her bare breasts against his chest. He bent his mouth to her neck, tracing her muscles with his tongue, as she explored his rain-slick body with her hands.

His sweet mahogany skin became almost iridescent, as the rain flowed in silvery trails over his chiseled form. With her finger tips, Cara chased silver beads over the rich dark curves of his torso, her ardor increasing with the tempo of the rain.

The two stood close, holding each other as the falling liquid beat rhythmically on their backs. The woodsy smell of the rain mingled with the musky scent of their bodies, as their lips came together. Sipping, sucking, nipping, dipping, the sweet taste of the rain in his kiss teased her senses.

Finally, she'd had enough teasing. She lowered her hands to his belt. A.J. pulled her hands away, scooped her in his arms, and carried her to the patio sofa in the balcony's corner. Then he lay on his back, settling her on top of him.

As the rain continued to shower them, Cara straddled his waist and set about loosening his buckle. Again A.J. stilled her hands. Making a frustrated sound, she looked to his eyes silently imploring, *What's wrong now?*

He just pulled her down to his chest so her ear was against his lips. "I love you."

Cara's heart became buoyant in her chest, and she felt moisture sting her eyes. She'd never felt as loved by a man as she did at that moment. She opened her mouth to echo the words to him, but she couldn't manage to squeak past the lump in her throat.

"Shhh." He kissed her softly. "I know."

He began sprinkling kisses from her cheeks to her shoulders, but Cara couldn't let the moment pass. She had to say the words.

She held his head between both hands, bringing their noses less than an inch apart. "I love you, too," she whispered.

His arms tightened around her waist, as he slipped her beneath him. Their lips joined in a kiss that seemed to go on forever. Cara was nearly overwhelmed with the new sensations that were coursing through her.

Rain fell rapidly as A.J. removed the rest of his clothing. Cara moved to the side so he could help her off with hers, the downpour doing nothing to cool the heat in her body. When they were nude, facing each other, she remembered to ask, "Do you have . . . ?"

In answer he pressed a square package that he'd pulled from the pocket of his jeans into her palm. He placed a tender kiss on her forehead, as she opened it and put the protection on him.

She lay back on the sofa so he could move over her, but was startled when his hands gripped her around the waist, lifting her on top. Cara couldn't suppress the elated smile that curved her lips as she stared down at him. He wanted her to take the lead.

Rain streamed over her skin as she positioned herself over him. Her eyelids fluttered, and she became submerged in the exquisite sensation of him filling her. Through the mist of her furor, she could see the heat in A.J.'s eyes as he grasped her hips to help with the sensual rocking of their bodies.

Tiny drops of sensation sprinkled through her, and like moisture gathering in a cloud, began to expand inside her. As she rocked over A.J.'s body, she felt the tension in his muscles grow. One of his hands left her hip and moved to finger the nipple of her breast. She continued to undulate over him, as his finger traced down to the joining of their bodies.

Her body became heavy with pleasure, and A.J. seemed to know just how to increase her excitement. She tried to balance her hands on the hard, slippery muscles of his chest as he arched his body up into hers, quickening the pace of their loving.

The storm continued around them, but the thunder she heard was in her own head as their bodies moved in perfect unison, and a burst of liquid fire cracked inside her like a bolt of lightning. She stilled for a moment before collapsing on top of A.J. He trembled beneath her as the aftermath of their mutual release rained down on them.

Almost immediately after their loving, Cara began to shiver as a chill replaced the fire inside her. A.J. picked her up and carried her inside. He set her on her feet in the master bathroom, then took a fluffy terry cloth robe off a hook and lovingly wrapped her in it. "Still cold?"

She shook her head. "This is much better."

He leaned down and kissed her forehead. "Good. I'll make us something to eat." Then he pulled a towel off the rack and wrapped it around his waist, pausing to give her a tender look before shutting the door behind him.

After he left, Cara sat on the toilet lid, trying to collect herself. It was thoughtful of A.J. to give her some time alone. She was lucky to have a man like him, and she could just kick herself for taking so long to realize it. He couldn't *be* more different from Sean.

Cara shivered as the water that had accumulated in her hair began to trickle down her back. She stood and went to the mirror. Her hair was a mess. The rain had frizzed her bangs and unraveled her braid.

Finding a brush on the counter, she loosened her hair and began to work through the long frizzy mass. Where was a curling iron when she needed one? Cara smiled at her reflection. Her eyes were shining and her cheeks had a rosier tint. She was happier than she'd been in a long time.

Making love with A.J. had surpassed her expectations. If she hadn't wasted so much time, they could have gotten started on the festivities a lot sooner. Her experience was limited, but she'd never known it could be like that. Now that she had a frame of reference, she realized that Sean had been a selfish lover. Sex was something that had been done *to* her rather than an activity in which she'd been an equal participant.

After all she'd put A.J. through, Cara was grateful he still wanted her. She'd tested him, blamed him for the sins of other men, and thrown his generosity back in his face time and again. And throughout it all, he'd stuck by her, made her laugh, and shared himself with her unselfishly. And best of all, he loved her.

Cara intended to put all her energy toward making up for lost time.

A.J. was pouring a mixture of ground beef, grated cheese, onions, and tomatoes into the skillet for the stuffed omelet he was preparing when Cara came out of the bathroom.

She looked adorable swallowed up by his big robe, her face scrubbed of makeup and her hair brushed away from her face. She walked over to him, and he reached out to touch her hair. "I never realized how long your hair is. Why don't you wear it down like this more often?"

"You like it like this?" she asked skeptically. And when he nodded she gave him a shy smile. "Then maybe I will."

She climbed on a stool near the kitchen counter. "Something smells wonderful. What are you making?"

He slid the omelet onto a large plate and set it on the table. "Omelet-á-la-A.J." He leaned over and kissed the tip of her nose. "You'd better like it because it's the only thing I know how to make."

"It looks fantastic. I'm sure I'll love it. Besides, I don't have a choice. I'm not much of a cook either."

He handed her the plate. "Take this into the living room. I'm right behind you." He grabbed a bottle of champagne and two glasses, then joined her on the sofa.

Cara's eyes widened. "Champagne? What happened to the wine from earlier?"

He gave her a knowing wink. "It was warm, so I poured it out. Besides, this is a special occasion . . ." Cara's eyes were starting to mist, so he gave her a kiss on the cheek. "And . . . my omelets taste better with champagne."

Cara didn't smile. Instead she gave him a very tender look. "I really do love you, you know that?"

He took the champagne out of her hands and pulled her into a tight hug. "The feeling is mutual."

She had definitely been worth both the work and the wait. Now that he'd finally gotten past her fears, A.J. knew everything was going to be all right.

Cara sat down across from Ronnie at The Big Squeeze. "Hi, Ronnie."

"Hey, stranger. This is the third time this week I've been in this place, and you were nowhere to be found. Girl, what have you been up to?"

"It's been hectic lately. A.J. and I are making a lot of progress with the CD-ROM, so I cut back on my hours."

Ronnie grabbed both of Cara's hands, turning them over and giving them careful inspection. "Well they don't *look* broken."

Pulling her hands back, Cara squinted at her friend. "What?"

"I thought your hands were broken, 'cause you sure haven't called."

Cara's cheeks warmed. "I'm sorry, Ron. I told you I've been busy."

"Uh-huh. *Getting* busy is more like it."

"Ronnie!" Cara slapped her friend's hand playfully. "Well, your hair looks great," she said, trying to get back in her good graces.

Ronnie flipped the long extensions over her shoulder. "I know, but don't try to change the subject. Ever since you and A.J. have gotten so tight, I hardly see you."

Cara became serious. She *had* missed her friend. She and Ronnie normally had more time together, but now she'd cut back to two days a week at the club instead of her usual five. She and A.J. spent the other three days working on her project.

Cara gave Ronnie's hand a squeeze. "I've missed you too, Ronnie. I'm sorry I haven't been there for you lately. We should make plans to go out to dinner some time soon. Just the two of us."

Ronnie twirled one of her braids, coyly. "I'll think about it," she said, then burst into giggles.

Cara straightened, suddenly remembering something. "Hey, catch me up. What happened with that letter you were going to write to the editor of the *Washingtonian?*"

Ronnie grinned wickedly, rubbing her hands together. "Ooh, it was sweet! In the letter, I said I was surprised that a quality publication would allow a reviewer to rehash personal vendettas in their magazine. I sent clippings of the positive reviews he'd given the Embassy in the past and me in particular. Then I demanded a retraction."

"Well . . . What happened?"

Ronnie tossed her head proudly. "Not only did they print a wonderful retraction, they fired Andre. That bum is out on the street, and I heard his new . . ." her lips twisted spitefully as she searched for a word.

"Ronnie," Cara said in a warning tone.

Her eyes widened innocently. "I was going to say *girl-friend*. Anyway, she dumped him."

Cara clapped her hands, leaning back, satisfied. "Well, it's true. What goes around comes around. It's about time that loser got what he deserved."

"Yeah," Ronnie said softly.

Cara looked at her watch. "Oh, I've got to run. I have a session with Wendy in five minutes. I promise I'll call you so we can make plans for dinner."

They said their goodbyes, and Cara dashed to the women's locker rooms to meet Wendy. Cara's heart filled with pride for the girl when she thought of all the progress Wendy had made. She'd lost twelve pounds and her self-esteem had grown significantly. Last Cara had heard, Wendy was going out on her first date. She really was a beautiful girl, and Cara was glad that Wendy had started to see that for herself.

Cara waved when she saw Wendy approaching. Everything in her life was going wonderfully. Her relationship with A.J. was incredible, Ronnie had finally gotten Andre out of her system, and Wendy had made unbelievable progress in such a short period of time. Who could ask for anything more?

Chapter Twelve

Angelique had just put her key into the ignition when she heard footsteps echoing in the parking garage. Jonathan Parker was headed for his old blue Honda parked in its usual spot at the far corner of the lot.

Angelique smirked. She had a pretty good idea what kind of money Parker made, and he clearly didn't invest it in his car. Or his clothes, for that matter. She shook her head, thinking of the cheap, wrinkled material he always wore. Apparently, he sank his wealth into his computer equipment. She'd bet that laptop he carried was worth more than his entire wardrobe and his car put together.

From the safety of a black BMW, hidden behind tinted windows, Angelique watched as Parker approached the two large men who were leaning casually on his car. They were dressed in suits to blend with the business crowd.

Angelique frowned, eyeing Parker's scrawny figure. Maybe she'd gone overboard; one guy probably would have been enough. Oh well, even though it was late enough that most of the building had gone home, the suits were a nice touch.

Parker was attempting to talk to them, but damn it, she couldn't hear what they were saying. She was twisting in her seat to get a better look when Parker whirled around and tried to run. One of the men grabbed him by the shoulder, and Parker lost his balance, sprawling at the feet of her hired thugs.

He started yelling, and one of the assailants kicked him in the stomach, effectively silencing his screams. Then, while that attacker emptied Parker's pockets, the other thrashed Parker's briefcase against a pillar until the lock broke. A shower of papers settled on top of Parker's quivering body.

Angelique scowled. She hated to see such a quality leather briefcase ruined. A.J. had spent big money on the case for Parker's birthday. She shrugged. Parker probably didn't have enough taste to appreciate it anyway.

The muggers gathered what they wanted, taking the time to laugh and curse at Parker's prone form as he quietly begged them not to hurt him. Coward, weakling, nerd—those were the most pleasant names that echoed through the garage.

With a malicious grunt, one attacker slammed his fist into Parker's face, causing blood to spurt from his nose. Then the thugs grabbed the case that contained Parker's laptop computer and ran toward the stairwell.

Parker trembled quietly on the ground, surrounded by a mess of paperwork and blood.

Smiling, Angelique backed Brad's car out of the space and headed home. There were thousands of ways for her to get what she wanted out of life, and she was just getting started.

* * *

Thanksgiving was coming, Cara thought, stepping out into the crisp November air. Absently, she felt around in her purse for her car keys. She hoped A.J. would spend Thanksgiving with her at her parents' house. Her mother asked her to invite him weeks ago, but she'd kept forgetting to bring it up. Now the holiday was two weeks away. She hoped it wasn't too late to invite him. Or maybe she hoped it was. She and her father hadn't been getting along as well since she'd changed her career. No telling how he might behave.

Not finding her keys right away, Cara stopped in the middle of the parking lot and gave the search her full attention.

Without warning, a pair of hands locked around her arms. Cara dropped her purse and tried to pull away. Instantly she was released, and she looked up to face her attacker.

"A.J." She placed a hand over her rapid heartbeat. "My God, you scared me. I didn't see you coming."

His brows were drawn together, and his jaw was tight. "You didn't see me coming because you had your head down."

Cara frowned at the reprimand in his voice. "I was looking for my keys."

A.J. shook his head. "You should always have your keys ready before you leave the building, and you shouldn't be walking in a dark parking lot by yourself."

"Well, I—" She placed her hands on her hips. "What are you doing here anyway?"

"I wanted to make sure you got home okay." His face was solemn, an unusual expression for A.J.

"What's with you?" She cocked her head to examine him closer. "First you sneak up on me, and then you lecture me on parking lot etiquette? What's going on?"

He picked her purse up from the concrete, then pulled her toward his car. "I have to tell you something."

Her vital signs immediately went on red-alert. "What's wrong? Has something happened?"

He didn't answer. Instead he opened his car door and motioned for her to get in.

She made a general motion toward the lot. "But I have my car."

"I just want to talk for a minute. Then you can go back to your car, and I'll follow you."

"Follow me? Why? Is there some escaped convict on the loose?" She got into the car and had to wait for A.J. to get in beside her before she got an answer.

"Parker was mugged yesterday."

"Oh no!" She covered her mouth with her hand. "What happened?"

A.J. shook his head. "Apparently, after our partner meeting yesterday, two men jumped him in the parking lot."

"Is he hurt?"

"They broke his nose, and he has a huge bruise around his ribs. They ruined his briefcase and stole his laptop. I think that's what hurt him the most."

"Poor Parker," Cara said, remembering how the last time she'd seen him, he'd been glowing with enthusiasm over his partnership at Capital. "I can't believe this happened."

"I didn't find out about it until this afternoon. Parker didn't want us to know. One of the techs saw his car in the garage and asked if Parker was around. So I called him. He sounded like crap on the phone. Little by little, I finally got the story out of him."

"How's he handling it?"

"I went over to see him, and he was a wreck. He didn't talk much. The whole thing really shook him up."

Cara sat quietly, shaking her head, and A.J. reached over to squeeze her hand.

She turned to face him. "Parker was mugged in the

parking garage at Capital? No wonder you were so worried about me.''

"I wasn't trying to scare you, but I nearly lost my mind when I saw you standing out there in the middle of the lot. Anyone could have grabbed you.''

Cara took a deep breath, looking out the window at the dark parking lot. She didn't want to think about what could have happened if A.J. hadn't been the one to sneak up on her.

A.J. turned her chin, so her gaze met his. "Now that you're only working two days a week, do you think you could do me a favor?"

"What?" Cara knew it had to be serious. She'd learned that A.J. didn't make a habit of asking for favors unless they were important.

"Let me take you home at night."

"Then how would I get to work?"

He thought for a minute. "You don't go in to the club until the afternoon anyway. I could take you to work on my lunch hour."

Cara shook her head. "That sounds like an awful lot of trouble."

"It's only two days a week. Besides, now that the data preparation for the CD-ROM is almost finished, taking you to work will allow me to spend more time with you. In a couple weeks, you'll start meeting with DataVision, and most of my part in it will be done. The Malloy deadline is closing in, too. We'll both be very busy."

"I don't know."

If Sean had made a suggestion like that, he would have made her feel like she was too helpless to take care of herself. Looking out for his "possessions" made him feel like more of a man. She knew A.J. honestly cared about her, and that he wanted to make sure she was safe because he loved her. The difference was clear.

A.J. gave her an intense look as her silence stretched

out. "It's not that I think anything will happen to you. I'd just feel better knowing that you're safe."

Cara smiled. She knew him better than she'd thought.

"Okay. But only because I don't want you driving your-self nuts worrying about me." She put her hand on the door handle.

"One more thing. My mother would like you to have Thanksgiving dinner with us."

"Oh, that's so sweet. I'm anxious to meet your mother." Cara frowned. "But my mom asked me to invite you to have Thanksgiving dinner with *us.*"

A.J.'s lips slanted as he thought. "I'd suggest that we combine both families and celebrate together, but I'd hate to inflict my brother on your parents."

"He can't be that bad."

He slapped his palm on the dashboard. "Okay, how about this? We spend the early afternoon with my mom, and we have dinner with your parents."

Cara smiled. "That's perfect."

"Great, then it's settled. Now I'll walk you to your car."

When they reached Cara's car, A.J. gave her a long slow kiss, and Cara couldn't help the amazement that spread through her. At times Sean had smothered her, but in A.J.'s warm embrace, she felt nothing but comfort.

Chapter Thirteen

Angelique picked up the phone on A.J.'s desk. "I told you never to call me here!"

"Relax, sweetheart. I just want to know when you're going to get over here."

Angelique rolled her eyes, touching the dark green lace on the negligee she wore under her dress. The garter-belt and stockings had better do their thing because she needed to distract him from her lack of progress.

"Bradley. Darling. I'm working." She barely maintained a civil tone. "I'm anxious to see you too, but you've got to give me time to finish up."

"Did you find what we need?"

"Maybe I could, if you'd get ... off ... my ... back," she bit out through clenched teeth.

A chuckle registered over the line. "You're a real pain in the neck, you know that?"

"That's why you love me," she answered, examining her manicure. What a toad he was. "Now, if you'd let me—"

"You're down twenty grand."

Angelique nearly toppled over on her spiked heels. "What!"

"You haven't brought me anything useful in two weeks. That's twenty grand."

"You sonofa—" she whispered, her anger melting the icicles his words had formed on her spine. "What about Parker's laptop?"

"There wasn't anything on it we could use. You know the deal."

"I took a lot of risks getting that computer. How dare—"

"Risks don't count, sweetheart, only results. See you tonight." The line went dead.

Angelique slammed down the phone, her body trembling with panic. Twenty grand! Times had been desperate before, but now they were dire. She scanned A.J.'s office. She was wasting her time here. He usually took his work home with him, anyway.

She stalked to the door and jerked it open only to close it again in a rush. A light went on down the hall. Someone was coming. It had to be A.J. He was the only one who worked late on Sundays. She had to think fast.

A.J. strolled down the hall, trying to push Cara from his thoughts. He wasn't making any progress working at home, and his office was one of the few places left where he hadn't made love to her. Hopefully, there, he might actually concentrate on *work*.

He walked into the dark office and sensed immediately someone was in the room with him. He could barely see. Only a thin crack of light came through the wall of curtains covering his window, but he knew someone was sitting in the chair behind his desk.

A.J. thought fleetingly that if this were a movie, the chair would slowly swivel around to reveal a sinister villain holding a gun on him. But judging from the strong scent of perfume permeating the air, he suspected the occupant was a woman.

Immediately his thoughts picked up where they'd left off moments ago, and he envisioned Cara sitting in that chair wearing nothing but a sexy negligee. Draped seductively over the leather, she'd be ready to remove his office from the dying list of places where they hadn't made love. A.J. took a step forward.

He felt his groin tighten as the chair slowly began to spin around. Seeing Angelique's lingerie-clad body draped over the chair instead of Cara's stabbed him with disappointment and pricked his temper.

"Hi, A.J.," Angelique purred, crawling on top of his desk. "What took you so long?"

"What the hell are you doing here?" His voice sliced the air like a razor.

She knelt on the desk with her hands on her hips. "What does it look like?"

A.J. slit his eyes at her, stepping forward. She looked like an overstuffed puff pastry—the kind that made your stomach ache and rotted your teeth—which made him long for Cara's naturally sweet curves all the more.

"It looks like somebody's going to get fired if *somebody* doesn't get off my desk." He grabbed her by the arm and hauled her to her feet. Then he snatched the coat and dress lying on the floor and shoved them at her.

Instead of taking the clothes, Angelique struck a pose. "Are you sure—"

"You're fired."

Her face went pale, and she immediately grabbed the clothes and put them on. A.J. couldn't ever remember seeing such genuine fear on a woman's face.

Now dressed, she clutched at his arm. "A.J., please. I'm sorry. Don't fire me. I . . . I can explain."

His temper cooled a notch. The desperation he saw in her eyes was real. "What the hell were you thinking?"

She took a deep breath, not meeting his eyes. "You don't understand how badly I need this job, A.J." She raised her gaze. "Things haven't been going well for me lately. And, on top of everything else, seeing you and Cara together, well, I guess it . . . got to me."

A.J. shook his head. "Come on, Angelique, your interest in a man is in direct proportion to his wallet. Don't try to make me believe you're jealous."

She gave him an imploring look. "Yes, A.J., in the past, money always has been important. But recently, I'd started to think that maybe . . . never mind. There's no reason for you to believe me."

She sounded so defeated, so unlike Angelique, that A.J. felt a twist of sympathy. "No, finish. What were you going to say?"

"My mother was a model in Europe. She raised me to believe that money and beauty are the only things a woman needs to be happy. Well, I have those things, but I'm not happy. Recently I found myself looking for something more . . . I don't know what exactly, but now I see I'm looking in the wrong places."

She gave her haphazardly tossed on dress and coat a deprecating look. "I can't explain what came over me. I can't afford to lose my job. I won't do anything to jeopardize it again if you let me keep it."

After a long silence, A.J. waved his hand at her. "Go on, get out of here. I'll chalk this up to a moment of bad judgment if you make sure this doesn't happen again."

Angelique didn't waste a moment making her exit, and A.J. sat behind his desk to catch his breath. That had been close. If he'd fired Angelique, it would have left a gaping hole in their staff that couldn't possibly have been filled before the Malloy deadline.

So much for concentrating on work. His evening had

taken a turn for the bizarre. Angelique had never hit on him before. Where was this coming from?

A.J. looked around the room suspiciously. Even though Angelique had been full of explanations a few minutes ago, there was one question she'd neglected to answer: how the hell had she known he was going to be here?

Thanksgiving day was bright and sunny, and Cara enjoyed the afternoon at A.J.'s mother's house in Northern Virginia. Unfortunately, it went by too quickly. Cara loved Alma Gray, and A.J.'s younger brother was . . . amusing. At two o'clock they stood at the door saying their goodbyes.

Alma gave her a warm hug. "Now don't you let that boy get away with not bringing you by more often, Cara. You two have to come over and go to church with me one Sunday."

Cara kissed her on the cheek. "I'll see that we do, Alma. It was wonderful to finally meet you."

Cara stood by the door while A.J. kissed his mother goodbye.

"Psst."

Her head snapped around to find Eddie motioning her over. She went to hug him goodbye. "It was nice to meet you, Eddie."

He hugged her back, then slipped something into her palm. When she pulled away, he gave her a smug nod, as if that said it all.

When they were outside Cara read the slip of paper. Her eyes widened. "He gave me his phone number."

A.J. looked over. "What?"

She passed the paper over to his side of the car. "Your brother gave me this."

A.J. looked at the number, chuckled, then threw it over his shoulder. "Believe it or not, that means he likes you."

Cara nodded. "I know."

"No actually, he likes you for *me*. It's kind of a joke between us. If he thinks I really like a girl, he gives her his number. He figures if she can resist him, it must be true love."

"You've got to be kidding."

A.J. chuckled. "It's just his way of letting me know he approves. Really, it's just a joke. I would have warned you, but I'd forgotten about it. It's been a while since I brought someone home."

"Wow, and I thought *my* little brother was strange."

But as it turned out, A.J. didn't think so. As a matter of fact, he got along well with her whole family. Her mother fussed over him, trying to make sure he got enough to eat. Her nineteen-year-old brother hung on his every word, and her father . . . well, it was safe to say that her father approved of A.J. Too bad her father's approval didn't extend to Cara.

The tension started after the pumpkin pie was served, when they were in the living room relaxing and talking, and her mother mentioned she was going to redecorate the house.

"I was watching the 'Home' show last week, and they were saying that each room should have a different theme. I've started planning some of the rooms already. Now I need to pick out patterns for the curtains I'm going to sew."

Cara raised her eyebrows. "That sounds like a big project, Mom. How long is that going to take?"

"Probably about eight to ten months."

"Eight to ten months? Won't you be spreading yourself a little thin?"

"No, honey. Why do you say that?"

Cara frowned. "Because you're starting work full-time at the bridal shop next month." Her mother had always enjoyed crafts and sewing, and now she had the opportunity to practice her hobby full time.

Her mother tilted her head. "Oh, I guess I didn't tell you. Your father and I discussed it, and I won't be going back to work after all."

Cara sat straighter. "What? Why not?"

Her father answered. "Cara, you know I'll be retiring next year. Why should your mamma start work again when we'll finally have more time together? That wouldn't make sense."

Cara blinked. "But Mom, you always said once we were grown, you'd be able to go back to work. I thought that was what you wanted."

"Sweetheart, don't get so upset. Your father's right. He and I would finally have more time together. What's the sense in my going back to work just as he's retiring?" She gave a little laugh. "I'll wait 'til he works my nerves so bad that I'll be glad to be out of the house."

Everyone laughed, but Cara. She knew her mother had been looking forward to helping out at the bridal shop. Cara knew what had happened. Her father had made up his mind that he wanted her home with him, and her mother, as usual, deferred to his wishes.

Her father leaned forward, smiling at A.J. "Well, I have to congratulate you, A.J. You got Cara back into computers where she belongs."

Cara couldn't believe her ears. "Excuse me? Dad? A.J. did *not* get me back into computers. It was a coincidence that I ended up at his consulting firm."

Her father waved his hand. "Whatever. Either way I'm glad you finally stopped playing around. I was worried about you for a while there. But now you have a man in your life again, and you've put your real career back together."

Steam started pouring out of her ears—or at least it felt like it. "There was nothing *wrong* with my career in the first place. And secondly, I'm *not* giving up fitness training.

I've just broadened my range a bit. How many times do I have to explain this to you?"

The room had grown silent, and heat warmed her face as Cara realized she was yelling. She hadn't wanted to make a scene in front of A.J., but this always happened when her father got started on her choice of careers. She got up and headed for the stairs.

"Where are you going, Cara?" her father asked. "It's not polite to leave your company."

"Well, he's perfectly welcome to join me in the bathroom, but I'm sure he'd rather wait here." She hadn't intended to be rude; it just came out that way. As she climbed the stairs, she heard her parents apologizing for her behavior. Cara rolled her eyes and tried to push through the thick cloud of humiliation that settled around her.

Alone in the bathroom she took a few deep breaths and washed her face, but she still couldn't muster the desire to go back into the living room. Instead she went outside on the porch. It was cold, and she hadn't brought her jacket, but the frigid air outside was preferable to the frigid atmosphere in the living room. She hadn't been sitting on the step more than a minute before A.J. joined her.

"Are you okay?" he asked, sitting beside her.

"I'm sorry. I didn't intend for this to happen, but my father and I don't agree on my chosen career."

He slid his arm around her shoulder. "I noticed. Do you want to talk about it?"

She shrugged. "There's nothing much to talk about. He's never going to change his mind about what I do. He still thinks it's just some kind of phase I'm going through."

"Have you tried to make him understand how happy fitness training makes you?"

"It doesn't matter. He thinks I'm just playing all day. He thinks I couldn't handle the stress of the computer field, so I copped out and got a job at a health club."

"What about your mom?"

Cara rolled her eyes. "What about her? She goes along with my dad. I think she understands, but she won't talk to him about it.

"*She* makes me angry, too. I *know* she wanted to work at the bridal shop, but she let Dad talk her out of it. On her own, she's pretty headstrong, but when it comes to important decisions, she allows him to have the final say. That doesn't make sense. They're married. They should make equal contributions in important decisions."

He gave her a direct look. "So who are you really mad at here, your father or your mother?"

Twice Cara started to answer and then stopped. Her first thought was to say both, then she wanted to say her dad, but when she really thought about it, she was more upset with her mom.

"I guess I blame my mom for not taking a stand with my dad. If she disagrees with his reaction to my career change, she should say so. If she really does want to work at the bridal shop, she should do it. Instead, because my father is 'the man of the house,' she goes along with what he wants. When there's a problem, it's his duty to solve it. He never treats her like her opinion is worth anything."

A.J. hugged her closer. "Cara, you have to remember they're from a different generation. Just tell me one thing, are they happy?"

Cara blinked. "Yes. The years only seem to bring them closer," she said, her voice taking on a tone of wonder.

"Then maybe you should accept that the choices your mother makes are right for her, even if they're not right for you." A.J. squeezed her shoulder. "And once your father realizes you're serious about fitness training, he'll come around."

"It's been four years. How long is it going to take to prove I'm serious?"

A.J. shook his head sympathetically. "Are you ready to

go back in? It's pretty chilly out here.'' He rubbed his arms.

"I'll be in soon. I just want to sit here for a few more minutes. You go ahead.''

He leaned over and kissed her softly. "Everything will work out eventually. I promise.''

He went inside, and Cara tried to pull herself together. A.J. was right. Maybe she had been too hard on her mother. She seemed to be happy, so Cara had to be satisfied with that.

And as for her father, she refused to fight with him over her career anymore. She didn't need his approval, and if he couldn't accept her decision, that was his problem. She didn't want to ruin what could be salvaged of the holiday atmosphere, so she would go in and apologize.

Taking a deep breath, Cara felt a little better. She was in control now. And neither her father nor any other man could take that away from her. A.J. had shown her, with his loyalty and encouragement of her independence, that not all men were threatened by a strong woman.

She wished things could be different in her parents' relationship. But there wasn't anything she could do about that. Thank God, she had A.J. At least she knew he valued her opinion and her contributions to their relationship.

Armed with her new sense of serenity, Cara went back into the house. The first thing she saw was A.J. and her father with their heads together in the kitchen. Their backs were to her. She went to stand in the doorway.

". . . Well, I think you ought to tell her that,'' A.J. was saying.

Her father shrugged. "We were always close. I'm sure she already—''

"What's going on in here?'' Cara asked.

A.J. spun around. "Hi, sweetheart. Malcolm challenged me to a game of Dungeon Rats. I'd better not keep him waiting.'' He squeezed her arm as he brushed by.

"Dad?" she asked.

He looked deep in thought and a bit uncomfortable. "Cara, can we talk for a minute?"

Her heart started beating faster. She didn't want to argue. "Well, I—"

"Please. I don't want to argue. Just talk."

He seemed sincere. She pulled a chair out at the kitchen table. "I'm sorry for causing a scene earlier. I didn't mean to—"

"I'm sorry, too, Cara. I wasn't trying to upset you when I brought up your job. You know that, don't you? It's just that you always were so damn smart. Smarter than your old man. I wasn't good at academics, never was.

"I went into physical education because I didn't have much choice. Back when I was young there weren't as many options as there are now. I played sports. That's what I was good at. When I couldn't do that anymore, I coached basketball. Then I taught PE at the elementary school. Those were the only choices that were open to a man like me."

"Dad, that's the point. I did have choices, and I *chose* to go into fitness. And there's nothing wrong with that. If it was good enough for you, why can't it be good enough for me?"

He squeezed her hand. "Because you can do better than good enough. When you showed more of an interest in athletics than academics, I thought I'd done something wrong. Raising you to play sports and all. But I was so glad that we had something in common. I couldn't really help you with your math homework, but you would watch the football games with me, or we would go outside and play softball. I loved those times, Cara, and I wouldn't trade them for the world. But A.J. made me see that I might have pushed you too much."

She wrinkled her brow. "A.J.?"

"I can't force you to want what I wanted for myself."

He looked away and mumbled, "I'm sorry if I wasn't fair to you."

Tears gathered in her eyes. "Thanks, Dad." They still had a lot more to work through, but this was a good start.

Cara and her father joined the others in the living room. Now, A.J. and her mother were in a heated battle on the video screen, and Malcolm stood on the side cheering them on. Cara sat and admired how well A.J. had fit into her family. Not only did her brother adore him, her mother thought he was "scrumptious," and her father respected him. His cheerful good humor added a special warmth to the holiday gathering. And he'd even managed to help things along between her and her father. She didn't know how she could possibly thank him for his support.

Still, she tried on the drive back to her apartment that night. "A.J., I don't know what you said to my father, but it really helped."

He reached over and squeezed her knee. "I didn't say much, but I'm glad you two were able to talk. I told you things had a way of working themselves out."

"Well, for whatever part you played in it, I'm grateful." She leaned across the seat and started nibbling on his earlobe. "How can I possibly thank you?"

"It's not necessary. I didn't really do anything," he said seriously.

Cara grinned. He wasn't getting her hint. She'd just have to be more obvious. "Well, it's still Thanksgiving, and I'm in the mood to . . . give *thanks.*" She slid one hand onto his lap, and used the other to stroke his neck. "Are you *sure* there isn't any way I can show you how thankful I am?"

He squirmed a bit, straightening behind the wheel. "Now that you mention it, I can think of a few things. If you insist."

She slipped her hand over his coat and inside his shirt, teasing his nipples with her fingernail. "Really? What?"

He groaned. "You're lucky we're only about two minutes from your house. I'm not sure if you're rewarding me or torturing me."

She moved back to her side of the car. "Well if I'm bothering you . . ."

He grabbed her thigh and yanked her back to his side. "Get over here. I haven't had enough of that . . . gratitude yet."

She giggled in his ear. "Well, make up your mind."

Less than a minute later they were back at her apartment, and not a moment too soon. Apparently A.J. had thought of a whole list of ways she could be thankful to him because he proceeded to whisper them in her ear on the elevator ride up.

They barely made it through the door.

Chapter Fourteen

A.J. often wished Whittaker were a computer because the old man was long overdue for an upgrade.

"I don't care how long you ran your own business," A.J. said, tightening his fingers around the telephone receiver. "That doesn't give you a right to override my authority."

"Why do we keep coming back to this?" Whittaker's tone made A.J. grind his teeth. "All I did was ask Angelique to direct status inquiries from a few clients to me first. You've bitten off more than you can chew. You're going to run this company into the ground if you don't slow down."

"That's ridiculous and you know it. I've never had a decision blow up in my face. I know what I'm doing."

He *had* overextended himself. He knew that, but now things were under control. At first, he'd resisted Cara's suggestion to delegate more responsibility, but the more he'd considered it, the more he realized he had no choice. He'd already divided most of his accounts between Whittaker and Parker so he could concentrate on Malloy and

Cara's project, but give Whittaker a bit and he wanted a megabyte. The old man wouldn't rest until *he* sat in the president's chair instead of A.J.

"Look, man, I didn't call to argue with you. I just want to know what we're going to do about Parker? It was hard enough getting him to pay attention when he was in the room, but now, when we only have phone contact with him, getting his attention is impossible."

"We'll just have to tell him that he has no choice. He has to attend meetings at the office."

"The only reason we tried the conference calling in the first place is that he's terrified to come back here. There's no way you'll get him out of that apartment."

"Then maybe we should reconsider his partner status with this company. Clearly, he's in no shape to live up to his duties."

"Now hold on a minute. Parker may not be good with people, but the guy's a genius with computers, and you know it. Since the mugging, he hasn't messed up one program. In fact, he's turning things over even faster than before. With the Malloy deadline so close, he's saving us a lot of time."

"That may be true, but his attitude is unstable. You can barely get a word out of him, on the phone or in person, and when you do, you can't predict his mood. One minute he's sullen and depressed, the next he seems bitter, almost angry. How would our clients feel if they knew about this?"

"It's none of their business. The point is that Parker gets the job done, better than you or I could without him. And as for his attitude, I'd like to know how fast you'd bounce back after getting mugged. Give the guy some time. If he continues like this, maybe we can get him into counseling."

"I don't see how that will help. I think he's too far gone."

"Just give me a chance to talk to him."

As soon as A.J. hung up with Whittaker, he called Parker. It took an unbelievable amount of time for him to answer. Finally he heard a sluggish "Hello?" from the other end.

"Hey, man, it's Gray. Listen, have you talked to Whittaker lately?" The line was silent for a minute. "Parker?"

"Nah, man, I haven't talked to him." He sounded distracted—well, *more* distracted than usual.

"Is everything okay?"

"Sure . . . fine."

"Okay." A.J. wasn't convinced. "Well, *I* talked to him and—"

"Who?" Parker sounded startled.

"Whittaker, man, Whittaker. I think he might—Parker, are you sure you can't come into the office for the partner meetings? We've been driving each other nuts these past couple weeks without a referee. I could pick you up or send a driver. I promise you'll be safe."

Silence.

"Are you still there?" A.J. asked.

"I have to go. I heard something." Parker hung up before A.J. could protest.

He stared at the dead receiver. Obviously, Parker wasn't even ready to *talk* about leaving his apartment yet.

With Whittaker on his back and Parker out of touch, A.J. was on his own—as usual.

While Sabrina was on vacation, Cara was in charge of the club. She had to stay late each night to let the cleaning crew in, then lock up. She usually finished around eleven forty-five, then A.J. would pick her up. That Friday, when A.J. came for her, they decided to go out for a late dinner.

They ended up at the International House of Pancakes with two large stacks of buttermilk pancakes in front of them. Cara watched as A.J. put butter on each cake, then cut the stack into perfectly sized, triangular pieces before pouring syrup over it.

"Do you always eat your pancakes that way?"

"Huh?" A.J. glanced at her pancakes, which she'd already started eating, cutting as she went. "Oh, yeah. I guess I picked it up from my mom. She always fixed our pancakes this way."

"You know, I think my mom used to do something similar, but I never had the patience to cut the whole stack first."

A.J. nodded. "My brother's the same way."

"So, what's Eddie up to these days?" she asked, sipping her hot chocolate.

"He quit his job at the record store last week." A.J. rolled his eyes, shaking his head. "The boy's twenty-four years old, and he can't keep a job for more than six months."

"Well, what's he interested in? Has he gone to school?"

"He went to community college for a year and a half then dropped out." A.J. quirked his lips. "He wants to go into the music business."

Cara leaned forward. "Really? Does he sing? Play an instrument?"

A.J. gave her a frustrated look. "No. He *raps.*"

"Is he any good?"

"Who cares if he's any good." He threw his hands up. "He'll never get anywhere without finishing his education. Instead he spends all his time and money in the studio. If he put half as much energy into school, he'd have his Ph.D. by now."

Cara tried to interject, but A.J. was intent. His eyes had become as dark as onyx, reflecting his anger and frustration in ways his words never could.

"He's going to end up just like our father. Going nowhere, doing nothing. They are so much alike."

"Now, A.J., I don't think you're being fair. A lot of

people become successful without a college education. It sounds like your brother is committed to his music. How do you know he's not any good if you've never listened?''

"I don't have to listen to know that it's taking the place of more important things in his life. He doesn't take responsibility for anything. He just thinks about himself and what he wants. Everyone else be damned.''

"A.J., I think you're blaming your brother for your father's sins. Eddie is young. Give him some time to find his place in the world. Or better yet, help him. Show him some support. Your father hasn't been an influence on Eddie's life—you have. I'll bet he looks up to you.''

A.J. shook his head. "No. He doesn't listen to me.''

"Then listen to him. My father wanted me to have a career in computers because he thought fitness training was frivolous. You saw what kinds of problems that caused between us. If you take Eddie's interest in music seriously, he may eventually take your advice about school.''

"No, Cara, it's not the same thing. Eddie can't go on thinking life is a playground, waiting for everyone to just hand him things. I've helped Eddie too much as it is. He's on his own now.''

Cara stabbed a pancake with her fork. She still thought A.J. was acting like her father, but he didn't want to admit that right now. His brother was a sore subject.

She studied the tense lines in his face. She'd noticed that he was on edge lately. The closer the Malloy deadline came, the more he was prone to sudden lapses of long silences. The only clue to his mood change would be the pulsing vein in his forehead.

"How is everything at work?''

"You know how it is.'' His brow creased. "It's always something.''

Cara put her fork down. "Do you want to talk about it?''

"No! I've had enough talking,'' he said sharply. When

she blinked at his abrupt reply, he turned on his sexy grin. "I'd rather lick that syrup off the corner of your mouth."

"No thanks. This napkin will do just fine." She swabbed her mouth, trying to wipe away the tension roused by his harsh tone.

"Lucky napkin." A.J. gave her a slow wink and a tingle vibrated up her spine.

They finished their pancakes and were headed back to A.J.'s car when Cara smacked her forehead.

"Oh, no! I left my overnight bag in my locker."

"We can pick it up tomorrow," A.J. said, unlocking her car door.

"But I won't have any clothes to wear."

He grinned. "I won't complain."

"No, really. I need my hair dryer . . ."

"Don't need it."

". . . and my makeup."

"Don't need it."

". . . and the new underwear I bought at Victoria's Secret."

"Okay. We'll stop at the club on the way home." He looked at her over the roof of his car. "No one will be there, right?"

"I'm sure the cleaning crew is gone by now."

Despite the emptiness of the health club at 1:00 A.M., the room was surprisingly bright from the random dotting of security lights and the moonlight reflecting off the lake through the large glass-paneled wall. The dim lights and the bulky exercise equipment created unusual shadow mosaics on the carpet, giving the normally sweaty environment a unique ambiance.

"Usually empty buildings seem so eerie at night, but right now, I feel like a kid with a huge playground all to herself," Cara whispered.

"Then by all means," A.J. invited, "let's play." He

stepped away from her and headed for a treadmill. "Hey, it works. I guess they don't shut down the power at night."

"A.J.! We're not here to play with the exercise equipment; we're here to get my overnight bag."

"Go ahead and get it. I'll be here when you get back." He'd moved onto a ski machine and was busy shooshing away.

Sighing, Cara went to the lockers to get her bag. It didn't take her more than two minutes, but when she returned to the main room, A.J. was nowhere to be seen.

"A.J.?" She received no answer save her echo. "This isn't funny! If you're trying to scare me, give it up!"

Determined not to let him sneak up on her, Cara turned in circles. She caught a movement in the mirrors behind the exercise bikes, and despite herself, she shrieked.

"Cara, relax. It's only me." A.J. stepped into view, and she flew into his arms. "I'm sorry, sweetheart, I wasn't trying to scare you. I went to the bathroom, and when I came back, here you were." He rubbed her back soothingly.

Her heart was racing but had begun to calm now that A.J.'s arms were wrapped around her. "I'm okay. You just startled me. I guess this place is more eerie than I thought."

"Well, let's see if I can't bring back that playground atmosphere." A.J. bent his head and captured her lips in a playful kiss, first nibbling her lips with his own, and then letting his teeth gently tug at them.

Cara let her overnight bag drop to the floor as she wrapped her arms around his neck. A.J. continued his sensual teasing, using his tongue to lightly flick over her lips before letting it disappear back into his mouth. Cara joined the game, trying to capture his tongue between her lips when it popped out to taunt her. But he was too quick. Before she could catch him, he'd branded one corner of her mouth, then the other, her top and bottom lips, and even her nose in his sensual tag. Cara giggled at their silliness. A.J. had seemed so tense earlier, she was happy to see him in a more lighthearted mood.

When her mouth opened to let another carefree giggle escape, A.J.'s tongue plunged in, surrendering the game of hide-and-seek and changing the mood once again. His arms pulled her closer, pressing her body tightly against his to reveal that a new playmate had come out to play.

Their mutual arousal was thorough and intense, and Cara could not stifle the groan that came to her lips. The excitement of the situation hit her full force. A.J. and Cara were alone in the health club in the middle of the night, and suddenly she wanted to make love to him right where she stood. The idea alone made her shiver.

Cara boldly slid her hand between their bodies as A.J.'s teeth and tongue played tug-of-war with her earlobe. She found the waistband of his sweatpants and reached inside his briefs to capture him. A.J.'s sudden intake of breath told her that he was eager to play.

"Cara, I want you, right now, right here."

"Yes," Cara whispered.

She released him to run her hands under his shirt, enjoying the feel of his hard muscles under her palms and his soft sprinkling of chest hair between her fingers. As her fingertips glided down his back, she felt the tension from the long day at work leave his muscles.

A.J. scooped Cara into his arms and crossed the room to a bench press machine, where he sat with her on his lap. She straddled him, clamping her legs tighter around his thighs so she could feel him pressed against her femininity. He leaned back, letting his lower body rock up into her. Repeating his rocking motions, he nibbled on her lips when his body came upward and withdrew his mouth as his body descended. Cara hungrily ground her hips into his, her impatience roused by the seesaw motion of his body.

She caught sight of their bodies in the mirror behind

him, and could not suppress the giggle that bubbled up inside her.

A.J. halted his teeter-totter-like motions. "What's so funny?" His voice was husky with passion.

Cara giggled again. "I can't help it. *This* is funny. We're making love on a bench press."

A.J.'s eyes glinted mischievously. "We may not get this chance again. Maybe we should try out all the equipment."

Cara snickered at the thought. She immediately envisioned the two of them hopping from machine to machine, entangling themselves in erotically impossible positions.

"Now, there's an idea." She met his mischievous look with one of her own.

Cara grabbed the bottom of his sweatshirt and yanked it chest high so she could tug on the T-shirt below. She pulled both shirts over his head and threw them behind her, watching as they landed on the handle bars of an exercise bike. They both laughed.

"Very good." A.J. said nodding at the shirts. "Now it's your turn." He reached for the hem of her shirt.

"Oh yeah?" She felt playful again and decided to give him a little chase. "You'll have to catch me first!" She jumped from his lap and sprinted away.

A.J. leaped up and was hot on her heels. Cara jogged down the stairs to the lower level where the rest of the Nautilus equipment was, but she didn't get far. A.J. plucked her off her feet and swung her into his arms. "I've got you now, and this time you're not getting away."

A.J. carried Cara over to the wall where mats had been spread on the floor for sit-ups and floor exercises. He lay her down and covered her with his body. It felt good to forget everything and lose himself in Cara and their play. For that moment, nothing existed outside the fantasy they had built inside the health club.

Bracing his arms on either side of her body, he lowered his head and engaged her in a long potent kiss designed to make her lose her head. Once he was certain he'd caught her full attention, he levered his body up from hers, using only the strength of his arms. Staring down at Cara's lovely face and her sexy expression, he almost lost control. But he had enough stamina left to continue their game.

Bending his arms slightly, A.J. lowered himself just enough for his body to graze Cara's, allowing his lips to hover within inches of hers. When Cara raised her head to bridge the distance between them, A.J. straightened his arms, lifting his body once again out of reach. Then he lowered himself again to repeat the routine.

Cara moaned with frustration at the erotic push-ups. She was no longer in the mood for games. Wrapping her legs around his back, she arched her body upward, molding her herself to his arousal. When he lifted his body this time, hers went, too.

Tiring of his game, A.J. collapsed on top of Cara, grinding his hips into hers and burying his lips in the silky skin of her neck. He was beginning to feel the burn.

Her arms locked around his back, raking his bare skin with her nails. "Please," Cara whispered. "Now."

He quickly stripped off her sweatpants and underwear, then yanked down his own just far enough to free himself. He sank into her, gaining his second wind as her legs intertwined behind his back. Pushing, pumping, dipping, and lunging in quick strokes, A.J. felt Cara begin to tremble beneath him, making sweet sounds in his ear. Soon after, he followed her over the edge.

It took them a few minutes to recover, then A.J. separated from her, rolling to the side to pull up his sweatpants. "What a workout!" Then he started chuckling.

Cara, who was fixing her clothes, paused. "What are you laughing at?"

"I was just thinking back to something I said to you the day we first met."

Cara narrowed her eyes. "What?"

"That thing about you helping me 'pump my iron,'" he said, his laughter gaining momentum.

"You!" Cara tried to hit him, but she missed. "Let's get out of here. You're going to pay for that remark when we get home."

A.J. grinned, running for the stairs. "Good! I could use a little 'personal training,'" he tossed over his shoulder, picking up speed as she chased after him.

At the start of her workweek, Tuesday, Cara tried not to let images of her and A.J. frolicking on the exercise equipment haunt her. It wasn't working.

A.J. and Cara had made love on nearly every flat surface in both their apartments. He'd even had a particular fascination with the leather chair in his office, and now they'd christened the health club equipment. Cara stifled a delicious, private giggle, but the mood didn't last.

Their playful romp in the club seemed to mark an end to their festivities. The tension she'd begun to notice in A.J. was increasing. All weekend he'd been anxious and irritable. Last night had been the worst.

She had awakened around three in the morning to find him in front of his computer, pounding away. His movements had been so stiff and jerky, she'd thought she could see the tension radiating from his body. Coming up behind him, she began to massage his shoulders.

He'd been so engrossed in his work, her presence startled him. "What are you doing up?"

"I could ask you the same thing. Are things so hectic at the office that you have to work at three in the morning? I thought you rearranged your workload so you wouldn't have to work these crazy hours."

He rubbed his forehead with his hand. "I did. I couldn't sleep. There's so much that needs to be done, so I came out here to work."

Cara stroked his temples. "Your body's so tense. You need to relax. Come on back to bed."

He pushed her hands away and turned back to his keyboard. "You go ahead. I have more work to do."

"This isn't good for you," she said, placing a hand on his shoulder. "At least let me work some of this tension out."

He roughly brushed her hand away. "No! Please! Leave me alone."

Cara stepped back as if he'd burned her. She stood silently staring at his back.

After a moment his shoulders sagged and he turned around. "I'm sorry, Cara. I shouldn't be taking this out on you." He reached out, and she walked into his arms.

They held each other for a long while, then Cara pulled away slightly. "A.J., please talk to me. Tell me what's bothering you."

"It's nothing I can't handle on my own."

Cara frowned at his words. He'd been shutting her out more and more lately. Now that work on her CD-ROM had shifted to DataVision's headquarters, she didn't see A.J. as much. She wasn't sure how many hours he spent at the office, but the stress was obviously getting to him.

"Sometimes talking about problems helps to vent the pressure." She took a seat on the couch, hoping he would join her.

He remained at the desk for a few more minutes, and the silence became so thick, it was stifling. She brought her knees up to her chest, winding her body into a ball the way the tension had wound her nerves.

Finally, A.J. joined her on the couch, unwrapping her limbs until she relaxed against his side, her head on his shoulder.

"At first we were having problems with some of the systems. Every so often one would shut down for some stupid reason or another. This happened frequently enough that we became concerned. If word got back to Ross, Locke & Malloy that our systems were unstable, it would blow the whole account."

Cara curled her hand in his. "Were you able to figure out what was causing the problem?"

"We cracked down on tech support, but they swore they were double-checking every system they set up. Anyway, we tightened security on our current accounts to guard against viruses, etc., especially on the Malloy account."

"Did it help?"

"It must have because we haven't had any more problems like that."

"I take it that means you've had other problems?"

"Whittaker."

She lifted her head from his shoulder. "What?"

"He called Angelique and told her to direct several accounts through him instead of me. Thank God she came to me right away."

"How loyal of her," Cara said sarcastically.

"So I confronted him. He claimed I was still spreading myself too thin. He thinks I can't handle the day-to-day responsibilities of being president, and he's all too anxious to relieve me of them."

"What's his problem?" Now she knelt on the couch, facing him. "You've already delegated a lot of your duties. Can't he appreciate how hard you're working?"

"He never wanted me to be president in the first place. He thinks I'm too young, and I take too many risks. He used to have his own consulting company, but his wife pressured him to retire. He compromised by taking a back seat when he joined Capital. But I think he still resents that he's not running the show. He's just waiting for me to screw up so he can take over."

"That's awful!" She squeezed his hand. "No wonder you're so tense, having to work under that kind of pressure."

"That's not all. Ever since Parker was mugged, he's more remote than ever. I've tried to talk to him about getting help, but he hardly ever leaves his apartment."

"Poor Parker." Her heart went out to the man. Parker was at least thirty, but he looked half his age with the emotional maturity to match. "I really feel bad for him. He's a nice guy, but I don't think he knows how to relate to other people very well. I got the impression that he'd like to be included more, but he just doesn't know where to start."

A.J. shrugged. "Ah, Parker likes it in his little world of motherboards and hard drives. He has very little interest in the business side of things, and it's just as well."

"He really respects you A.J. I think he looks up to you."

He shook his head warily. "Well, Parker looks up to me and Whittaker looks down on me. I guess that leaves me trapped in the middle. Being in the middle only gets you crushed."

"So you feel like you're in this alone?"

"That's not what's bothering me. It's just this feeling I have in my gut. The closer the Malloy deadline comes, the more I'm sure something's going to go wrong. With all the conditions in our contract, so much is riding on this one job. Things just aren't flowing like they should be."

Cara reached out to hug him. "Well, no matter what happens, I'll be there for you."

A.J. hugged her back, but for some reason, Cara wasn't certain that he believed her.

Chapter Fifteen

As Angelique dialed her cellular phone, she admired her new marquis-cut emerald ring; it wasn't yet paid for, but it would be.

"Everything's in place," she said when Brad picked up.

"Finally," he said, clearly unimpressed.

She refused to let him crush her mood. Her money was secure. "The system will shut down the first day it's in commission, and the virus won't show up until it's too late for them to do a damn thing about it."

"You sound very confident. If this plan is so secure, why didn't you come up with it *three months ago*."

Angelique bristled. She wasn't about to tell him about her ally. Even though the fool expected a cut, she didn't intend to share a penny of her money or an ounce of the credit. Besides, if she let Brad know exactly how this plan had come about, he'd think she'd screwed up again.

"It takes time to set this kind of thing in motion. It wasn't easy to crack the system."

"Well, I must say you came through just in time." His

voice was bored, as though picking lint from his suit would be more interesting.

"What do you mean by that?"

"I was about to take matters into my own hands. But it didn't come to that. I'm glad. It would have been inconvenient to find another mistress."

Angelique ground her teeth. Once she got the rest of her money, she would take great pleasure in dumping him. The fantasy of her walking through his penthouse apartment, cleaning him out of everything valuable from his Armani suits to the silk sheets, filled her with pleasure.

"I would have missed you, too, Bradley."

Oh, she'd miss him a lot, when she was reclining in some remote location, draped only in the finest fabrics while her new lover admired her beauty.

"Good, you can prove it tonight while you tell me all about your little scheme."

Cara arrived at the club earlier than usual, fighting the growing sense of dread rising in her stomach. Sabrina had called her at home that morning to inform—or warn—her that Wendy's parents were so pleased with the progress she'd made, they wanted to meet the trainer responsible.

Wendy *had* made a lot of progress. Not only had she lost the extra pounds and gained new confidence, she also smiled and laughed with a sassy wit Cara had come to admire. She was proud of Wendy, but thinking back to their early sessions, when Wendy would become a nervous wreck at the slightest provocation, caused the dread in Cara's stomach to boil over. Wendy had been able to gain the self-assurance her parents hadn't instilled in her, but what were these people going to be like?

It didn't take long for her to find out. At the time Cara usually met with Wendy for their session, Sabrina called her into her office to meet the Townsends.

As soon as Cara walked in, she noticed the striking couple. They looked like cover models for the good life. Mrs.
Townsend had long, wavy auburn hair that looked as if
it belonged in a shampoo commercial. She wore a crisp
designer suit with a tasteful accent of what appeared to
be very expensive jewelry. Mr. Townsend was the typical
version of tall, dark, and handsome. They both looked as
plastic as Barbie and Ken dolls.

Sabrina made the introductions. Cara wasn't sure what
to expect, but she got the distinct impression she wasn't
quite what they'd envisioned. Oh, they were nothing if not
polite. Too polite. So enthusiastic about meeting her, but
their plastic smiles never reached their eyes.

"Cara, it's just so wonderful to meet you." That was Mrs.
Barbie.

"Yes, Cara. Wendy just loves you. You've been a great
influence on her," Mr. Barbie said.

They went over Wendy's workout plan in detail, but the
Townsends wanted to see her progress chart.

"I have a copy in the training office. I'll be right back."

As she left, the Townsends were singing her praises, and
Cara began to wonder if she'd judged them too harshly.
It really wasn't so unusual for an adolescent to be self-
conscious, and Wendy had overcome it with relative ease
after she'd begun losing weight. Cara remembered the
initial conversation she'd had with A.J. about Wendy. He'd
thought Cara was overreacting to the Townsend's concern.
People with their social status often *did not* pay much attention to their children; instead they paid someone else to
do it for them. At least the Townsends were showing a
genuine interest in Wendy's well-being. They'd taken time
out from their busy schedules to come and meet Wendy's
trainer. Obviously they cared about their daughter, and
Cara may have been too hard on them.

She retrieved the paperwork from a file drawer, determined to return with a new attitude. She'd grown to care

about Wendy, and there wasn't any reason why she shouldn't like her parents as well.

Cara approached the office, noticing that the door had been shut after she'd left. It remained open a crack and Mrs. Townsend's voice carried into the hallway.

"Yes, that's clear, but Alex and I really feel Wendy needs a role model she can relate to."

Sabrina's voice was confused. "Cara and Wendy have already established a rapport. Why would you want to interfere with something that works?"

"Look, Sabrina," her tone was cajoling. "You've done an excellent job of meeting our needs in the past, so this really is a simple issue. We want another trainer for Wendy."

Cara's heart pounded heavily in her chest. A wave of hurt and anger blazed through her as she realized what was going on.

"I'm sorry Mr. and Mrs. Townsend, but I'm very happy with Cara's relationship with Wendy, and I really feel changing her trainer at such an early stage would impede future progress. That's my professional opinion, and you really haven't given me one valid reason to the contrary."

"Sabrina," her tone was stern, now. "We know what's best for our daughter. I just want you to do what I've asked."

Sabrina was quiet for a long time. "Are you interested in a different trainer because Cara's Black?"

There was a nervous laugh from the Townsends. "Alex and I are *not* prejudiced. We realize that her people are ideal for this sort of thing, but Wendy is at a very impressionable stage right now. She talks all the time about how she wants to be just like Cara. It's more important that Wendy be influenced by the *right* people. That's the reason we joined a club like this."

"I'm sorry Mr. and Mrs. Townsend, but Tower Vista does not tolerate racism. If you aren't happy with the staff we

have here, then I suggest you take your business else-
where."

Cara didn't hear another word and wished she could
see what was going on inside. Then she heard chairs shuffling, and she was startled as the door swung open. The
Townsends brushed past without even looking at her.

The next second Sabrina was in the doorway, cursing
under her breath. "Oh, Cara! Um . . . how long have you
been standing there?"

"Long enough."

"Did you . . ."

"Yes."

"Damn! I'm sorry." Sabrina ran a hand through her
thick blond hair. "I didn't want you to hear that."

Cara gave her a tepid smile. "Thanks for supporting
me."

Sabrina opened he arms and they hugged. "Anytime."

After Cara left Sabrina's office, she couldn't shake the
mixture of hurt and anger rising inside her. Tears of frustration pricked her eyes. No matter how hard a person
worked for something, there was always someone out there
trying to take it away. Sometimes it was easy to forget that
there were still people who disliked her just because of
the color of her skin. Immediately stripped to the lowest
common denominator, she became nothing more than a
color.

Most of the time, she was able to go on. She'd never
allowed statistics to define her life, to tell her what she
could accomplish, or how much she could succeed. But
there was always someone ready to remind her that, in
their eyes, no matter how far she went, no matter what
she achieved, she would never be anything more than a
color.

Cara didn't want to let the incident with the Townsends
get her down, but her heart felt heavy, and she couldn't

seem to shake it. She walked out into the lobby, so intent on her thoughts that she ran right into A.J.'s back.

He spun around and gripped her shoulders. "Hey! Cara?" He looked at her eyes. "Honey, what's wrong?"

She took a step forward and buried her head in his chest. "I just need a hug."

His arms wrapped around her. He guided her over to a secluded corner of The Big Squeeze and sat her down across from him.

"What happened?"

Cara looked at the concern in his eyes. He would understand. Then she frowned. "What are you doing here? I thought you weren't coming in until later?"

"I have a late meeting at Ross, Locke & Malloy. I just dropped by to make sure you could get home safely tonight. Never mind that right now. Why do you look so down?"

She took a deep breath. "I met Wendy's parents today."

He nodded. "And it didn't go well? Did they criticize your training program?"

"No, it was worse than that. They're pulling Wendy out of Tower Vista."

"They're moving?"

"No, but they want her to have a different trainer. One that she can 'relate' to better."

A.J. nodded. "One that's white."

"You got it."

He exhaled a string of expletives. Finally, he said, "How does Wendy feel about all this?"

"I don't think she knows. She wasn't at the meeting when the decision was made. For that matter neither was I."

"What do you mean?"

"They sent me for some paperwork, and on my way back I overheard them talking to Sabrina."

"Did you say anything?"

"At first I was stunned. Then Sabrina told them what they could do with their attitudes and they stalked out. Wendy is going to be crushed. I just hope she gets out on her own before her parents ruin her any more."

A.J. squeezed her knee. "What about you? How are you holding up?"

"I know I shouldn't let them get to me, but I was blindsided. I've gotten so comfortable here with my clients and coworkers that I've let myself forget this was possible."

He leaned over and kissed her on the forehead. "It never gets easier."

She looked into his eyes. "When was the last time something like this happened to you?"

A.J. gave her a sad smile. "It used to happen a lot when I was first starting out. People had a hard time believing I had advanced degrees and might understand something a little more complicated than the physical labor of inserting card A into slot B." He shook his head. "The funny thing is, the farther I've gotten, the more I've realized that only one color rules this world, not black, not white, but green. Money talks. High and mighty businessmen can see their way clear to doing business with anyone if it will improve the state of their wallet."

Cara sighed, twining her fingers through A.J.'s, as he continued.

"What I find more frequent than discrimination these days is just the opposite. People trying to prove just how 'down with the bros' they are. Inviting me to shoot a couple of hoops on the weekend or saying things like 'How 'bout that new Ice-T CD,' and trying out their versions of the latest homeboy slang. I guess I like basketball and rap music as much as the next guy, but when they assume that's *all* I like, I can't resist the urge to stretch the truth a little."

Cara smiled. "What do you mean?"

"Well, one guy was really ticking me off. He said come

over for a fried chicken dinner, we can shoot hoops afterward, and my son has the new L.L. Cool J album."

"What did you say?"

"I said I'm trying to lay off fried foods, golf is my sport of choice, and who is L.L. Cool J?"

Cara burst into giggles. "How did he react to that?"

"His mind was boggled. He just stared at me."

"Good for you. Those kinds of stereotypes are just as bad as the negative ones. They all come from the idea that people know who you are based on a glance."

For a minute they settled into silence, and Cara realized that her heart was no longer heavy.

"Thanks, A.J. I feel better now."

"I'm glad, sweetheart." He looked down at his watch. "I've got to go. Are you sure you can make it home okay?"

"Yes, I'll be fine. You didn't have to come all the way down here for that . . . but I'm glad you did." She gave him a hug.

"I'll call you tonight after my meeting, okay? I'll probably need to hear your voice."

"Is everything okay? You look worried."

"We're still having some problems with the systems at Capital. I'm just praying that when Malloy called this unexpected meeting, it's not because they want an explanation. I need to keep a lid on this. I don't know what I can say if it *has* gotten back to them."

"Well, I have my fingers crossed for you."

"Thanks, honey."

After A.J. left, Cara went through her normal evening routine but her spirits were higher. A.J. always managed to be there for her, despite his problems at work. Actually, she felt partially responsible for his problems. If he hadn't spent so much time on her project, he would have had more time to focus on the Malloy account.

He was always looking out for her best interests. He'd helped her get her CD-ROM off the ground, he'd helped her smooth things out with her father, and most important, he'd proved that it was possible for her to love a man without burying her identity. Now he was going through some rough times at the office, and it was her turn to be there for him. But she wanted to do more than just offer kind words and emotional support. She wanted to do something tangible.

As Cara bounced, leaped, and turned through her aerobics class, the question *What could she do?* bounced, leaped and turned in her head. A.J. knew more about his company than she did. If he didn't know who was behind his problems, how could she find out?

After aerobics, Cara had to give a new client a fitness test. As she counted the woman's sit-ups and timed her on the exercise bike, Cara ran the list of all the people she knew at Capital. Whittaker and Parker were A.J.'s partners; if they were up to no good, A.J. would have a better chance of finding them out than she would. Who else? Chavez was the only person she knew in tech support. She hoped it wasn't him.

Cara frowned. She really didn't know too many people at Capital. Since she'd mainly worked with A.J. early mornings and weekends, she'd rarely seen anyone else. The only other people she'd had contact with were A.J.'s secretary, Leslie, and Angelique.

After completing the fitness test, Cara had a few minutes to herself. She sat at The Big Squeeze, considering her options. Of course A.J. and his partners would have explored all the possibilities. It wasn't likely that she would come up with any ideas they hadn't already thought of, unless she approached it from a completely different angle.

First, A.J. and his partners were men; second, they were computer jocks. Male computer jocks would be looking for other male computer jocks. Cara had learned early in life that men often underestimated women. After careful thought, Cara concluded that Leslie and Angelique were not only the only women in the company, but they were also the only non-computer jocks.

That gave her a place to start. Cara liked Leslie a lot, and she didn't really believe that the woman would do anything to hurt A.J., but Angelique, on the other hand, had been nothing but trouble from the beginning. Cara remembered the day she'd overheard Angelique on the telephone. She'd been certain there was more going on there.

Well, there was only one way to find out. She'd learned enough from her old job at MCS to perform some routine background checks, but Valerie might be able to find something faster. Valerie had been the one to direct her to Capital in the first place. She could probably give her some pointers on what to look for.

When Cara's break was over, she returned to work smiling. Finally she was going to do something as special for A.J. as he'd done for her.

Chapter Sixteen

He couldn't trust anyone. That truth flashed repeatedly in A.J.'s brain like the cursor on his computer screen. The Malloy deadline was two weeks away and someone was trying to sabotage the project. Not knowing who was behind it ate at him the way a computer virus ate RAM. It was definitely an inside job.

He couldn't turn to his partners. Whittaker was obsessed with challenging A.J.'s authority, and Parker was so neurotic, he didn't have a clue what was going on. A.J. would have to sort through the tangled wires on his own.

Who had the most to gain? The obvious answer was RSI. They would get the contract if Capital couldn't deliver. The less obvious answer was Whittaker. He might try to take over if they lost this job. Still, would he jeopardize his own income just to push A.J. out? It didn't make sense.

Maybe an employee was being paid off. All the technicians were under scrutiny, although there was room for error since Parker was too rattled to supervise them himself. It could be anyone . . . Chavez, Angelique, someone from accounting or security.

He didn't have time for guesses and speculations now. Everything was on the line. Capital's reputation. His authority. The future of the company. What happened next was on him.

He had to nail whoever had been hacking in the company computer, and fast. It was time for him to do a little hacking of his own.

Cara stepped into the elevator at Ronnie's building. They had a dinner date that night, and she was anxious to catch her friend up on the latest events in her life. It was one of Ronnie's rare evenings off, and they'd been planning this dinner for two weeks.

Getting off on the third floor, Cara walked down the hall, rang the doorbell, and waited. And waited. She looked at her watch. Yep, six o'clock. She hoped Ronnie was ready, Cara was really hungry.

She pressed the bell again. Ronnie had to be home. She couldn't forget dinner . . . could she?

Finally, the door opened a crack, and Ronnie peaked through. "Oh, damn!"

"Veronica Howard, don't you dare tell me you're not ready."

The door parted another inch. "Um . . ."

Cara could see her friend was still wearing her bathrobe. "You're not sick, are you?"

Ronnie averted her eyes, looking guilty. "Not exactly."

"Well, then let me in. I'll wait for you to get dressed." Cara tried to push the door, but Ronnie held it firm.

"Cara?" ronnie looked behind her then back at Cara, not meeting her eyes. "I don't think . . ."

Now Cara knew something was wrong. It wasn't like

Ronnie to forget a dinner date or hide things from her. "Spit it out, girl. What is it? Do you have a man in there?"

Ronnie gave her a weak smile. "Actually . . ."

"Oh. Anyone I know?" Cara grinned. "Just kidding. I get the hint. I'm leaving. Just tell me one thing before I go. Who is he, where'd you meet him, and why didn't you say something sooner?"

Ronnie's face fell. "I don't want to lie to you Cara, but you're not going to like this."

Cara narrowed her eyes. "Who is he?"

Ronnie stepped back and Cara walked in, looking around. She didn't see anything unusual. "What's going on? Did you forget about dinner?"

"I'm sorry, Cara. I've had a lot on my mind recently."

Then Cara saw the luggage. "Someone moving in or out?"

Ronnie had that guilty look again. "In."

Cara went over and looked at the suitcases stacked by the hall closet door. She picked up the travel label. It was marked with the initials A.R. Cara closed her eyes.

"Please, God. Please tell me these initials don't stand for Andre Roberts."

"He had nowhere else to go."

A chill skied down her spine. When was Ronnie going to learn? Cara looked toward the closed bedroom door.

"Is he here now?"

Ronnie nodded.

Cara spun around and headed for the door.

Ronnie followed her. "I'll call you tomorrow, okay?"

Cara just stared at her friend, then closed the door.

As the elevator descended, so did Cara's hopes. She didn't know how she could stand by and watch her friend go through this hellish cycle again. Before Andre, it had been that loser Derrick in college. He used Ronnie to get through cooking school, then dumped her. Before Derrick, there had been a basketball player, a track star, and a guy on the student council in high school—each made from the same mold. They'd all hurt Ronnie, and Cara had been there to pick up the pieces.

Unfortunately, Ronnie still fell in love with the wrong men. At least in the past she'd picked *different* men. Now she'd gotten stuck to one in particular, and she couldn't shake him off. Cara knew she couldn't do anything more except be there for Ronnie when she finally realized Andre was bad for her.

Cara stared at her computer screen. She'd gone as far as she could go on her own. Valerie was supposed to call her back with the results of the background checks some time that morning. Then maybe the information she'd gathered by herself would start to make sense.

She'd done some networking with computer consultants on the Internet and made discreet inquiries about the CEO of A.J.'s main competition, RSI. According to his peers, Bradley Kincaid was little more than a spoiled rich kid in the body of a corporate executive. He didn't like to lose, and he didn't know the first thing about playing fair.

Several of her online contacts who'd worked with Kincaid said they'd suspected him of dirty-dealing but had never been able to trace anything back to him. It was more than likely that Kincaid was somehow connected with A.J.'s problems. But what was the link?

When Valerie finally called, Cara picked up the phone on the first ring.

"Hi Val, I knew it was you. Have you finished the background checks?"

"Yep. Leslie Kruegger. No story. Unless you care about the fam tradition of marrying docs?"

Cara laughed. "Nope. I figured Leslie would check out.

She's a nice lady, and she and A.J. are pretty close. What about Angelique?"

"Michaels? Piece o' work. Whattaya after?"

Cara's heart started beating faster. "Why? What did you find?"

"A rap sheet longer than my arm."

"For what?"

"Electronic intrusion, data theft. She's a real cyberslut."

"A cyberslut?"

"She'll hack any system for money."

Cara grinned. Why wasn't she surprised? "This is very interesting. A.J. told me Angelique had virtually no computer experience when he'd hired her."

"Well, hon, she lied. Some kinda child prodigy. Multi degrees in Comp Sci and an addiction to big bucks."

"Ah, I knew it. Do you have any idea what she's up to at Capital?"

"The name RSI mean a thing to ya?"

"They were in competition with Capital for a big account. They lost, but there still may be a turnover if the job doesn't pull through."

"That's it then. Bradley Kincaid. CEO. Angelique's current cyberpimp."

"Oh God, that's how they're connected. I have to tell A.J. They've been having problems for months. Who knows how much damage she's done by now. You're a lifesaver, Val. Can you fax me the results of your research so I can show A.J. hard evidence?"

"Sure, Care. No prob. ASAP."

Cara hung up the phone and ran to get dressed. She had to get this information to A.J. right away.

A.J. sat behind his desk massaging his temples. He couldn't believe he'd let his company get so far out of hand. He stared down at the paperwork before him, trying to think past the nerve throbbing in his head. His entire skull seemed to vibrate with his headache.

He leaned back, cushioning his head on the cool leather chair. This time he'd almost blown it. Why had it taken him so long to see the truth right under his nose?

If his head weren't already pounding, he would have slapped his hand against his forehead for his carelessness. Delegate responsibility. He'd known that wasn't a wise decision. If he'd stayed on top of everything as he had in the past, things wouldn't have gotten so far out of control.

Thank God he'd finally gotten everything back on track. Bradley Kincaid's plan had failed, and Angelique had been arrested that morning.

Cara was climbing the elevator walls. She wanted to jump out of her skin, she was so anxious to get to A.J. The doors finally opened on his floor after what seemed like an eternity. It was all she could do not to run down the hall. Instead she managed a slightly more reserved skipping motion.

When she got to his door, she breezed past Leslie with a wave, who she knew was used to this behavior by now, and pushed open his door without knocking. He'd forgive her once he heard what she had to say.

"Cara!" He lifted his head out of his hands and began massaging his temples.

She smiled sympathetically. He looked like he was having a really bad day. She slammed the fax papers down on his desk.

"A.J. I have something very important to tell you."

He looked at her warily. "You're pregnant?"

"No." She frowned. The thought was so foreign it took her a moment to recover.

"Well, then it can wait, honey. Things are really crazy around here today. You won't believe—"

"No, A.J., you have to look at this now." She smoothed her hands over the papers.

"Sweetheart, I'll take you to lunch in, say, an hour. Then we can talk about whatever you want. But I really have to get back to—"

"Please. A.J., you don't understand. This is about Angelique. She's behind all the computer problems you've been having. You see, Bradley Kincaid is her uh, I guess you could call him her employer. He's been paying her to make sure the Malloy project doesn't go through on time."

A.J.'s expression remained blank. The poor thing, he was probably in shock.

"If you don't want to take my word for it, everything is right here." She pointed to the paperwork. "I had it faxed over to me."

Cara waited anxiously while A.J. read each document. She knew it might take a moment for everything to sink in, but she was impatient for a reaction. When she finally got one, it was not what she'd expected.

A.J. put down the papers and gave her a level look, then he burst into laughter.

Oh my God, Cara stared at him in shock. *The man is hysterical.*

"A.J., are you all right?"

He shook his head in amusement as his laughter slowed to a chuckle. He waved the papers in the air.

"How did you get all this?"

Cara frowned. "My former coworker, Valerie. She ran some background checks."

A.J. nodded. "That's cute. You put on your little private detective cap, called in a few favors, and started an investigation. This is great. I wish I'd thought of it."

His mocking tone made Cara grit her teeth, and she felt the stinging heat of annoyance rise in her cheeks. Then her body relaxed as she began to realize what was happening. Of course he was upset that she'd uncovered this information before he had. With his strong sense of responsibility, she should have foreseen this. She just had to make him see that he'd been under so much pressure that no normal human being could be expected to know everything. She reached out toward him.

"I'm sorry, A.J., I understand how you must be feeling right now. You've been under a lot of stress lately. No one would expect you to—"

He shook his head, still chuckling. "No, I'm honestly impressed. Here I was doing things the hard way. It never occurred to me to involve outsiders . . ."

Cara's mind was whirling. So *that's* why he was acting like this. Of course he didn't like the idea of a stranger being brought in on his private business. She'd have to assure him that Valerie could be trusted. Still, she wished he would address all this later and take care of Angelique before it was too late. Her mind was going so fast it took her a moment to comprehend what A.J. was saying.

". . . finally caught Angelique in the act and had her arrested this morning."

Cara's jaw dropped. "She . . . she's in jail, *now*?"

"Yes."

"I don't understand. What happened?"

A.J. took a deep breath and leaned back in his chair. "I started rechecking all the accounts that had system crashes within the last four months, and one of the major factors they each had in common was that they were a part of the core group of accounts Angelique brought to us after she was hired. I'd also found her in the office on several occasions that weren't logged on the books. So I started watching her.

"I figured if she was behind the system problems, she was trying to gain access to the Malloy account. Security is tight on that system, and only Whittaker, Parker, and I have clearance. I was pretty sure she hadn't broken our encryption codes yet, so I set her up. I told her we were under a crunch and gave her access to a phony section of the Malloy account. Then I monitored the system to see if she'd altered the files. Of course she had, and when I confronted her, she was willing to cut any kind of deal to save her ass. She's in pretty deep with a list of prior offenses that should keep her in jail for a long time. She gave us enough to bring RSI up on solid charges, too."

Cara, having lost her adrenaline rush two seconds into his explanation, sagged into a chair.

"Oh, A.J. Why didn't you tell me?"

"I would have if you'd given me the chance."

"But the last time we talked, you didn't have any idea who was behind these problems. I thought Whittaker was your prime suspect."

"Oh, I had my suspicions. Just nothing concrete to base them on."

"I'm sorry I had too little too late," she said sheepishly.

Now she understood his initial sarcasm. She cringed, thinking of how she'd gone on and on when he'd known about Angelique all along.

A.J. grinned. "Well, it was a sweet thought, honey, I'm just sorry you wasted your time."

He folded the papers she'd given him and handed them back to her.

She stared down at the papers. "I'm sorry for barging in like this, A.J. I just hated to see you suffering. You were always so tense and stressed, yet you still found the time to be there for me when I needed you. I wanted to be there for you, somehow."

He came around the desk and kissed her on the forehead. "Thanks for thinking of me, sweetheart, but next time don't worry. I work better when I handle things my own way. I think I could have figured this mess out a lot sooner if I'd followed my gut. Delegating responsibility doesn't work for me. I need to stay on top of things."

Cara raised an eyebrow. It had been her idea for him to delegate some of his work.

"But, A.J., you admitted that you were pushing yourself too hard. No one has to shoulder all the responsibility alone."

He started rubbing her back. "That's true, honey, but sometimes it's hard for other people who aren't as familiar with all the dynamics to really understand how things need to be done. When too many people try to get involved, it may just confuse things."

Cara squinted at A.J., trying to hear what he wasn't saying. "Do you mean me? Are you saying I should have stayed out of it?"

He squeezed her shoulder. "Nooo. It was sweet that you wanted to help. I think it was really cute that you went to all this trouble."

Cara finally started paying attention to the words he was using. Sweet. Cute. These were words for small animals and children.

"Cute? You think my investigation was cute? What about the fact that I didn't have access to half the information you did, and I still figured this out. In a lot less time, I might add. My research may have come too late, but I hit the target dead on."

"That's right, sweetheart. All I'm saying is that you don't have to worry about my company. I've got it covered." He wrapped his arms around her. "There are a lot better things we can worry about . . . together."

Cara pushed out of his arms. "A.J., stop humoring me. You may as well be speaking in one syllable words and patting me on the head. I get the message. You think by concerning myself with your business, I'm just interfering."

"It's not that you're interfering." He shrugged. "It just isn't necessary."

Cara put her hands on her hips. "Was it necessary for you to involve DataVision in my fitness project? Or for you to do all that extra work so they wouldn't drop the project? Was it necessary for you to involve yourself in my problems with my father? Or pick me up after work at night?"

A.J. sighed. "That's different, Cara."

She crossed her arms over her chest. "Why is it different? Because that was my life and this is yours? Remember that time I tried to give you advice about your brother? You wouldn't even listen to me. I tried to explain that you were treating him just like my father had been treating me, but you weren't trying to hear that. You blew me off by saying 'that's different, Cara.' Well why is it different? Because I *need* someone to help me through my problems, but you don't?"

"I didn't exactly say that," A.J. said, shaking his head.

"That's okay because I heard what you did say. I thought our relationship was a partnership. Give *and* take. I just thought it was my turn to start giving a little more. But apparently that was never what you wanted anyway. You wanted to step in and be the hero in my life. Solve all my problems. But when things aren't going right in your life, how dare I assume that the all-mighty hero could possibly need help from a mere woman."

"Cara!"

"You never took me seriously, did you? Not for one minute. When I came in here with information on Angelique, you literally laughed in my face."

"This is ridiculous, Cara. You're blowing this out of proportion. This is business. My whole company's on the line here. You can't expect me to—"

"I don't expect a thing from you. You really had me fooled, letting me think you were different when all along you played a better game on me than Sean ever did. I was just one more responsibility for you to fulfill."

"Maybe we both need to just cool off and discuss this later. We'll meet at my apartment tonight and finish this."

"Oh, believe me," she said, giving him a long look. "It's finished."

Then she turned and left his office without another word.

Chapter Seventeen

A.J. glanced at the clock. Ten minutes before six. Maybe he should just take the work home. He needed to smooth things over with Cara. She must have cooled off by now. He didn't understand how things had gotten so out of control, but he'd make it up to her tonight. He'd pick up groceries on the way home and cook dinner. She loved it when he cooked for her.

He opened the office door and almost ran into a tall, sweaty bicycle courier carrying a box. A.J. immediately moved back. The air had suddenly become very thick.

The courier stepped forward. "Hey, man, you Mr. Gray?"

"Yes," A.J. said, trying not to draw back again.

"Then this is for you." The courier shoved a box into his hands, unfolded a wrinkled sheet of paper, and tapped a blank line for A.J. to sign.

A.J. took one look at the dirty, gnawed-on pen the courier offered and reached into his breast pocket. "No thanks, I have my own."

As A.J. was signing the form, he felt the courier watching him. He looked up. "What?"

The courier was shaking his head and looking him up and down. "Man, what did you *do?*"

"Huh?" A.J. handed him back the paper.

The courier just pointed to the box, shaking his head as he left the office. "All I got to say, man, is you better get you some flowers, quick."

A.J. rolled his eyes at the courier's back. *Sure, man, and you better get some deodorant, quick.*

A.J. had carried the box to his desk when he noticed the handwriting on the note taped to the outside. It was Cara's.

Here are the things you left at my apartment. Please return my belongings via courier. Cara.

A.J. stared silently at the box. What was happening? Was she telling him it was over? He reread the note. This had to be wrong. Why would she break up with him over a silly little argument?

Mindlessly, he ripped open the box. Familiar items stared back at him. His electric razor. Three silk ties. Toiletries that used to sit in the bathroom next to her makeup. Then something else caught his eye. The souvenir he'd bought her on their tour of D.C. She was returning his gifts, too?

Now he was digging through the box. Everything he'd ever given her was there. The stuffed whale from the Aquarium at the Baltimore Inner Harbor, rose-shaped earrings, and even the stick figure drawing he'd made for her on a day neither of them had felt much like working. Until now, she'd kept it tacked above her computer.

How had they gotten to this point? He mentally reviewed their argument, trying to pinpoint exactly when their relationship had taken a fatal turn. She'd been upset because he hadn't thought her investigation was necessary. Then she'd asked him if the things he'd done for her were necessary. He'd said they were different, and then things had gotten crazy.

A.J. groaned. She must have misunderstood something he'd said. He'd been having a bad day and probably said things he shouldn't have. They needed to talk. He had to explain.

Cara paced around her apartment feeling miserable. The more she tried to avoid thinking of A.J., the more he clung to her thoughts.

She flopped down on the couch and began flipping channels with the remote. Finally, she settled on a sitcom rerun, but before long she was wondering why she'd never noticed how much the lead actor resembled A.J. She flipped to an all news station, thinking she'd be safe, when the anchorman started discussing an increase in the use of computers for crime.

Cara flicked off the T.V. and went into the kitchen for something to eat. She opened the refrigerator. She hadn't been shopping in a while. All she had was some milk, eggs, half of a carton of orange juice, and a few carrot sticks. Cara reached for the eggs, then paused, remembering omelet-à-la-A.J. Then she shook her head. If she avoided eating everything A.J. had made for her, she might never eat again.

She put the eggs on the counter, certain she could fix a perfectly good omelet for herself.

After she'd dropped her third eggshell into to the mixing bowl, then spilled the entire mess down the front of her shirt trying to get it out, Cara gave up.

She went into the bathroom to clean up and was struck by an overwhelming sense of emptiness. Now her shampoo bottles and nail polish stood alone on the shelf they used to share with A.J.'s razor and shaving cream. Suddenly Cara felt the full impact of what she'd done.

It wasn't like her to be so impulsive. Sure, she was still upset with A.J., but why had she packed up all his things as if the relationship were beyond repair?

She'd panicked. A.J.'s condescending attitude had combined with her frustration over seeing Ronnie repeat her mistakes with Andre. She hadn't wanted to play the fool. She was afraid of repeating *her* past mistakes. But in her urgency to save herself, Cara had forgotten a couple crucial facts. A.J. wasn't Sean. And she loved him.

After she'd stepped out of the shower, Cara heard someone leaning on her doorbell. When she pulled the door open, A.J. nearly fell over her threshold. Then he quickly picked up a box and pushed his way into her apartment as if he expected the door to slam in is face at any moment.

"Cara, I'm not going to let you just walk out of my life like this. We can work this out if you'll just talk to me. Please, give me a chance to . . . to . . ."

Shutting the door behind A.J., Cara took in his frazzled state. His forehead was creased, and he clutched the box as if he held the weight of their entire relationship in his arms.

"You're right. I overreacted. I shouldn't have packed up all your things and sent them back to you."

A.J. dropped the box at his feet, sagging against the corner of her sofa. "I'm so happy to hear you say that."

Cara twisted her braid between her fingers. A.J. had been through enough turmoil for one day, and she didn't want to add to it. But she wanted him to understand how she was feeling.

"I know you were under a lot of pressure, and I shouldn't have run out of your office the way I did, but—"

He'd crossed the room, and within seconds, Cara was engulfed in A.J.'s warmth.

"I'm so glad you understand." He kissed her on the

cheek, then started tugging at the neckline of her robe. "Let's just put the whole thing behind us."

Cara summoned all her willpower to pull away from the comfort of A.J.'s arms. Then she went over to the box she'd sent him and started picking things out. The D.C. souvenir, the stuffed whale, the earrings, and the sketch.

"Here. I'll keep these things." She pushed the box still full of his clothes and personal items at him. "And you keep this."

"Why? What are you saying?"

"I'm not breaking up with you." She went to sit on the sofa, drawing her knees up to her chest. "But I do think we've been moving too fast lately. Maybe we need some time to ourselves to make sure that we know where we're headed."

A.J. put the box aside and sat in front of Cara on the coffee table. "Just what is it that you're unsure about?"

"Today really opened my eyes about our relationship," she said, pulling her braid over her shoulder.

"Why? Because we fight like normal couples do? Come on, Cara. That wasn't our first fight, and I'm sure it won't be our last."

"I know that, but I don't think I was looking at our relationship realistically. I thought that we had this perfect partnership where we work together and share things."

He shook his head. "I think we do."

"Not really. In all honesty, A.J., it's been kind of one-sided." She unfolded her legs and leaned toward him. *"You* are always doing things for *me.* Making sure my career is on solid ground. Making sure my relationship with my father is stable. Making sure I get home safely every evening."

"Cara, I'm not trying to—"

"It's your nature to look out for people, and I respect that. You're not like Sean. If he did something for me, it was for purely selfish reasons. You do nice things because you care. I know the difference. But what about the fact that you aren't willing to accept any kind of help from me?"

"Cara, if this is about your investigation, I'm sorry I said it was unnecessary. I had a headache, and I was on edge." He reached out to squeeze her knee. "I appreciate the fact that you tried. I really do. Like you said, you hit the target dead on."

"This is exactly my point," Cara said, nodding at his hand on her knee.

A.J. looked at his hand and frowned. "What?"

"When I came to you about Angelique this afternoon, you were so condescending to me. Isn't that sweet, Cara. Isn't that cute. As if I were a child who'd made a mess of the kitchen trying to make her parents breakfast. That's not how you treat someone you view as an equal."

"Cara, I apologize if I made you feel like a child. I told you, I was having a rough day."

"But you also acted like it was foolish to even think you would need help. You kept saying, 'I had it covered.' 'I work better doing things my own way.' Okay, my timing was a little off this time. You did have everything under control by the time I got there, but what if my research had come earlier? Would you have been able to accept the fact that you hadn't figured everything out all by yourself?"

A.J. was silent for a moment. "This is ridiculous, Cara. I don't know how I would have reacted if things had been different. But honestly, I doubt I would be too happy to know that I was lax in my responsibility to Capital."

"That's my point, A.J. I really don't think you know how to lean on another person. It requires that you trust someone else enough not to let you fall, and I don't think you have that trust in me yet."

"Of course I trust you, Cara. I don't understand what the problem is. We're happy together. Where is this coming from?"

Cara sighed in frustration. She knew he wasn't getting it, and she didn't know how to make him understand. Maybe she wasn't making any sense.

"A.J., everyone has an idea of what their ideal relationship should be. To me, love is mutual trust and sharing. I'm not the kind of woman who can sit back and let her man take care of her. I need to know that I can contribute as much to this relationship as I can take from it. I want you to need me."

He reached for her hands. "I do need you."

"Not in the way that I mean." She shook her head. "I feel shut out of your life."

A.J. was silent as he let go of her fingers. He looked as if someone had just punched him in the stomach.

"Look, maybe this will change with time. Maybe it's just the way I look at things. Right now, all I'm asking for is a little time to think."

His eyes were full of confusion when his gaze met hers. "And in the meantime?"

"In the meantime," she said, taking one of his hands between hers, "I'd still like to see you. I still want to go out. I just want us to slow down. Spend some nights in our own beds. Alone."

A.J. took a deep breath, shaking his head. "Okay. If this is what you want."

Cara wrapped her arms around his neck. "Thanks, A.J. I know you don't understand, but thanks for trying."

"What are you doing up there?" Cara asked for the umpteenth time as Ronnie snipped away at her hair.

She held her breath, trying not to focus on Ronnie's own hair. It was wound into huge spiraling twists and had been dyed the same color as a brand new copper penny. Maybe she should have reconsidered this decision.

"Be quiet. Now that you're finally letting me cut your hair, it's too late to stop."

Cara tried to reach up, but Ronnie smacked her hand away.

"Stop fussing. I'm almost done. I know what will get your mind off your hair. This is good news."

Cara held her breath. Ronnie had better not tell her she and Andre were getting married. She'd held her tongue this long, but she refused to stand by and watch Ronnie make the biggest mistake of her life.

"I gave Andre the boot. For good this time."

Cara raised her eyebrows but she didn't raise her hopes. She'd heard this before. She'd thought the magazine incident would've been the end of him, but even then, Ronnie had taken him back. Cara finally accepted that Ronnie might not ever let him go.

"Girl, I know what you're thinking—I've said this before. But believe me, this time it's really different. I'm tired of his trash, and I finally realized that I deserve something better."

"That's great, Ronnie." She hesitated to say anything more.

"Honestly, Cara, I knew how you felt about him moving in, but I appreciate the fact that you didn't say anything. That look you gave me was enough. It really started me thinking. Your reaction made me feel guilty, and I felt that way because I knew I was wrong. But, if you'd said something to me, I probably would have felt obligated to defend him. At least this way, the truth finally sank in. And it sank in good this time."

"Oh, Ronnie, if I could, I'd hug you."

"Don't you dare move. I'm finished cutting. Now I'm going to curl it."

"Can I see?"

"No, it doesn't look like anything yet, and you'd probably pitch a fit. Tell me what's up with you and A.J."

Cara was silent. Where did she start?

"That bad?"

"We had a fight yesterday."

"Over what?"

"Well, I told you that he was having some problems at work, and that I asked Valerie to do some background checks for me."

"Yeah."

"Well, once I got proof that Angelique was behind his problems at the office, I went straight to A.J."

"And what happened?"

"I ended up looking like a fool."

"Why?"

"Because not only did A.J. already know about Angelique, he'd had her arrested that same morning."

"Oh, Lord!"

"Basically, he laughed at me. He thought it was so 'cute' that I thought I could help him. He treated me like a three-year-old."

"You're kidding? That's testosterone for you."

"He wasn't taking me seriously. He thinks everything is *his* responsibility, and he has to take care of everything all by himself. He doesn't want my help or my advice. I was so upset, I packed up all the stuff he had at my apartment and sent it back to him. He came over later to apologize, but things still aren't quite right.

"Just like Sean couldn't stand to let me do anything for him, A.J. will never let himself need me."

Ronnie stopped curling her hair and came around to face Cara. "Damn, if you two aren't made for each other."

"What are you talking about? Weren't you listening to me?"

"Sure, I was listening. Were you?"

"What do you mean?"

"It's no wonder you two keep clashing," Ronnie said,

waving a brush at her. "You both want to control each other."

Cara sat up straight. "I've never tried to control him."

"Yes, you have! By fighting so hard *not* to let him control you. I won't date you—I will date you—I won't date you."

Cara shook her head, dislodging the comb Ronnie had planted in her hair. "That's not true."

Ronnie picked up the curling iron and went back to work. "Sure it is. He needs you, but he doesn't realize it. He's just as convinced as you are that he needs to be in control all the time."

"I've gotten past that."

"Not completely. What you've been saying is that in order for you to feel like you're not losing control in this relationship, you need to know it's not one-sided. He has to accept your help just like you accept his, right?"

"Yeah, I guess."

"And for him to feel in control, he needs to know he's taking care of his responsibilities. But by accepting help from someone else, he feels like he's not being responsible."

"Exactly. That's the problem."

"What you both need to realize is that you can't always be in control in a relationship. But that's a good thing. You always have someone to watch your back when you're not able to. You should be happy that you two look out for each other. The rest of us have to deal with guys who are too selfish to bother."

"You're right, but if he shuts me out every time he has a problem, how can we ever really be close?"

"I'm sure that will change with time."

"Maybe, but what if it doesn't?"

Ronnie was silent for a few minutes. "I'm done. Are you ready to see your new fly hairdo?"

"Let's see. Give me a mirror, quick, before I lose my nerve."

Ronnie lowered the mirror over her head, but it was so close, Cara couldn't see anything past her nose. She grabbed the handle and pulled it back. Her hair was still long but now curling toward her face and around her shoulders in a lighter, fluffier style. She caught her breath.

"It's . . . pretty." She caught Ronnie's eye in the mirror. "But, can I do this myself?"

"I cut it so all you have to do is curl the ends every now and then. Very low maintenance. Believe me, I don't want you backsliding into that braid. Now the sides are too short. The worst you can do is a ponytail."

Cara blinked at her reflection. No more French braids? "Ronnie, how long before it grows back?"

A.J. slammed down the telephone. Mitch had just finished a meeting with Cara at DataVision. He'd wanted to ask him how was she doing. How she looked. But A.J. couldn't let Mitch know he saw more of his girlfriend than A.J. did.

Lately, he and Cara hadn't had any time together. She wouldn't let him pick her up at the club anymore, and with the Malloy deadline closing in, he didn't even have time to work out. He called every chance he had, but they usually ended up playing answering machine tag. The few times he had caught her on the phone, their conversations were short and strained.

A.J. felt a nerve in his forehead begin to throb. Why had their relationship suddenly gone flat? If he understood what she wanted, he'd give it to her. But she hadn't made any sense. He couldn't change what had happened in his office, and his apologies didn't seem to be enough.

Rubbing his temple, A.J. opened his bottom desk drawer. Blindly, he felt around for the familiar shape of his aspirin bottle. Instead his fingers wrapped around a small plastic case. He pulled it out. A cassette tape?

He read the handwritten label. *Boogaloo Sounds.* His brother's rap group. A.J. sighed. Eddie had given him the tape months ago. But A.J. had been frustrated with him for one reason or another and had stuck it in the drawer without listening to it.

He started to toss it back when something Cara had said came back to him. How did he know Eddie was wasting his time if he'd never listened to his music?

A.J. shook his head. He had deadlines to meet. He didn't have time for this. He threw the tape back into the drawer and turned to his computer, but he stopped typing mid-sentence. Cara had said he was treating Eddie the same way her father had treated her. Was she right?

No. A.J. swatted the air with his hand. That was different. Then he paused. The day he and Cara had argued in his office, she blew up at him over those exact words. Was she right? *Had* he blown off her opinion without even considering it?

A.J. pulled Eddie's tape out again. He looked around the office. He didn't have anything to listen to it on. Then he remembered that Leslie kept a portable radio at her desk.

After he had Leslie's cassette player plugged in, he popped in Eddie's tape. He leaned back in his chair to concentrate on the music. He'd only planned to listen to one song, but when the entire cassette had played, A.J. found himself turning it on again.

Cara had been right about Eddie and his music. Could she have been right about a few other things?

Around the time she normally met with Wendy, Cara sat at The Big Squeeze feeling down. Since Wendy's parents had pulled her out of the program, Cara not only had a hole in her day, she had a gap in her life. She really missed Wendy. Every time Cara thought about the girl's parents, she became angry and frustrated all over again. Not only because they were robbing Cara of Wendy's company, but because they were robbing Wendy of so much more.

Wendy had finally found something to give her confidence. Something that allowed her to see the person she really was, not just the person she saw through her parents' distorted eyes. Cara hoped Wendy would find another program somewhere else. She hated to think of Wendy losing all the progress she'd made. Cara wished she knew how the girl was doing.

"Hey Cara."

Her head snapped around to see Matt walking toward her.

"Hi, Matt."

"Do ya got a minute?"

She glanced at her watch, laughing sadly. "I've got thirty minutes. What can I do for you?"

"I wanna show you something."

"What is it?"

"A surprise."

She followed Matt downstairs, and he pointed to one of the meeting room doors. She looked at him suspiciously as she pushed it open.

Wendy sat inside, waiting. As soon as she saw Cara, the girl jumped up to give her a hug.

"Wendy! What are you doing here," Cara asked, giving her a tight squeeze. "Let me look at you."

She looked great. Her red hair, no longer frizzy, was long and thick, curling in beautiful waves. "Look at that hair!"

"I got a perm. Do you like it?"

"I love it. And that's such a cute outfit," Cara said, admiring her ivory cashmere sweater and matching leggings.

"Thanks. Once I lost weight, my mother insisted on

buying me a whole new wardrobe. She said I never had the figure for nice clothes before.''

Cara stiffened as she tried to hide her disdain.

Wendy grabbed her hand. "Sit next to me. I want to talk to you. I missed you so much, I had to sneak a visit."

"I miss you, too, Wendy. But I don't want you to get in trouble."

"Oh, I don't care what they say. That's partly why I'm here. My mom wouldn't tell me what happened, so I called Sabrina. I want to apologize for how my parents treated you. I feel just awful."

"Don't worry about it, Wendy. It's not your fault."

"I threw the biggest fit of my life when they told me they didn't want me to come back here. I told them I would come whether they wanted me to or not, but I didn't have enough money for the membership. This summer I'll get a job so I can pay for it myself. I'm not going to let them tell me what to do."

Inside, Cara's heart was bursting with joy. Wendy's inner strength was shining through. She was so proud, she wanted to hug her.

"Not five minutes ago I was sitting at The Big Squeeze worrying about you, and here you are looking better and happier than I've ever seen you. Are you keeping up with your workout?"

Wendy smiled devilishly. "No way. My mom tried to enroll me in the health spa at her country club, but I refused to go. I'm threatening to gain the weight back just to spite her."

Cara raised her eyebrows.

"Don't worry. I won't. I'm doing sit-ups and stuff at night in my room after they go to bed. It wouldn't matter if I did gain some of it back though. Jimmy says he'd like me either way."

Cara's heart smiled. Wendy had finally caught on. It

didn't matter how she looked on the outside. What mattered was how she felt about herself.

"Ooh. Who's Jimmy?"

"My new boyfriend," she said with an excited giggle.

Wendy told her all about Jimmy, and Cara was enjoying their girl-talk until Wendy brought up A.J.

"Things aren't going too well between us right now."

"Why not?"

"We just don't see eye to eye on something important."

"Do you want to talk about it?"

Cara felt very close to Wendy, so she told her the PG version of what had been going on.

"A.J.'s the kind of person who likes to do things for other people, but he doesn't like for people to do things for him. I told him that makes me feel shut out of his life. But he misunderstood me."

"What do you mean?"

"Well, it's his nature to want to fix things. So yesterday I received a box from Federal Express. It was full of his High School yearbooks, family photo albums, and old home videos. He thought that if I knew more about him, I wouldn't feel shut out."

"But that isn't what you were looking for?"

Cara sighed. "No. Unfortunately, I don't think it's something that can be fixed that easily. He has spent so much time doing things his own way, depending only on himself, there's nothing I can do for him. He doesn't need me."

Wendy stared at her for a long time, and then she started laughing.

Cara frowned. "What's so funny?"

"You and A.J. are so much alike," Wendy said, shaking her head.

"That's what Ronnie said."

"Cara, A.J. does need you."

"How do you know?"

"Because he needs you to need him. Just like you need

him to need you. That's why he's always doing things for you. That's his way of showing he loves you."

"Yes, but what about him? He's so self-sufficient. He won't let me do the same for him."

"Why is it so important that you solve his problems for him? You two are happy together, and you both work hard to make the other person happy. Why isn't that enough?"

"I don't know . . . that's something to think about." She gave Wendy a hug. "Ya know what, kid? You're pretty smart."

A.J. rested his chin on his palm. He still wasn't making any progress with Cara. He'd been thinking about the things she'd said to him. After he realized she'd been right about his brother, he figured she must have been right about him holding back from her. He tried to fix that. The yearbooks and photos were to help her understand where he was coming from.

But when he'd talked to her on the phone that morning, she'd said that wasn't what she'd meant by feeling shut out. He didn't know what else to do!

The phone rang on his desk, and when he answered the line, he heard his mother's voice. "A.J. I got tired of waiting for you to call. I haven't heard from you all week."

"Sorry, Mamma. Things have been really crazy around here." He filled her in on what had been going on at work.

"Well, you've had quite a week. I didn't know things had been so hectic. I called because I talked to your brother this morning."

"Oh yeah?"

"A.J., it meant so much to him that you went to see him at the studio last night. He couldn't stop talking about it."

"I'm glad I went. You know, Mamma, he really knows his stuff. He gave me a tour and showed me all the equipment. I've never seen him so serious about anything. We even talked about the music program at Howard University. He actually said he'd think about taking a few courses.''

"Oh that's wonderful, A.J. What made you finally decide to give him a chance?''

"It was something Cara said to me.''

"How is Cara? You two should come over for dinner some night next week.''

"I don't know, Mamma. I haven't seen too much of her lately.''

"Don't tell me you and Cara are having problems? She's my future daughter-in-law. Don't you go messing up with that girl, ya hear? What happened?''

"I'm not sure. We had an argument.''

"About what?''

He told her how the fight had unfolded. "When I went to her place that night to work things out, she'd calmed down a lot. But she was still upset. She said she wasn't sure where our relationship was headed. That I don't need her. That I didn't trust her enough to lean on her, or something. But that doesn't make sense.''

"It makes a lot of sense. I should have known this was going to happen sooner or later.''

"What? Why?''

"There's something I should have said to you a long time ago. Anthony-James, you are not your father.''

"What does *he* have to do with this?''

"Ever since you were a child, you've gone around taking care of everybody. Me. Your brother. All your friends. I know because your father was never there for you, you felt like you had to be self-sufficient. When you were growing up, I tried to get you to open up to me. But you never wanted to ask for help when you had problems.''

"That's not true, Mamma. I always came to you for advice. I still do.''

"No, A.J. You tell me about your problems after you've

solved them. You never give me an opportunity to help you. For instance, this is the first I've heard that you'd been having difficulties at Capital. But this has probably gone on for weeks, right?"

A.J. took a deep breath. "Months. I'm sorry, Mamma. I hadn't realized I was shutting you out, too."

"As your mother, it was hard to come to terms with the fact that my baby didn't need me. But you're my son, and you'll always be a part of me. That makes it easier for me to accept, but Cara doesn't have that kind of bond with you. She *needs* to know that you need her."

"Well, Mamma, now I'm asking. What should I do? I don't want to lose her."

"It's simple, A.J., just open up with her. Let her see that you haven't got all the answers. Don't be afraid to let her help you."

"Thanks, Mamma. I have a lot to think about."

Chapter Eighteen

"A.J. What are you doing here?" Cara asked when she opened the door Sunday evening. She hadn't been expecting him but felt like an addict suffering from withdrawal. Her eyes drank in the sight of him.

Apparently, her new hairstyle had caught him off guard. He stared at her for a moment before answering.

"I . . . Your hair looks great. When did you do this," he asked, reaching out to touch the soft waves.

"A couple of days ago. I finally let Ronnie do her thing."

"I love it." He let his hand drift down to rest on her shoulder. "I was hoping you'd let me take you out to dinner. I've missed you, and we need to talk."

"Uh, okay." She glanced down at the old sweatshirt and shorts she'd been wearing to clean the bathroom. "Just let me change."

She came out wearing gray slacks and a clingy white sweater. "Is this okay? Where are we going?"

"That's perfect. I thought we'd go to Bish Thompson's."

"Oh, seafood. Sounds great."

Their small talk was strained on the drive over, and by the time they were seated in the restaurant, they'd abandoned all attempts at conversation.

Cara's heart ached when she looked at A.J. and realized how different things were now. Was this her fault? She knew she couldn't expect him to change. Could she be happy with things the way they were?

The waiter placed some hush puppies on the table, and Cara was grateful to have something to do with her hands—she no longer had her braid to fidget with.

When A.J.'s hands grazed hers in the basket, their gazes met. Too bad physical attraction alone wasn't a strong foundation for a lasting relationship. If it were, she and A.J. would be partners for life.

"Cara, there's something I wanted to tell you."

She leaned forward to hear him over the loud voices coming from a raucous family sitting behind her. "Yes?"

"Um . . . I saw my brother the other day."

She leaned back, feeling a bit disappointed. She'd hoped he wanted to talk about their relationship. "Oh, yeah? How's Eddie doing?"

"Great." A.J. picked up a fork and began to twirl it between his fingers. "I found an old demo tape of his in a drawer, and I listened to it."

Cara raised her eyebrows. "Really? Was it any good?"

He continued to spin his fork until finally it landed on the floor. He retrieved it and set it at the end of the table, picking up his spoon.

"Actually, it was very good," he said, tapping his palm with the spoon. "But if you hadn't said something to me about it, I might never have known."

Cara's heart beat faster. "What do you mean?"

A.J. tapped his spoon until it slid through his hands and under the table. He picked it up and placed it next the fork, then reached for his knife.

Cara grabbed his hand. "A.J., stop. You're not going to

have any silverware left to eat with." She squeezed his fingers. "Now, what is it you're trying to tell me?"

A.J. took a deep breath and folded his hands in his lap. "When you told me about my brother, I didn't listen to you. I was so sure I knew what was best. But, after our last fight, I started thinking about what you'd said about me blowing off your advice. You were right. When I took my brother's music seriously, he and I really started to connect. I went to see him at the studio, and I gained a lot of respect for him. He's really working hard at trying to make it. We even talked about him taking some music courses at Howard."

"A.J., that's great. I'm so glad."

He gave her a serious look. "Cara, I'm not going to lie. When we first started having problems, nothing you said made sense to me. All I knew was that we'd been happy together, and I didn't see how one argument could change all that."

"A.J., I just—"

"Wait. When I realized you were right about my brother, I started wondering if there was more that I was missing. I tried everything I could think of to fix things between us, but I still didn't understand until I talked to my mom."

"Your mom? What did she say?"

A.J. toyed with his napkin. "She said she'd often felt the same way you're feeling, Cara. I hadn't realized that she'd been feeling shut out for thirty-five years."

He didn't meet her eyes as he began smoothing wrinkles on the table cloth. "I thought I was making things easier for her. She had so much to worry about already. Lord knows, my father was never there for her. I thought if I worked things out on my own, that was one less problem. I didn't know she felt like I didn't need her."

A.J. finally looked in her eyes. "When I told her about us, she told me that was how I was making you feel. And I'm sorry, Cara. I didn't mean to. Hell, I thought if I did the opposite of everything my father did, I couldn't go wrong."

Cara reached across the table to hold his hand. "Where do we go from here?"

"I'm willing to work on this if you'll bear with me. It's going to take some time for me to learn to lean on someone besides myself."

"I understand."

His eyes searched hers. "I don't want this to come between us."

She stared into his eyes. She could see that he was sincere, but for some reason she still felt unsure. What if A.J. couldn't let her into his life completely? She loved him, but she didn't want to be like Ronnie—repeating past mistakes over and over. How could she be sure this was right?

A.J. was waiting for a response, and Cara still didn't know what to say.

"Cara, please—" His sentence was interrupted by the shrill beeping of his pager. "Damn! I'm sorry, I've got to check on this. The final Malloy presentation is tomorrow, and I told them to page me for any little problem. I'll be right back."

When A.J. returned two minutes later, she still wasn't any closer to an answer. She looked up when he came to stand by her chair. "What's wrong?"

His brow was furrowed. "I'm really sorry, Cara, but we've got to leave. There's an emergency at the office."

"Oh no! What is it?"

"Chavez didn't say. He said he's calling the other partners. I need to get over there ASAP, but I don't have time to drop you at home. Do you mind going along for the ride? If it's something I can wrap up quickly, we can still have our dinner. If not, I'll send you home in a cab."

"Sure. No problem."

A.J. left a wad of bills on the table, then grabbed her

hand and led her out of the restaurant. He must have broken some speeding laws on the way to Capital because they arrived in record time. She followed him through the building, and they found everyone collected in his office.

"What's going on?" A.J. asked.

Chavez, Parker, and Whittaker were already there, along with another technician Cara didn't recognize. Parker and A.J. were both dressed casually, probably as they normally would on a Sunday evening, but Whittaker had taken the time to put on a three-piece suit.

Not wanting to get in the way, Cara leaned against a wall in a corner of the office. No one mentioned her presence except for an inquiring look from Whittaker, to which A.J. replied, "She's with me."

Chavez walked up to A.J. "I hate to tell you this, man, but we found a virus in the Malloy system."

A.J. swore. "Did you clean it up?"

A film of sweat covered Chavez's forehead. "We can't."

"Why the hell not?" A.J. looked around the circle of faces for an answer.

Chavez nudged the younger blond technician next to him, signaling him to respond.

"Um . . . we were just doing the Final QC on the accounting program when the virus showed up. We ran the anti-virus software, but not only wouldn't it remove the sucker, it couldn't even detect it."

Chavez fidgeted with the baseball cap on his head. "Yeah, man. Danny and I tried everything. The system doesn't show any unusual files or clusters."

A.J. looked puzzled. "Then what exactly is the problem?"

The two technicians exchanged looks. "Well, instead of loading the accounting program, the machine keeps pulling up a video game," Chavez said.

"That's impossible," Whittaker said. "You must have loaded the wrong disks."

Chavez shook his head. "Nah, man. We tried several copies. None of them work."

A.J. turned on his computer. "Let me see the disks you used."

They handed him the disks, and A.J. tried them all. Sure enough, a video game kept appearing on the screen.

"Damn. Has anyone notified the people at Malloy?" A.J. asked.

Whittaker stepped forward. "We can't do that. If they find out about this screw up before we fix it, the job will go down the tubes."

A.J. shot him a dirty look. "The job is already down the tubes, old man. The accounting software is the most crucial segment. If we can't get it to work tonight, there's no way we'll pull off tomorrow's presentation. Parker, have you taken a look at this yet?"

Parker's head jerk up at the sound of A.J.'s voice. "Uh, uh what?"

"I said what do you think? Have you taken a look at this yet?"

"Of course," he said with confidence.

Cara bit her lip from her forgotten corner as everyone turned expectant gazes on Parker. Chavez and Danny were whispering excitedly to each other, Whittaker and A.J. were waiting for a response, and Parker, who seemed to become more flustered by the minute, didn't utter a word.

"Well?" Whittaker prompted.

Parker just shrugged his shoulders and shook his head, his eyes darting around the room.

A.J. sighed. "If Parker's stumped, we've got real trouble."

Whittaker smoothed the front of his suit. "Obviously, Angelique is behind this."

A.J.'s head snapped around. "How could she be behind this? Only—" He stopped mid-sentence to scan the room. His eyes fell on the two technicians who were watching the exchange intently. "You two can go. We'll take it from here."

Chavez looked disappointed. "Are you sure? We don't mind staying to help you figure this out."

He shook his head as he walked them to the door. "I think I have this under control. But stand by. I'll call if I need you."

Cara thought she would be the next to be dismissed, and was about to volunteer to call herself a cab. More was going on here than just the virus, and A.J. didn't seem to want an audience when he got to the bottom of it. But to her surprise, he met her eyes for a brief moment, then he turned back to Whittaker who was loudly protesting.

"What gives you the right to dismiss them? We may need their input. After all, they were the first to discover the virus."

A.J. gave the man a hard look. "We don't need them because the person behind our problems is still in this room. It can't be Angelique because, number one, she has been arrested, and number two, only the three of us have the kind of network security clearance to tamper with the system."

Whittaker blinked at A.J. "What are you saying?"

"I'm saying," A.J.'s voice became menacing, "that you can cut the act. You were the last person to work on the accounting program, and you're the only one who would have anything to gain in this situation."

Whittaker stroked the knot of his tie as his face began to redden. "Now see here—"

"Don't bother denying it, old man. It all just became crystal clear. Angelique wasn't supposed to be arrested five days before the Malloy deadline. If she hadn't been, no doubt she could have taken the heat for this before turning up missing."

He advanced on Whittaker. "No one would be able to blame you once we discovered she was working for Bradley

Kincaid and had prior arrests for hacking. Then it would be conceivable that she hacked through the security system. But since she has already confessed to everything else, we know this is an inside job. If we lose this account, you'll get what you've been after. Proof that I'd run the company into the ground and a basis to take over yourself. Right, old man?''

Whittaker was lobster-colored and blustering. "This is preposterous! How can you suggest something so outrageous? I have more to gain if this deal succeeds than if it fails. Why would I risk everything? You're blaming me to divert attention from your incompetence. You can't cover up your blunder by shifting the blame.''

The two men continued to argue—loudly—and Cara was afraid they might come to blows. She was about to step in and try to calm them down when she caught sight of Parker. She'd been watching A.J. and Whittaker so closely, she'd almost forgotten about him. Why didn't he try to get involved? Instead, he seemed to become more agitated. He was leaning against a wall, his body so tense it almost trembled. His eyes were bouncing from one man to the other, with an anxious, almost wild gaze. Cara shook her head in sympathy. Parker wasn't taking this well at all. The commotion between the two other men was upsetting him. She hoped the near violence wasn't bringing back memories of the mugging.

"Stop it!" Parker shouted, startling everyone into silence. "Look at you two. Arguing. Arguing. You're always arguing. Stop it. Just stop it.''

"It's okay, Parker. Calm down," A.J. said, reaching for his arm.

Parker jerked away. "What are you doing?"

"Nothing," A.J. said, backing off. "I just wanted to—''

"I didn't do anything wrong." Parker ran a shaky hand through his shaggy cut.

Whittaker huffed impatiently. "Calm down, you idiot.

We haven't got time for your paranoid games. No one has accused you of anything."

Parker's eyes became wide for a moment, then they narrowed. "You both think you're so clever. Why?" His laugh bordered on hysterical. "Why couldn't I have done this?"

Parker looked directly at A.J. "Betcha didn't think I could do it, did ya? Well, I did. Right under both of your noses. You never knew. You never thought I was cap-able. Damn. You both thought I was obliv-ious. Hell. Well I wasn't. I was smarter than both of you." His voice rose in pitch, and he began speaking faster. The more he talked, the more his voice cracked and he cursed. Soon it was almost impossible to understand what he was saying.

A.J. stepped toward Parker. "Man, you're hysterical—"

"You stay away from me," Parker yelled, his arms flailing. "Both of you. I don't—"

Whittaker grabbed Parker's shoulder and socked him in the face. Parker crumpled to the floor instantly.

Cara, who'd been clinging to the wall in stunned silence rushed to Parker's side. A.J. and Whittaker were gathered around him.

"Man, Whittaker. What the hell did you hit him for?"

Whittaker looked a bit regretful as they tried to shake Parker's limp form back to consciousness. "I just wanted to calm him down."

A.J. quirked an eyebrow at him. "You *slap* someone to calm them down! You only *punch* someone if you want to knock 'em out."

Cara knelt close. "Look, he's coming around."

Parker opened his eyes, whimpering. He began muttering unintelligible words and repeating over and over again, "I just . . . wanted . . . to be . . . somebody."

Cara touched his cheek. "Parker, are you okay?" She repeated the question several times, but he wouldn't answer her. His eyes were unfocused as he continued muttering and whimpering.

A.J. looked into his eyes. "I think he's okay physically, but mentally . . . he's gone."

Whittaker stood, still looking guilty. "What should we do with him?"

"Call the police. Explain what happened and have them come down and pick Parker up. I'll give my statement later." A.J. looked toward his computer. "Right now, I've got a crisis on my hands."

Whittaker snapped to attention, some of his color returning now that he had a task to complete. While he dialed police, Cara helped A.J. lift Parker's listless form onto the sofa. Whittaker joined them in the hall, and they locked the door to A.J.'s office.

Cara followed the men to the technical support office filled with computer terminals. A.J. sat in front of one and Whittaker pulled up a seat beside him. They logged onto the system, and within minutes, the two of them were cursing up a blue-streak. Cara looked on over their shoulders.

Elaborate video graphics of crashing buildings and animated, crying computers taunted them from the screen. At least Parker had a sense of humor. She almost giggled as the image of a sinister, amoeba-like creature chased a track-shoed PC terminal across the monitor. The words, *Type Go to Play,* scrolled across the bottom of the screen.

A.J. looked at Whittaker. "Do you have any more copies of the accounting program?"

"I probably have some in the car."

"Good. You get those and I'll try to load mine."

While Whittaker retrieved his copies, A.J. systematically tried each of his disks, all of which displayed the virus game. When Whittaker returned, his disks showed the same problem.

"I don't understand. These worked just fine before I

left this evening," Whittaker grumbled. "How could the virus have gotten to them?"

"My disks were fine, too. Obviously the virus is on the network and is invading all the backup files we try to install." A.J. massaged his temple. "Let me try restoring the program from the tape backup. It might not be the most updated version, but it will give us something to work with."

While A.J. tried to restore the backup file, Whittaker went to talk to the police officers who'd arrived for Parker. Cara hung back, watching A.J. work and feeling more useless than she ever had in her life.

She could see the tension in his hunched shoulders as his fingers moved over the keyboard. She wanted to walk over and smooth the tight muscles at the base of his neck, run the back of her hand over the soft stubble on his chin, or just wrap her arms around him. But Cara knew that wasn't what he needed right now.

When he relaxed against the back of his chair, waiting for the file to upload, she moved to his side. "A.J., maybe I should go home. I don't want to be in the way."

"No." His fingers closed around hers and squeezed. "Please stay. I need a friendly face close by right now."

It might not have been much, but it was something, so Cara pulled up a chair. A.J.'s tension became her own as she watched the blue status bar of the program uploading to the hard drive reach 100 percent.

A.J. began typing commands and let out a soft curse just as Whittaker appeared in the doorway.

"Parker's been taken into custody," Whittaker said, pinching the knot in his tie. "Any luck?"

A.J. pushed the keyboard away in frustration. "Damn it! I don't know how he did it, but Parker managed to get to the tape backup as well."

Whittaker folded his arms. "Then we have to get Parker back here to fix this!"

A.J. snorted. "Parker has taken every precaution to see that we can't restore this program in time for tomorrow's presentation. Do you really think that after we've had him arrested, we could trust him to fix this? For whatever reason, Parker wanted us to lose this contract, and it looks like he may get his wish."

Parker rested his head on the back seat of the police car, feeling the pain of his split and swelling lower lip.

He'd screwed things up badly. He'd had the world in the palm of his hand, and he'd managed to ruin everything.

Angelique had been his last chance. He'd thought he'd been so clever. For months, Gray and Whittaker had wondered about the system glitches. Once he'd set his mind to it, *he'd* found out within a matter of days. A simple trip wire in the Malloy system, and he'd caught Angelique red-handed.

Then he'd held all the power—for the first time in his life. Power over Angelique. Command of Capital's fate. Control over his own future. It was all in his hands. He could have turned in Angelique and been a hero at Capital. Could have saved the Malloy project and finally had the respect he deserved from his partners. But Angelique had promised him something better.

After the mugging, he'd sworn never to be exploited or underestimated again. He'd thought Angelique had understood him. She made him believe Gray and Whittaker didn't deserve his hard work, that they used him for physical labor and took all the credit.

Parker slumped against the seat, trying to ignore the cuffs chafing his wrists. Angelique promised that he'd head an entire *branch* at RSI. Power, money, prestige—at his fingertips, and all he had to do was bring down Capital.

What a fool he'd been. Angelique had been caught and now so had he. Now he could see that he'd blindly accepted promises that would never be kept. That's what he deserved for betraying the only company where he'd ever belonged.

"We have to try *something,*" Whittaker said, moving up behind A.J.

A.J. started typing, and Whittaker grabbed his arm. "What are you doing?"

"I'm trying something. We may as well see where this game leads us." He typed the word "go."

"Stop. You might make it worse." Whittaker pushed the keyboard out of A.J.'s reach. "Right now, all we're missing is the accounting program. By the time you're through, everything could be destroyed."

"We haven't got too many options here. What else can we do?"

Suddenly the computer started beeping and the words *Time's Up* flashed on the screen. Apparently, while A.J. and Whittaker argued, the game had gotten tired of waiting.

The video graphics returned to the screen, this time periodically interrupted by the message **Two Chances Left,** flashing in bold letters.

"Now look what you made me do." A.J. slapped the table. "Once you tell it to start, you're under some kind of time limit. We only have two more chances to work through this. After that, it will probably crash the entire system."

"Maybe Angelique knows something about this. We can call the jail and—"

"That's a stupid idea," A.J. cut Whittaker off. "Hasn't she caused enough trouble already?"

"Well, we haven't got any other choices. We have to try."

"What if she doesn't have the first clue what to do? And who knows if she'd tell us if she did?"

Whittaker crossed the room to the phone. "There's only one way to find out."

It was cold. Angelique figured this was what the world would be like when hell froze over. And without a doubt, she was in hell.

Alaska. After some pleading and cajoling, her mother flew in from Europe to bail her out of jail. Drab prison garb and menial labor were not for her. Been there, done that. And she wasn't doing it again. She couldn't go back to Europe. No doubt she was wanted there, too. Through the underground hacking networks, she'd uncovered a safe place to hide out.

But Alaska! Why couldn't her contact have found her someplace warm like Florida or California. These polar temperatures would be murder on her skin. She burrowed deeper into her hunter green parka, gingerly stepping out of the van. She hadn't taken two steps before she was flat on her backside.

A pair of arms wrapped around her and hauled her to her feet. "Didn't they tell you to wear sensible shoes?" The man eyed her leather boots with disdain. "You won't last long with those prissy things. And you'll have to by more substantial clothing." He fingered the flimsy material of her cashmere pants. "Some strong materials. Flannel and wool."

She hadn't worn flannel in all her life. "Who the hell are you?" She tried to knock his hand away and almost lost her balance again.

"Icepick," he said, quoting the screen name her contact had given her. "I am to look after you. You and I will get along . . . very well. I like feisty women." Then, eyes full of suggestion, he scooped her into his arms and carried her toward his home.

Angelique gazed up at the fur-lined face of the man

who held her. He had chubby Eskimo cheeks and a wide squashed-looking nose. He stared down at her with a gap-toothed grin.

Angelique groaned loudly. This was indeed hell.

Whittaker sat next to A.J. with a stifled curse.

A.J. looked at him. "What did you find out?"

"Angelique jumped her bail three days ago. The police are still looking for her."

A.J. shrugged. "Well, I say goodbye and good riddance."

"How can you be so cavalier," Whittaker groused. "She might have been able to help us."

"I doubt it. We'd be fools to let her touch the system again, anyway."

Cara, who been quiet throughout the exchange, finally spoke. "Actually, I can't guarantee that it would work, but I've been watching the pattern of this program. It reminds me of a virus I saw at MCS."

Whittaker looked at her as if he'd never seen her before. "What the hell is MCS, and why should we care?"

"Whittaker," A.J. said in a warning tone.

"Monumental Computer Securities. I used to work there."

"I thought you were an aerobics instructor."

"Fitness trainer."

Whittaker shook his head. "You used to be a security agent. And now you're a fitness trainer?"

"Well, I wasn't actually a security agent." Cara looked down at the keyboard. "I was in training."

"And we're supposed to listen to you?" he asked with a bitter laugh.

A.J. ignored him. "What do you think, Cara? Did you work with this virus before?"

Whittaker looked exasperated. "Don't tell me you're actually going to listen to her?"

"I didn't work with this exact virus," Cara said. "But it was similar. I can't promise anything, but maybe if I take a closer look, I can figure out how to get rid of it without losing everything."

A.J. gave her a long look. "At this point, we've got nothing to lose. Let's go for it."

Whittaker shouted, "Are you crazy? We only have two chances left."

A.J. met her eyes. "Go ahead, Cara."

She rebooted the system and began examining the files. "The virus is stored in the Master boot record. That's why the anti-virus programs can't trace it. It's on the hard drive of the network server. All your network files are still on the system, and they seem to be intact."

He squeezed her shoulder. "That's good news."

"I knew Parker couldn't be all bad. The virus is just holding your files hostage. Apparently, you have to either wipe out the whole system and start from scratch, or play the virus game and win. Knowing Parker, he'd at least have left you a chance to salvage everything."

He leaned forward. "So you're saying we have two choices, rebuild the system or play through the virus?"

Cara took a deep breath. "Yes."

A.J. rubbed his forehead. "It could take days to reinstall all the software. Not to mention rewriting three months of programming for the Malloy system."

Whittaker swore. "Maybe we can call in a virus expert to clean this up."

"It's Sunday night. No one's going to come out here now. We won't be able to get anyone until tomorrow morning. By then it will be too late. If we had that kind of time, we could clean it up ourselves."

"So what do we do? Pack it in?"

A.J. looked at Cara. "There's only one thing we can do. We have two chances left. We have to play the game."

He scooted his chair over and turned the monitor toward Cara.

Whittaker was confused. "What are you doing?"

"I'm going to let Cara play."

Chapter Nineteen

"You want *me* to play?" Cara felt goose bumps rising on her arms.

He kissed her on the cheek. "I trust you."

"What if I mess up?" she asked, her stomach muscles clenching.

"At this point, we're looking at not only losing the Malloy account, but completely rebuilding the system at our expense. You're better at these games than we are. I've never done anything like this before." A.J. glared at Whittaker. "And *he* sure as hell hasn't."

Behind her, she could hear Whittaker cursing under his breath, but it didn't matter. A.J.'s future was in her hands.

"Okay. I'll give it my best shot."

He squeezed her hand. "Let's do this."

Cara's hands were trembling so badly she could barely type on the keyboard. It took her three tries just to spell the word *Go* correctly.

She glanced over at A.J., shaking her head. "I'm going to mess this up. I can't even—"

A.J. massaged her shoulders. "Just relax. Take your time. I know you'll do just fine."

Cara took a deep breath and turned back to the screen. All along, she'd wanted A.J. to lean on her, and now that he was, she couldn't let him down. She at least had to try.

When a complex, but familiar, puzzle appeared on the screen, all her worries disappeared. "Myopia!"

"What?"

"I've played this game before—at Parker's."

She quickly solved the first puzzle and another appeared on the screen.

"Damn. How many do you think there are?" A.J. asked.

"I don't know," she said as her fingers flew over the keys. "Let's just hope he didn't upload the entire sequence. I only played the first few."

Cara didn't have any trouble with the first six. But new puzzles continued to appear. "A.J., I haven't played this one before."

He squeezed her shoulder. "Don't panic now, honey. You're doing great. Just take your time."

Cara stared at the colorful grid swirling on the screen. Each block had a series of numbers and she had to figure out the correct sequence before she ran out of time.

Her palms began to sweat as she stared at the keyboard. What should she do? A.J.'s voice kept echoing in her ears. He was counting on her. He'd never placed this kind of trust in *anyone* before. The weight of that knowledge pressed so heavily on her mind she couldn't concentrate.

Five minutes passed, and she still hadn't solved the puzzle. Cara was about to take a wild guess when the words *Time's Up* flashed on the screen. Then the animated graphics returned.

One chance left.

Cara sagged in her chair. "Oh no. I took too long."

A.J. wrapped his arms around her. "It's okay, sweetheart. You did great. We still have one chance left."

Whittaker, who'd been quiet in the background, spoke up. "Let me try this time."

"No." A.J. turned back to Cara. "Do you feel up to giving it another shot?"

Cara took a deep breath. She still felt shaky from the last round. "Maybe you or Whittaker *should* try this time. Everything's riding on this last chance."

A.J. gave her a quick kiss on the cheek. "That's why I'm depending on *you*."

Cara heard Whittaker groaning, but she didn't care. This time she had to win. She typed the word *Go* and began solving the puzzles again from the beginning. This time, when she came to the problem she hadn't been able to solve before, she went with her instincts. With A.J. behind her, she felt like she couldn't go wrong.

She continued to make decisions with confidence, and knocked off the succession of puzzles with less difficulty.

Then the screen started blinking again. A list of files opened on the screen and began to disappear one by one.

Cara panicked. "What's going on? I thought I won!"

A.J. hugged her. "It's deleting itself from the system. The virus is cleaning itself!"

He looked over her head to Whittaker who was pacing the room clutching his chest. "You all right, old man?"

Whittaker took a deep breath. "All this excitement is too much for me. I think it's time for me to retire."

The three of them burst into laughter.

The next day, Cara fumbled around A.J.'s apartment. *Everything was out of control.*

As she opened the balcony doors to clear out the black smoke veiling the room, she heard A.J.'s key in the door.

Just as he passed through the door, the smoke alarm went off.

"What the hell—" A.J. said, stopping to cough.

Cara continued to wave frantically at the smoke, and A.J. turned off the alarm.

"Cara?" he called.

"I'm out here on the balcony." She slumped onto the patio sofa when A.J. came out to join her. She sighed miserably as she took in the dark circles under his eyes and the lethargic slant of his shoulders. She was hoping to surprise him with a romantic dinner, and instead she'd surprised him with a small house fire.

"What's going on?"

"I'm sorry, A.J. I knew you'd have a hectic day, and I wanted to have dinner ready for you when you got home."

He laughed. "I guess the smoke means you burned it?"

"I bought a beautiful chicken to roast, but while I was waiting for it to cook, I fell asleep on the couch." She rested her head on his shoulder. "I ruined everything."

A.J. wrapped his arms around her and pulled her close. "Forget dinner. I'm too tired to eat anyway, but *you* are a sight for sore eyes. It's a pleasant surprise just finding you here."

"Yeah, sure, and I almost burned down the apartment building."

He chuckled, and then turned her face to his. "Does all this mean we're okay?"

Cara smiled. "We're better than okay. I love you and you love me. That's all that matters."

"You know we never did finish our conversation yesterday. Last night I learned something. It felt good to have someone in my corner. Not to have to face problems alone. I think we make a good team."

"We make a great team. With you behind me, I feel like I can do anything. It's the one time when I truly feel in complete control. I really think you and I can work through anything as long as we're together."

"I feel the same way. You're a part of me."

"Oh!" Cara pulled away from their embrace suddenly. "Tell me how the presentation went."

"It was excellent. As far as they know the project was completed without a hitch, and Ross, Locke & Malloy offered us a long-term contract."

"Fantastic! So all your hard work was worth it."

"A little peace of mind would be worth more. I can't keep driving myself crazy over this company. I told the boys at Ross, Locke & Malloy that if they want to work with Capital in the future, they have to draw up a new contract. One without any stipulations. Our work will speak for itself."

"Did they agree?"

He flashed her his crooked grin. "They agreed. And you and I are taking a much needed vacation."

Cara playfully placed her hands on her hips. "Oh, yeah? Are you asking me or telling me?"

A.J. answered her playful question with a both tender and serious look. "I'm begging you."

Then he took her hand and led her into the bedroom.

Epilogue

Cara stood next to A.J. in a corner of the Nautilus room at Tower Vista. Although she no longer worked there, she and A.J. were still regulars.

She worked with A.J. now and Capital was known as Gray & Gray Computer Consulting. Whittaker had indeed decided that the consulting business was too dangerous for him and had retired, letting A.J. buy him out. Whittaker was happily touring the country with his wife.

Unfortunately, Parker was still recovering from his nervous breakdown at a private institute. But he was doing better and making progress. Cara and A.J. went to visit him to make sure he was doing okay.

Cara smiled. Married life definitely agreed with her. Her CD-ROM had just hit the shelves and was a big seller at the fitness conference that summer. And she and A.J. thoroughly enjoyed working together. They still disagreed frequently, but that was part of the fun.

Even Ronnie had a new man in her life—one Cara approved of. His name was Baxter, and he was a big German Sheperd. Ronnie claimed that Baxter was the only kind of dog that was allowed in her life anymore. She had decided to give up the two-legged version for good. Ronnie would be very selective with the next man she dated—Baxter would see to that.

And Wendy. Cara giggled as she looked across the room to watch Wendy in action. True to her word, Wendy had gotten a summer job—at Tower Vista. Wendy turned around to wave at Cara and A.J. and promptly dropped the free-weight she was carrying directly on the foot of a handsome brown-haired hunk to her left.

Cara and A.J. exchanged shocked looks as the young man howled in pain, and Wendy escorted him to the first aid center. Later they ran into Wendy at The Big Squeeze.

A.J. raised his brows at the young girl. "We saw what happened with the weights. Did you get in trouble?"

Wendy tossed her red ponytail sassily. "Nah. He wasn't hurt too bad. I was careful not to drop it too hard."

Cara and A.J. exchanged quizzical glances. "You dropped it on purpose? Why?" Cara asked.

Wendy grinned devilishly. "Well, dropping the free-weight on A.J. worked out so well for you two, I figured I might be able to snag myself a hunk the same way. It worked, too. I have a date with Todd just as soon as he can walk again."

About The Author

After graduating from college with a degree in psychology, Robyn Amos discovered that writing about the suspenseful and romantic lives of the people in her imagination was more fulfilling than writing scholarly research papers. Through Washington Romance Writers, she joined two loyal critique groups. With their help, Robyn sold her first two novels to Pinnacle's Arabesque line. Now she continues to write about characters from a variety of cultural backgrounds, hoping her stories of romance and adventure will transcend racial stereotypes.

Robyn Amos would love to hear from her readers:

> P.O. Box 7904
> Gaithersburg, MD 20898-7904
> RobynAmos@aol.com
> http://www.erols.com/robyna

I have also included the synopsis for COME MIDNIGHT

Robyn Amos

Look for these upcoming Arabesque titles:

ENJOY THESE SPECIAL
ARABESQUE HOLIDAY ROMANCES

HOLIDAY CHEER   (0-7860-0210-7, $4.99)
by Rochelle Alers, Angela Benson,
and Shirley Hailstock

A MOTHER'S LOVE   (0-7860-0269-7, $4.99)
by Francine Craft, Bette Ford,
and Mildred Riley

SPIRIT OF THE SEASON   (0-7860-0077-5, $4.99)
by Donna Hill, Francis Ray,
and Margie Walker

A VALENTINE KISS   (0-7860-0237-9, $4.99)
by Carla Fredd, Brenda Jackson,
and Felicia Mason